THREE LIVES

OF

TOMOMI

ISHIKAWA

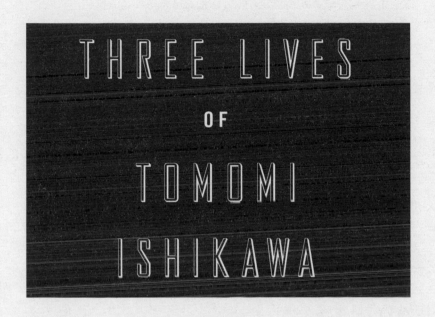

THREE LIVES
OF
TOMOMI
ISHIKAWA

BENJAMIN CONSTABLE

GALLERY BOOKS

New York   London   Toronto   Sydney   New Delhi

G

Gallery Books
A Division of Simon & Schuster, Inc.
1230 Avenue of the Americas
New York, NY 10020

First Gallery Books trade paperback edition June 2013

GALLERY BOOKS and colophon are registered trademarks of Simon & Schuster, Inc.

For information about special discounts for bulk purchases, please contact Simon & Schuster Special Sales at 1-866-506-1949 or business@simonandschuster.com.

The Simon & Schuster Speakers Bureau can bring authors to your live event. For more information or to book an event contact the Simon & Schuster Speakers Bureau at 1-866-248-3049 or visit our website at www.simonspeakers.com.

Designed by Davina Mock-Maniscalco

Manufactured in the United States of America

10   9   8   7   6   5   4   3   2   1

Library of Congress Cataloging-in-Publication Data

Constable, Benjamin, 1968–
    Three lives of Tomomi Ishikawa / Benjamin Constable.—First Gallery Books trade paperback edition.
        pages cm
    1. Treasure hunt (Game)—Fiction. 2. Friendship—Fiction. 3. New York (N.Y.)—Fiction. 4. Paris (France)—Fiction 5. Adventure fiction. I. Title.
    PR6103.O58T48 2013
    823'.92—dc23
                                                                                2012050506

ISBN 978-1-4516-6726-4
ISBN 978-1-4516-6728-8 (ebook)

Contents

An Introduction to All This—December 2006   1

Part One—March 15 to August 17, 2007

1. A Surprising Letter from Butterfly That Changed Everything   7

2. Tomomi Ishikawa's Computer   21

2½. Tomomi Ishikawa's Writing   31

3. Tomomi Ishikawa's Apartment Is Mysteriously Cleared   37

4. Tomomi Ishikawa's Dead   47

5. Stranger (?–2001)   55

6. Tomomi Ishikawa's Paris   63

7. Jay (1970–1998)   73

8. Looking Underground   86

9. Resistance   97

10. Treasure Hunting   107

Part Two—August 20 to August 28, 2007

11.	Arriving in New York	119
12.	On the Steps of the New York Public Library	127
13.	The Book in the Piano	140
14.	Komori (1942–1999)	151
15.	Mr. C. Streetny	163
16.	Beatrice's Good Mood Starts to Seem Strained	173
17.	Tracy (1966–1997)	184
18.	Yogurt and the East Village Gardening Association	196
19.	Guy Bastide (1942–2000)	208
20.	McCarthy Square	224
21.	Daddy (1942–2001)	236
22.	Unfinished Things and a Goodbye	249
23.	In Which Some Unsaid Things Are Said	263
24.	A Meeting in the Park at Midnight	284

Part Three—September 2007

25.	Incessant Nagging	291
25½.	Cigarettes and Water	302
26.	A Sticky Situation	311
27.	An Ending	326
	A Letter to Tomomi Ishikawa—November 2008	335

THREE LIVES

OF

TOMOMI

ISHIKAWA

An Introduction to All This

'I'd like to write a book where the two main characters are me and you,' I said to Tomomi Ishikawa, and absentmindedly organised the objects on the table.

'Oh good,' she said, and started to cough. 'I could have consumption. And we could go and live in Italy and you would spend your evenings drinking absinthe with women of ill repute, and you'd write terrible, terrible romantic poetry that you'd read to me on my deathbed and I would tell you it was the beauty of your verse that was killing me.'

I stopped myself laughing. 'That's not really what I had in mind.'

'Really?' She sounded surprised. 'Why, what were you thinking of?'

'It's the story of two people who hang out and talk about stuff.'

'Uh-huh, yes, good,' said Tomomi Ishikawa. 'And what's the angle?'

'There is no angle. There's no romance, no adventure, no—'

'Wait, wait, wait, you must be mistaken. That would be boring. A book like this should have at least a betrayal, a stolen painting and a talking dog, or a monkey.'

'Oh.' I thought she would have been impressed with my idea. 'Well, perhaps there could be a mystery. Like a series of killings we have to solve.'

'I see,' said Tomomi Ishikawa, 'but who could have done them?'

'You!' I grinned.

'Me? Oh, Ben Constable, thank you. I will change my name to Mimsie and then the book can be called *M Is for Murder*!'

'Ow!' Now I laughed. 'No. I'll be called Ben Constable and you will be called Tomomi Ishikawa.'

'But those are our real names.'

'That's the point.'

'Oh, OK. You could still call me Butterfly, though; it's less formal—*B Is for Murder*.'

'It'll be like a nickname,' I assured her. 'And the twisty plot will beckon the reader through the streets of Paris, and New York too.'

She leaned in across the table. 'Will Ben Constable perhaps be the final victim?'

I leaned in as well. 'I'm not fond of that idea.'

'Don't you even want my help?'

'Well . . .'

'Do you think . . .' We both stopped to see who would speak but Tomomi Ishikawa took the conch. 'Do you think you might spare me the gallows? It's such a dismal end after the glamour of a criminal's life.'

'There won't be gallows,' I said. 'I'm not even sure that there'll be murders. You're not imagining the same book as I am, Tomomi

Ishikawa. I want to write about an unusual friendship. I don't want to ruin it with fanciness and gimmicks.'

'But you said—'

'It's about things like now, this conversation.'

'So they talk and they drink and laugh late into the night.'

'Exactly,' I said. 'Our reality's as gripping as any fiction.'

'Sure it is.' She smiled. 'But maybe at the end of the evening the fictional Tomomi Ishikawa could stalk some women who were in the same bar'—she shot a glance at the people at the next table, then lowered her voice—'and kill them one by one, leaving their entrails draped across their naked bodies.'

'Maybe you should write your own book,' I said.

She considered this for a moment. 'Yes. Maybe I should.'

PART ONE

March 15 to August 17, 2007

▌

A Surprising Letter from Butterfly
That Changed Everything

Dear Ben Constable,

You may well be curious to know why I have sent a letter and not a text message or an email; why didn't I just call for the pleasure of laughter, or wait until we were seated at a table in the corner of a busy café, turned sideways on our chairs with our backs to the wall so as not to blow smoke in the other's face, our coats on a stand by the door with the distant smell of rain, and droplets tracing watery furrows down the window as we turn to face each other directly, because the conversation has, perhaps, become more intense, and we carefully place our elbows so as not to upset the coffee cups or, better still, wineglasses? And why, you may ask yourself, is it a typed letter, not handwritten (more intimate), with the delicate and honorable craft of calligraphy?

I'm sure it has crossed your mind that the time taken to write and the effort to deliver such a letter suggest a message or a purpose greater than idly occupying myself on a sleepless night, more urgent than to flatter with evidence I was thinking of you.

But what about the tactile delight of paper, Ben Constable? Why should I not write simply for the multisensory pleasure it gives, to bask in the gratification of the words, or for the weight of a thousand of years, no—much more, thousands, of letter-writing tradition?

You are right, of course; there is an explanation, although it is one I am loath to give, because you will not want to hear it. If only I had something to say that was joyful or could gently overwhelm you with images and sensations of wonder, but this is not that kind of letter, I'm afraid. And I become tangled as I try to dilute it, coat it in sugar. Would that it were possible to make you smile in spite of me.

And now, with such seeds of apprehension sown, I should no longer skirt the issue. But the point is choked up somewhere between the lump in my throat and my stumbling fingertips. If I could avoid it long enough, maybe it would go away or drift into memory like a bad dream. But alas, this point will not fade so easily.

Oh, how bad can it be? I'm not your girlfriend, so you can't be dumped. I'm not your boss, so you're not fired. You have done nothing wrong, you have not hurt me, I am not angry, I love you (and that's not the point either, by the way. I'm not about to embarrassingly prostrate myself before you, begging that we live out our tiny lives in tedium and grow old and frail in each other's arms).

And if the reason for my writing is still enigmatically shrouded in drivel, what I imagine is becoming clearer is my method for postponing the inevitable. As well you know, I have long taken shameless pleasure in the avoidance of the crux of any matter. "The point" is so often a delicacy to be savored, its anticipation a tantalizing delight, teasing its way closer with agonizing lethargy, in its every delay a mounting of the tension and a prolongation of the bliss.

However, what I have to say is important and sadly carries with it little pleasure. (Parenthetically, this style of never getting to the point is in some ways an appropriate reflection of our friendship. We are neither of us a stranger to the eternal flow of conversation, twisting its way across the floodplain, dallying in the shallows, splashing over small rocks, resting calm in deep pools, spinning in eddies and forming unlikely currents, because the experience of the journey has been the joy, and to reach the ocean is to signal the end. And maybe we had the remote idea that time could never run out and that we would never be bored, that the river would never stop flowing, as if the parenthesis could be endless and the brackets would never need to be closed and the opening clause never resolved, leaving the point to be continued at another, nonspecified time until eternity, and even then the sentence would just finish with an ellipsis . . . And I almost feel as though we could have gotten away with it too if it weren't for one overriding fact that spoils the whole thing. It's an obvious fact, and one that you know about, Ben Constable. The fact is that death will finish our conversation long before eternity even comes close.)

And this sadly brings me to the point, if only I could have said it earlier, and I did once try before I knew you too well; it seemed easier then. Do you remember, Ben Constable, you were drinking with your friends in a bar a few streets from here and I rang you to say hi (I wasn't feeling too good)? You told me to come and join you, and I didn't want to cramp your style, I would have left quickly, but you talked mostly just to me, and after a while your friends went on to a party, and you and I stayed drinking wine until close. Then we walked up Ménilmontant and I showed you the cobbled street at the top where there is a secret place to sit and we smoked a cigarette or two, and the point was becoming distant. I was just happy to be with you and we laughed in lowered voices so as not to disturb the neighbors and I wasn't sad anymore and the point drifted out of reach. Perhaps that was the beginning of this overly worded, endless sentence that is all our conversations (the carefree tangents, my avoidance). I'm so proud; it seems I've managed another paragraph without telling you why I'm writing.

But now I'm not playing because, this one time, the point isn't the last thing. It's the trigger for something new, the beginning of something bigger, the start of an adventure, Ben Constable. So here it is (I hesitate, trying to think of some other urgent distraction, but there is none): the point is that I'm going to die.

Of course, death comes to us all, but I'm dying more quickly. And I'm not going to drag it out, desperately clinging to the fading crepuscule of my life; I'm going to kill myself.

Sorry. I don't imagine that this is in any way entertaining for you. But I wanted to say goodbye.

I also wanted to introduce you to an idea: you are the inheritor of a thing, or many things, I've been making for years, since long before I knew of your existence—since my childhood, in fact. I can't tell you what it is yet; that would spoil it. It's a surprise.

But by the time these pages find your hands I will have been dead for a few hours. And as I'm writing, Ben Constable, I am sad because I miss you already. It seems such a shame to finish it all. But I'd like the dignity of control in my ending. I think you can understand that, because you know that endings do not always come last, and that they are only a question of definition, a place to change activity, theme or pace.

Hey, can I tell you some stuff? Stupid stuff, nothing exciting. But even at this of all moments, my attention snags on things that I like, things I think of as treasures. I'd love to show you. I'd love you to know about them.

The first treasure is the view while I write. I like the sketched lines of the trees at nighttime and looking down through their bare branches at the square below, where on sunny days people gather around the ornate drinking fountain or sit outside the salon de thé, smoking. I love the grand stairway leading up to the doors of the church, towering over the neighborhood like a sentinel. And I love to look at the collected objects around me, each with a story that will die on my parting, and the stopped clock on my wall saves me precious seconds. Its hands point to twenty past three, optimistically suggesting time for one last thing. I will miss my clock, and in my imagination the clock will miss me too.

And as I note these words I'm reminded how much I love the activity of writing. I might have drawn this up by hand for you to admire my spidery scrawl, and it is true there is something more intimate in the scratching of nib spreading ink, but while in front of my computer I prefer to type, for in the rapid flow of syllables so many words come out, in the click of each letter I find myself, and for this moment I am whole.

There's a fine mist of rain coming down outside, making golden halos around the streetlights, and I wish I were outside walking, with the water soaking into my hair and eventually running down to the tip of my nose, from where I would try to blow the drop or wipe my face with my sleeve as ladies shouldn't, but then I never said I was a lady (although perhaps one time I did). Paris and the rain also have places in my treasure chest of loved things.

Do you remember the day the sky went black and you called me from somewhere high up, Montmartre, I guess, and told me you could see a storm coming toward my house, and that you could see the lines of rain pouring down as they moved across the city? As we talked you gave me a commentary, saying it would start raining in two minutes, one minute, thirty seconds and then counted down from ten, and when you got to zero you asked whether it was raining yet, and I said no and then, a moment later, oceans fell from the sky outside my window and you probably beamed with pride, or at least that's how I imagined you because, let's face it, everybody likes being right. I was impressed.

There is another thing that I love as well, an improbable thing. On metro line 7bis, between stations Buttes Chaumont and Bolivar heading downhill, the tracks swing round to the right, and after maybe a hundred or a hundred and fifty yards there is a garden on the left-hand side of the tunnel. "Garden" is admittedly an overstatement; it has only one small plant, more like a weed, in fact, that has pushed through, or taken root in the wall beneath a light, but it's the only plant I know of that grows underground. I can never get to see it properly, but it's there. Sometimes I go up and down that line six times in order to get a good look. I love the idea that you will go and find a way to photograph it, or maybe even that you will hide in the metro station until it's closed and sneak down onto the tracks to touch its sun-starved leaves, and it will be an adventure and security guards will see you on closed-circuit screens and come looking for you and you will be on the run and have to find a secret way out of the metro through tunnels and come out of a manhole cover on some poorly lit side street, triumphant!

All that remains is to press print and place these pages into an envelope. Then, when you have left for work, I will go to your apartment and slide them beneath the door. But there is so much more to say; so, so much more. Or maybe there is nothing. Maybe I have to accept that the letter is over and the hypnotic purring of the keys will stop, and the sentence will never be finished, the opening clause never resolved, and I wish I could just keep this moment a little longer. Maybe because I'm a coward and if I carry on writing forever, then I won't die, but I don't actually know what to say. I don't think I can tell you how I came by my two leather chairs, or list the plants in my window box. The window box, yes, another improbable garden—a green place for me to linger. Oh, did I tell you about . . . and did I tell you about . . . ?

It's twenty past three (still) and there's a little more time, but I have to go now.

Ben Constable, there are adventures awaiting you and I'm sorry you will never get the chance to tell me about them and that we won't get drunk late at night and walk in the rain and shelter under trees on tiny cobbled streets and sit in our special sitting place, smoking cigarettes. I miss you already.

Goodbye.
Butterfly X O X O X

Fridays make me smile. I catch myself laughing in the mirror as I wash the week from my hands before leaving work. I love the weekend and the surprises that fall from nowhere. I call out good-bye, then pace along the road and skip down the escalators into the metro. I let people pass in front of me and help a woman with heavy bags on the stairs, a beggar gets my loose change and I leave my seat for a stranger. I stand with my back against the side of the carriage and consider getting out a book, but I prefer watching people come and go and eavesdropping on snippets of their conversations taken out of context.

The phone rang in my pocket.

'*Et alors?*' When conversations start like this on Fridays it means: 'So, have you had a good week?' and it means: 'So, are you ready to come out and play?' This evening, I was informed, we (me and friends) were going for a meal, then on to a party where there would be music and dancing, and people we'd never met. We were going to meet up at seven thirty for an aperitif and would be a little drunk by the time we got to the restaurant, where we would laugh and argue about politics and art. That gave me time to go home, have a quick siesta, shower, get dressed while listening to music, look for a random fact on the Internet that would spring to mind and seem like an urgent task, then turn up at about nine. Being late has never been a conscious intention; I just like to do things at my own pace. Rushing is not my thing. Today, for no particular reason, I am happy. But that's not uncommon.

When I got home, I waited for the lift and my fingers tapped impatiently in my pockets as it laboured up the six floors. I looked at my tongue in the mirror because that's surely what mirrors in lifts are for.

Cat was sitting outside my door, which surprised me because he doesn't need me to let him in or out.

'Hello, Cat, what are you doing here?' I said to myself, and watched him while I opened the lock. 'If you're bringing me bad news, I don't want to know.' He stood up and brushed against my leg and I felt a sudden uncertainty because Cat generally only comes for a good reason. As the door opened, there was the sound of paper dragging over wood—something pushed under the door. Cat moved past me and strolled in like he owned the place and I bent down and picked up a fat envelope with my name scrawled on it in a familiar hand. It was from Tomomi Ishikawa (who is also called Butterfly), although I couldn't imagine why she would have written to me and come all the way to my apartment to put the letter under my door while I wasn't there. But then Butterfly was full of surprises.

I hung up my coat, walked into the bedroom and flopped down on the bed. I kicked off my shoes and toyed with the envelope for a couple of seconds before ripping it open. Inside was a wad of printed pages.

Cat jumped onto the bed next to me and I hoped his paws were clean. He stretched out like a sphinx, much too big for a normal cat. I stroked him with my foot, but he ignored me and stared out of the window. I started to read.

Tomomi Ishikawa was my friend. Tomomi Ishikawa was dead in my hands. My brain locked up as I read the pages. No thoughts could get out. My eyes were heavy with tears, but they wouldn't fall. I watched my chest to see what my breathing looked like. It was slow, steady and strong. I could see my heart beating, big, powerful beats. It was fast. Very fast. Tomomi Ishikawa was dead, and like a deep and terrible wound, I knew I was hurting, but I couldn't feel anything.

I was trying to remember the five stages of grief: shock, denial, anger, depression and acceptance? What about guilt, is that one of them? This must be shock. I was in shock. I didn't know what was happening. I didn't know my mind and I didn't know what I was going to do. Why hadn't I called her yesterday? I could have called so easily. We could have gone for a drink. I looked at Cat and he turned his head and looked in my eyes. I wished he were the kind of cat that would come and sit squashed up next to me and absorb all my negative ions or whatever cats do. But Cat isn't like that for a couple of reasons. The first is that he isn't a domestic cat. He's some kind of wildcat or lynx (or something), the size of a dog, quite a small dog, but much bigger than a cat. He has big claws and doesn't much care for being stroked. He's not my cat. He just comes and hangs out sometimes. The second reason is that he doesn't exist. He's an imaginary cat, but that's kind of a secret.

I stood up, looking for my phone, and found it in my coat pocket. My thumbs scrolled down the contacts to Butterfly (fr); I pushed the green button and held it to my ear. There was silence for a second and I took the phone away from my head and looked to make sure it was connecting, then I listened again and it was ringing. 'Come on, Butterfly, answer the fucking phone. Answer!' After five rings or so it went to a recorded message and her familiar voice told me in French that she wasn't available and that she would ring me back as soon as possible. And I could hear myself laughing in the background because I'd been with her when she recorded it. I hung up.

'What do I do, Cat?' Cat looked at me. As an imaginary cat, one would think he wouldn't be restricted by reality, or the laws of science. But Cat is. For example he can't speak, or at least he never does. Sometimes I think I know what he's thinking and I sometimes imagine what he would say if he could speak to me, but that's imaginary imaginary. Cat is very much tied to the world of real imaginary.

'Oh Cat, help me, I don't know what to do.' I put the tips of my fingers on my eyelids as if this would free my brain to think clearly. I lay down on the bed, pulled a pillow over my head, and squashed it down onto my face. I hadn't been paying much attention to Butterfly of late. She had been occupied with other things and I'd just been . . . doing stuff. She must have desperately needed help, but I was doing stuff. Stuff. Fuck. I felt Cat's weight as he walked over me, squashing my legs uncomfortably down.

I picked up my phone and rang Tomomi Ishikawa's number again, but it went straight to voice mail. I rang it seven times in a row and each time there was a moment's silence and then her recorded voice. That's not normal; it rang before. How could it have gone out of range or stopped working in the few minutes between me ringing the first and second times? Maybe it had run out of battery. What if someone had turned it off?

I pulled a small box of interesting things from a shelf. I looked through it and pulled out a key on a short piece of red ribbon. I had a key to Tomomi Ishikawa's apartment to water the plants when she was away and in case of emergencies.

I put on my shoes, grabbed my coat and went out, slamming the door a little harder than I intended. I hoped I hadn't chopped off Cat's imaginary head, but he was standing by the lift. 'Let's take the stairs,' I said to myself, and Cat was happy because he doesn't really like the lift. He doesn't like the metro either, but he followed me down and into the carriage and settled between my feet. It's a tricky business being an imaginary cat on the metro, because people can't see you and they often infringe on your personal space, but he came with me anyway and I appreciated the gesture.

In the street outside Butterfly's door, I fumbled with the key panel, trying to remember the code. I typed in various combinations of four numbers I had in my head and the letter *A* until there was a click. We went in and climbed the stairs. I knocked, but there was no answer, so I pulled out the key from my pocket and let myself in. Cat went ahead because he is braver than I am in this kind of situation. I called out hello, but no one made a sound. Everything looked normal apart from a note on the table with a stainless steel click-on/click-offable pen on top of it. I walked into the bedroom. It was normal and the bed was made. In fact it was very tidy. I checked the bathroom, but there was no one there, then I picked up the note and read while Cat sat down and licked his right paw.

> *Ben Constable,*
>
> *It's twenty past three and it seems that everything is done. I won't be here when you arrive; I found a place to do this where nobody will have to get dirty hands (death can be a messy business). I've organized for somebody to come and deal with*

my things so you can leave them as they are, but the computer is
for you—please take it. There's stuff in the fridge as well if
you're interested. The yogurts are past the date, but everyone
knows that yogurt's just out-of-date milk, right? There's some
fruit as well if you can be tempted. (What the hell am I nagging
you about food for? Sorry—I just hate to see it all go to waste
and what with you not being the fattest person in the world, I
always imagine that you could use a few pies.) (There are no
pies.)

I hope you're OK and I'm sorry for all this. I have to go
now because I still have one more letter to write. (To you,
stupid.)

XOXOX Butterfly.
P.S. Hey, you should have this pen as well, it's an old favorite.

I picked up a banana and ate it. I stood for a moment looking at
the clock on the wall. It had faithfully kept the time of twenty past
three since I'd known her, but why she'd keep a stopped clock at
all was a mystery to me. Cat got up and stretched. Where had she
gone to 'do this' and who was the somebody who was going to deal
with her things? A lawyer? Some kind of removal person? Had she
booked herself into a special suicide clinic in Switzerland that offers a full sorting-things-out-after-you've-gone service? Does that
kind of thing even exist? It seemed hard to believe that she was
that organised. She would have gone to the clinic's website, noted
the clean lines of the building, thought of the architect Albert Frey,
and then started reading about desert modernism and the moment
would have passed.

Cat sat facing the door so that I could be in no doubt he was
ready to leave. I found a jug in the cupboard and filled it with

water, then went around pouring a little into each plant pot. I put Butterfly's shiny laptop, the note and the pen into my bag and left, depositing the banana skin in the dustbin at the bottom of the stairs.

Tomomi Ishikawa was dead and I didn't know what to do. I turned off my phone and went home.

2

Tomomi Ishikawa's Computer

For a moment when I woke up I was brand-new. The sun had risen over the buildings on the other side of the road and the shadows of ornate metalwork overhanging the window were crisp and clear on the curtains. I didn't know where I was. The air was cool but smelled dry like central heating. The quilt was clean and I liked the feel of cotton on my skin. I liked the room. I don't know what it reminded me of. It seemed exotic. I could hear cars somewhere, not too near, and I could hear birds. It sounded like spring. Everything was still. Everything was all right.

It wasn't whispering because it didn't make a sound, but something was quietly telling my head to stay like this. *Don't move. Don't think. Stay a while.* Answers were seeping through the fabric to form droplets (to questions I hadn't even asked). They splashed down onto my face. I was in the apartment I rent in Paris, France; the room was my bedroom. *Shhh.* It was Saturday, March 17, 2007. *Shhh, no more.* I'd been asleep for a long time;

maybe ten hours. *No, not yet, wait, wait.* I looked at my phone and it was switched off. That surprised me. The fabric tore and my life came flooding in. I closed my eyes. I wished I were asleep. Tomomi Ishikawa was dead and we would never sit, talking and laughing, again.

I stayed in bed for as long as I could, looking at nothing and thinking about nothing. She had told me several times that she was depressed. Eventually I got up because I was hungry. Sometimes I would listen to her, or put my arm around her. I made scrambled eggs and buttered some of yesterday's bread. Sometimes I made jokes. I poured a glass of grapefruit juice and drank it straight down, then poured myself another. One time I told her to snap out of it. I looked in the bathroom mirror for clues, but there was nothing. I looked out of the window and the weather was brighter, more blue than should be allowed. I dug my fingernails into my arm to see whether I could feel pain. I could, but it didn't mean anything. I scrunched my eyes. I thought about breaking something, the mirror maybe, but the prospect of cleaning up afterwards put me off. Besides, if I trod on a shard of glass, it might hurt my foot. I climbed back into bed, covered my body with the quilt and watched the ceiling. Yesterday she had slipped a letter under my door. She had been here, alive. She had walked down the street and smiled at somebody who perhaps held a door open. She had given a cigarette to somebody who asked her by the entrance to the metro, and she bought something from a shop.

At two in the afternoon I got dressed. I found hummus in the fridge and crackers in the cupboard.

I cupped the crumbs with my hand and pottered aimlessly into the living room. I sat down and pulled Tomomi Ishikawa's computer onto my knees and opened the top. The screen was shinier than mine. I pressed the on button. It lit up for a few seconds, then turned itself off—the battery was flat. I hadn't brought the power supply. I tried to plug in the charger for my computer, but it wouldn't fit. I could go out and buy a new power supply, or I could go back to Tomomi Ishikawa's apartment and get the one I'd forgotten. I didn't want to leave the house at all, but if I was going to Butterfly's I should do it now, before somebody came and cleared the place. Who knows, that could be soon. It was only a short metro ride away. What else was I going to do with my day? I found small things to do to delay leaving: the washing-up and cleaning my teeth, but finally there were no more excuses.

I got off the metro at Ménilmontant and my body weighed down as I climbed the steps from the station. I crossed the boulevard and turned up rue Étienne Dolet. I remembered the code from yesterday and typed it in, then dragged myself up the stairs to Tomomi Ishikawa's door and waited. 'Cat,' I called softly so that only he would hear. Nothing happened. I guess he was somewhere else hanging out with lady cats. 'Cat!' I called slightly more insistently, and he padded reluctantly down the stairs from the floor above. 'What were you doing up there?' He didn't answer and I said, 'Well, thanks for coming anyway.' I turned the key in the lock.

Cat went first and stopped dead in his tracks, listening. 'What is it, Cat?' He padded silently into the bedroom and poked his head behind the open door, then came out and walked into the kitchen area and looked in the bathroom. Something was different, the apartment smelt different; someone had been here. It was none of my business—this was what Butterfly had organised—but since I was here yesterday, small things had changed; I don't know what, imperceptible things. I've not been gifted with those kinds of observational powers, but somebody had been here, I was certain. All of a sudden I felt upset. There was nothing here to remind her of me. I had never given Butterfly anything. I had never even lent her a book. No wonder she felt so alone.

And these thoughts got stuck in my head and I scratched my skin as if I could scrape them away. I could have called more often, spent more time with her. I could have helped her. I looked in the bathroom. There were no products on the shelves. No shampoo or shower gel, no toothpaste, no creams. There was a small towel hung over the shower cubicle. I guessed it was used as a mat to step out onto. I touched the hard cotton and it was damp. Somebody had showered here and taken Tomomi Ishikawa's bathroom things.

My skin felt dry and I searched for some product I could put on my face, but there was nothing. Surely Butterfly had endless piles of creams and makeup remover and stuff. She was a girl after all. Why would she have taken them with her? Were they here when I came yesterday? How could I have possibly noticed? It's not the kind of thing that would strike me when going into a dead person's apartment. I looked in the bedroom. I thought about rummaging through the cupboards to see what I could find, but that would have been intrusive. The computer and the pen were for me. She'd told me to leave the other stuff alone. All this was none of my business. But whoever had come here had showered and taken Butterfly's creams and bathroom things. Maybe Butterfly had left them a note instructing them to do exactly that, in the same way that she had told me to help myself to the contents of the fridge. Then my eyes filled up and my throat closed because Butterfly had no creams or cosmetic products. I could have bought her some. Something nice to make her skin feel good. Even if it was a bit expensive. I could have easily saved some money to buy it.

Cat jumped up onto the windowsill and stood staring down at

the square below. The trees showed the first signs of coming green. A man was sitting on a bench near the drinking fountain. He turned and looked directly up at me and I stepped back out of sight. The clock on the wall said twenty past three. I looked around and the computer power supply was on the floor, plugged into the wall next to the table. I coiled the cable and put it in my bag. Cat jumped down and waited impatiently by the door, wanting to leave. I thought about staying for a moment and sitting still so that I could think, but not without Cat, so we went. When we were outside the man on the bench had gone and there were some children running round, chasing each other. Cat started walking off in the direction of Belleville and then looked back at me. I'd like to think that he was saying, 'Just give me a shout if you need anything,' but I don't know. Cat's remarkably uncommunicative. He disappeared round the corner and I walked back to the metro and went home.

Now, plugged in, the computer booted up without problem.

There were a few icons strewn messily on the desktop (which I find irritating), files saved there because she was too lazy to find a proper place for them. There was a letter of resignation from a job dating from over a year ago, and some kind of reference addressed to the prefecture from 2005. There were two folders imaginatively named 'untitled folder' and 'untitled folder 2' with nothing in either. I put them in the bin. I clicked on 'Documents' and expected to find hundreds or endless files, badly named and in no particular order to make them easy to lose and difficult to find, but that wasn't the case. There were five neatly labelled folders: 'My Brain', 'My Dead', 'My Paris', 'My Stuff' and 'Things I Like'. I quickly checked the recycle bin but there was nothing other than the icons I had dragged there seconds earlier. It had been emptied. Butterfly had cleaned up her computer. Perfectly normal, I guess.

'My Dead' and 'My Brain' were the folder names I was most interested in, and 'Things I Like' too. I clicked on 'My Stuff' to save the best for later. There was one file, whatever had once surrounded it now deleted. I imagined she decided at the last moment to leave just one thing for me. I clicked and a video started, cutting in in midsentence. The image was of me walking along slowly, filmed from the side.

'—one thing,' I said, 'but you might like it.' I was smiling as if I thought I was about to say something funny. 'The design for the whole of Paris was based on a Victorian resort in the northwest of England.'

'Uh-huh.' I could hear Tomomi Ishikawa's voice as she filmed.

'Napoleon III instructed Baron Haussmann to build the new Paris in the style of Southport in Lancashire.'

'Really?' There was noise from passing cars and buses.

'Have you ever been to Southport?' I asked.

'Nope,' she said.

'It's a quite nice seaside town, but it's hard to imagine that it inspired Paris. Anyway, they say it did, and that's everything I know about history and architecture.'

'Uh-huh.'

'Maybe Gustave Eiffel got all his ideas from Blackpool,' I said, and looked round at her. 'Are you listening to me, or are you just playing with your phone?'

'I'm not playing with my phone,' she said, 'I'm filming you.'

'I was making a joke,' I complained.

'I didn't get it,' she said. 'Sorry.'

'Blackpool's the town next to Southport.'

'Oh.'

'What could there be at Blackpool that, in a joke, Gustave Eiffel could have gone to see for inspiration?'

'Er, a tower?'

'Hurray!' I said, and we both laughed at my total comic failure.

'Tell me another joke,' she said. 'This time I'll get it, I promise, and I'll laugh and you will be very funny indeed for my film.'

'I don't know any jokes,' I said. 'Can I see?'

'OK,' she whispered, and I reached out my hand towards the screen and that was the end.

I went to the folder called 'Things I Like' to see whether there was anything about me in there. Inside were more folders than would fit on the screen and each was full of photographs. I waded patiently through snapshots of cities I couldn't quite place. Flash photography of faces I didn't know. Old people, young people, Asian people, white Europeans, black people, Native Americans, mountains, clocks, roads, gardens, plants, buildings, plants, buildings, flowers, buildings, towers. Stained-glass windows, Georgian windows, Napoleonic windows, shop windows, doors (big, small, double, ornate), gates, more people, churches, statues, windows, pillars, doors, Roman arches, doors, gardens, clocks, Gothic arches, windows.

I liked the brainless tedium of looking through pictures of no importance to me. I scrolled through the images as fast as the computer would bring up the next one, moronically clicking on the right-hand arrow over and over until my legs felt as if they'd been on a long car journey. I got up and drank a glass of water, went to the toilet, then came back to my systematic trawling of the photographs. There were occasional pictures of me. Several where I was talking to people, some of them familiar, most not, during soirées I remember. I don't remember the faces; I'm bad with faces. Even with people I know well. For example, Tomomi Ishikawa and I never met in a particular place and we had no allocated time. Sometimes we saw each other once or twice a week, sometimes once a month, sometimes less. But if I didn't know where to look out for her, I couldn't recognise her. She would do tests and walk by me in the street or sit at the next table to see whether I'd say hello. Most of the time, though, she would grin and wave so I would know it was her. I appreciated that. It reminded me of a thing. I went in the bag that follows me everywhere and got out a notebook, then scratched around for something to write with. All I could find was Tomomi Ishikawa's on/offable pen. I did a quick scribble on the page to see whether it worked and the blue ink looked strange coming from my hand; I normally write in black.

'Hey, how come you never recognise me?' Tomomi Ishikawa asked. *'I'm not sure whether I should be offended.'*

'Don't take it personally,' I said. *'I can't recognise anyone.'*

'I thought maybe all Japanese people look the same to you because we don't have lots of distinguishing lines like you limeys.'

I shifted in my seat with feigned discomfort and tried to catch my reflection in the window to see whether I was covered in lines. 'I just hardly ever recognise faces,' I said. 'I once passed my mum in the street and she said hello. I smiled and carried on walking, I had no idea who she was.'

'Really?' Now her eyes lit up.

'Really. I've got hundreds of embarrassing stories about not recognising people I ought to. Family, friends, famous people, dates—it's never good not to recognise your date.'

'You fucking freak.' She burst out laughing. *'That's*

awesome. Have you always been like that or has it come on due to brain abuse?'

'I've had it as long as I can remember,' I said. 'It's all about context. If people act like they know me and they're in the kind of place I might expect to see them then I'm usually OK. But out of context is a problem. People often get offended.'

'Oh my God. Are you sure this isn't something you've just made up so you can be different from everybody else?'

'No, it's a real thing. It's called prosopagnosia.'

'Wow, it must be real, it's got a Greek name!'

'Yeah, it might be Greek.'

'Oh, it definitely is. "Prosopon" means "face" and "agnosia" means "not knowing",' she said. And then, 'Wait, wait, wait, if you had a girlfriend you could have all the excitement of thinking you were sleeping with strangers, without any of the disadvantages, and all the comforts of a stable relationship.'

I laughed. 'It's actually a bit like that.'

'Oh my God, and it would be even better the other way around. You could use your proso thing as an excuse to sleep with loads of people on the basis that you thought they might be your girlfriend. I think you need to start putting out in a major way.'

'All right,' I said, unconvinced.

'But it would be a waste not to,' Tomomi Ishikawa insisted. 'And besides, you're single; it wouldn't harm anybody. You have to sleep with thirty women this year. OK?'

'Thirty sounds like a lot to me, but I'll try.'

'It's not that many. Think about it: there are fifty-two weeks in a year so you have to sleep with one woman a week

*and there would be twenty-two weeks when you didn't have to
if you couldn't find someone suitable.'*

> *'I don't have to do anything, Butterfly. I'll only sleep with
people I want to. Anyway, why would I think that thirty
women were my girlfriend if I was single?'*

> *'Oh, please, Ben Constable. Make an effort.'*

> *'OK, but only if it's true love every time. It might actually
be quite sad. My heart would be broken every week.'*

> *'Oh, oh, oh, wait—you could write an epic poem that
would detail your heartbreaking encounters and explain that
you are in fact a victim of love (not being able to recognise
people), and I could have consumption and we could go and
live in Italy!'*

> *'All right. You've convinced me.'*

> *'What, you're going to do it? Really? Oh, I knew you
would. Can I tell people?'*

I flicked through the pages of my notebook for the one Butterfly
had filled with the word 'prosopagnosia' over and over without telling me, while I'd gone to the toilet or the bar or something. The
words went along the lines and then round the side of the page,
between the lines and upside down.

$2^{1}/_{2}$

Tomomi Ishikawa's Writing

I looked at the folders. 'My Brain', 'My Dead', 'My Paris', 'My Stuff' and 'Things I Like'. Again, I managed to resist the more gratifying titles and clicked on 'My Paris'. There were fifty or so files. I looked at one called 'Time for Everything'.

When it comes to superlatives, Gare Saint-Lazare comes nail-bitingly close to deserving many, without ever quite getting a cigar. It's one of Europe's busiest stations, with rush-hour trains arriving and departing every thirty seconds. In passenger numbers it comes second in France with 100 million a year, and it's Paris's oldest station, although not the oldest in France.

Originally opened in 1837, it was built to house the Paris end of the line serving the nearby town of Saint-Germain-en-Laye, the current edifice was designed by Juste Lisch and completed in 1889 in time for the Universal Exhibition that year.

For a period, Claude Monet was the station's unofficial artist in residence. He was fascinated by the changing light and the clouds of steam.

The façade overlooks two squares: the Cour de Rome and the Cour du Havre. The former is home to a striking glass-domed metro entrance by Jean-Marie Charpentier. Both squares have sculptures by Armand Pierre Fernandez, who worked under the chisel name of Arman and was one of the original signatories of the declaration of Nouveau Réalisme in 1960. *Consigne à vie* is a tower of precariously balanced suitcases in bronze. *L'heure de tous* is a collection of stopped clocks, each showing a different time.

Tomomi Ishikawa saw Paris as a series of facts, dates and architects. She had obviously spent much of her spare time researching. The next file I clicked on was called 'Arcades' and looked like this:

By the middle of the nineteenth century, Paris had around a hundred and fifty covered streets (*passages couverts*). They are not uniquely Parisian—functionally descendants of the great bazaars of the Arab world and precursors to the modern mall—but the Parisian versions have in common an eerie and deserted feel, ghosts of an ill-remembered past. They are lined with small shops and covered by glass roofing, but unlike the later and grander arcades of Milan, Brussels, and Moscow, they are narrow and dimly lit.

There are approximately twenty *passages couverts*

accessible to the public (the rest were demolished to make
way for Haussmann's restructuring of the city in the 1850s).
They frequently resist attempts to revitalize them and many,
in their neglect, have taken on remarkable and unique
identities. Passage du Ponceau in the 2nd arrondissement is
dedicated solely to candy makers, Passage du Caire is
predominantly occupied by clothing wholesalers, Passage
Brady in the 10th is lined with Indian, Pakistani and
Bangladeshi restaurants. It smells of spices and casts a
doubt in one's sense of place.

These texts were all good and interesting, but they didn't feel as if
they were written for me. I backed out of 'My Paris' and allowed
myself the satisfaction of clicking on 'My Dead'. Inside there were
seven folders named as follows: 'Tracy', 'Jay', 'Daddy', 'Guy Bastide', 'Komori', 'Stranger' and 'Ben Constable'. Why was my name
included in a folder called 'My Dead'? I thought of all the times
when I've lost a file because I've accidentally dragged and dropped
it into another folder and not noticed. It's not an everyday occur-
rence, but it does sometimes happen and can be frustrating. But I
didn't belong among the dead, that much was certain.

In the 'Ben Constable' folder was a collection of files, all dated
in the American format with the month first. They were emails either to or from me. Piles of them. This one was entitled 'WORK-
ING TO PLAN':

> MR. CONSTABLE,
> Are we meeting today as planned?
> I'll be waiting for you like Samuel Beckett
> with little idea of the day or even time.

And if you arrive we can wait together.
Am miserable, Ben Constable,
but I won't be when I see you.
ISHIKAWA

Why had Butterfly given me her computer? She knew I liked hers because it was shiny, but I had a computer already—albeit a little the worse for wear—and I had no urgent need of IT charity. She'd erased nearly everything, leaving just a selection of tat. Why was this for me? What was I supposed to do with a collection of photographs of buildings and people I don't know? Some emails I already have stored in my email account? Extracts from a guide-book to Paris that she never got round to writing? Is this my inheritance? Thanks, Butterfly. There must be something for me in all this junk.

I had a sudden idea and logged on to the Internet. Maybe the password to her email account was saved on the computer. Butterfly loved email. Her default account opened automatically. There were thirty-seven unopened emails. Customer service communications, phone bills and special offers. This was her account for official things, not personal letters. But the last unread email in her inbox (and thus the first posted) was from an address I recognised. I had received many emails from this sender. This was Butterfly's real email account, where friends and personal business were kept. She'd sent something to herself.

Well, Ben Constable, if you have started to suspect there
is some vague and wayward method in the madness I have
left for you, then you are smart as can be. Maybe though, you
have not yet gone through enough of my shit to notice that

there is a story here. These are pieces of a puzzle, and a quest. This is your call to adventure! The adventure is, unfortunately, not brilliantly worked out, so you may have to add your own details, pinches of salt to render more palatable the inconsistencies in my ill-conceived plot.

Part of the reason I've gone to such lengths is the secret desire we all have to confess, and so part of the prize is to know me better (perhaps for worse), for much of what I have left you is spilled ink from my pen, giving form to the darkest corners of my conscience. But there is also an idea to draw you from what has seemed a long winter wrapped securely in the world of the known. Arise now, Sir Knight, for it is springtime and there are brave deeds to be performed, and I will be your faithful squire (though I hope the battles you fight are strictly with windmills and imaginary foe), and maybe you will win the beautiful Dulcinea, for the prize is the experience, the treasures are things to see, do, taste, smell; plus a small mass of written material that, maybe, you would use as inspiration for a novel, store as a keepsake, or burn to keep you warm on winter evenings when you're writing in poverty in your garret room and dying of diphtheria, as I hope for the sake of your artistic credibility that you do. You deserve a romantic death, don't you think?

You are, of course, in no way bound to complete the labors I have set for you, but there is plenty here to keep you going should you feel so inclined. And I shall look down from heaven (or up from hell, more likely) and smile and laugh with you, like I am almost certainly doing right now as you read this. Shit, I hope you don't find unnerving the thought that I'm in the room with you. Put that thing away, you dirty boy—no, only kidding; leave it out—no, sorry, I really am only kidding. I've taken this whole thing too far. Goddamn.

Now, go back and read some of the stuff on my computer. There should be some ideas for things to do, not that I think you're looking for things to do, but that's the starting point.

Butterfly.
X O X M X Y X X X B X R X A X I X N X O X O X

3

Tomomi Ishikawa's Apartment
Is Mysteriously Cleared

I left the computer and paced between the rooms. I stared long-ingly at my bed and thought about getting undressed to feel the crisp cotton cool against my skin. I thought of Butterfly's ghost in the room with me and I was embarrassed at the thought of being naked. If she wanted to hang out even after death, surely it didn't mean that she had to watch everything? Or maybe having attached oneself to a living person, ghosts are there for the whole ride and can't get off, and she would be forced to witness even my most intimate and potentially embarrassing moments.

I flopped down on the bed and tried not to think. I wondered whether she had cried when she did it, or if she was calm. I won-dered whether there was a moment of panic when it was too late and she had a doubt, or changed her mind. I imagined her lying on her side facing me, her arms around the pillow with her head rest-ing on it, her eyes watching me. 'Sorry,' she said.

I got up and put my shoes on. 'I'm going to the shop,' I told her. I washed my face and then ran down the stairs, out of the door and into the *épicerie* on the street below. The wine selection isn't great, but I found a couple of bottles that seemed passable and bought them both.

The next time I woke it was morning and I was drunk and fully clothed. There was the pungent odour of a full ashtray by my bed, delicately more noxious for the half-finished glass of wine next to it. In the mirror my teeth were stained purple. I took the ashtray and the wineglass to the kitchen, then came back for the empty bottles. There was something unwholesome about having got drunk by myself, but under the circumstances I could allow myself to run off the rails a little. That's what I wanted. To run off the rails.

I showered and spent a good five minutes brushing my teeth until they were passably tooth-coloured again. I opened the windows and let the cold air blow in, leaving the curtains closed. I got back into bed, still damp, and slept.

When I woke again it was three in the afternoon. I didn't feel drunk anymore and I had a towel wrapped round my waist. I got up and slipped on some shorts without exposing myself. Damn it, Butterfly. I don't even believe in ghosts or the afterlife or anything, but I still turned my back to the room as I pulled on my jeans.

I would have liked some instant food, but there was nothing. I chopped shallots and mushrooms and fried them quickly with lardons and plenty of black pepper. I stirred in crème fraîche and waited for water to boil for spaghetti. I mixed the sauce and pasta, threw in a raw egg, sprinkled Parmesan and gorged a big bowlful. It wasn't quality but at least there was quantity, and with a similar amount left in the pan I wouldn't have to think about making food for the rest of the day. I finished the grapefruit juice.

I sat down on my bed and indulged myself in the fantasy of letting my life go to ruin. I'd like to let everything fall apart and become a tramp, and live in the street and die from hypothermia one winter's night in a couple of years. I cleaned the kitchen sink and washed the floor. Next, I scrubbed the toilet, the shower, and the bathroom floor. I got out the vacuum cleaner and whisked round the apartment. In the living room, Butterfly's computer was watching me. I turned it on and looked in the 'My Brain' folder.

I drank half a bottle of pastis to get myself drunk, but rather than achieve the cloudy abandon I so desired, I passed directly to the hangover I knew I'd regret before I even started. Now it is 3:20 a.m. and my head is throbbing, I recommend consuming more than just yogurt before hitting the hard liquor. An unlit cigarette hangs from my lips. To my left is a tumbler still containing a healthy couple of fingers, to my right an ashtray, between the two, my loquacious hands flutter on the keyboard. Hrrrrr.

I write out of habit, Ben Constable, much like people who talk just to hear their own voices. This is not for you, today you are just the named outlet valve for my brain, an imaginary person to listen to my wandering thoughts.

If I should die and you should live . . . I can't sleep. I keep dropping off, sitting, standing, and the sandman comes to give me dreams, but I recognize him. He is the reaper come to take me, and I wake in fear because, for all I long for death, I run from it like the coward I am. I drink in the hope of one day finding the courage to let go.

If I should die and you should live and time should gurgle on . . . my head nods involuntarily, and as my consciousness slides the image of a place comes to mind. I wonder whether you know it. As you walk down from Gambetta there is a small leafy island, where many roads meet. One of them runs down alongside Père Lachaise and two rise steeply, then drop off, cutting their continuation from view so you could imagine anything over their horizon, plunging cliffs or the sea. And there he is, the sandman standing, calling me, and my body spasms back to life with a jolt. To the right there used to run a street called rue de la Cloche (which, as you know, means bell). The eponymous cloche is not from a church, nor does it toll from the nearby cemetery, it is a dome hollowed out beneath the ground where the bedrock has been dissolved by subterranean streams. They demolished the street and its neighbors to prevent it subsiding. I'm sure there is a lesson to be learned there.

If I should die and you should live and time should gurgle on, and morn should beam and noon should burn as it has usually done . . . Emily Dickinson has infected my brain (although I can't remember the rest of that particular poem). Oh, Emily Dickinson, what have you done to me? Look at me holed up writing diaries and letters and hiding from the world. Is this what you would have had me become? Who am I kidding that I could sit around writing and regain my innocence like trying to regrow virginity? I do not measure up to my literary heroes. Maybe that's why I turned bad. Maybe that's why I must die and life can carry on much better without me. I only hope that there is no eternity. To think that we would have to forever live and never cease to be.

It's still 3:20 a.m. and I don't know whether stopped time exists to impede my coming fate or to emulate it. Did you know that Paris has many stopped clocks? There is the clock in the form of a dragon-slaying knight in the Quartier de l'Horloge—its two faces do not agree on the moment at which time should stand still. Another favorite is the clock hidden behind the church of Notre-Dame de Bonne Nouvelle in the Sentier. And as you open the box of my delights after my demise, you will see many stopped clocks. Which reminds me of my mission before these words so rudely interrupted it. I need to find places to hide things for you. What have we got? Stopped clocks? Places from dreams. Hmmm . . . I have an idea.

I'm going to stop writing. I feel happy to be hanging out with my imaginary you, but there are things to do to avoid self-pity and that terrifying sandman calling me to sleep, but I will not come, no, not yet.

This was a bit like a letter addressed to me that had never been sent. I wondered how many pieces of writing like this could exist somewhere in the world. I stretched out on the sofa and the sandman came to haunt me for the umpteenth time that weekend. It was Sunday evening. I had the opposite problem to Tomomi Ishikawa. I had spent no more than ten hours awake since I got home from work on Friday.

Early-morning grey shone through the curtains. I could hear rain so I left them closed. I ate the rest of yesterday's carbonara cold from the pan and I wished I'd saved some grapefruit juice. I thought of going back to bed, but there were insistent questions I wanted answers to. Where was Tomomi Ishikawa's body? Had she committed seppuku and was she lying in a bloody mess somewhere? Who else knew about this and how could I contact them? I checked her email again. There were another ten unread messages from nobody of interest. Then I checked my own email.

There were twenty-two new messages, including three from my work which I thought best to ignore, seeing as it was Monday and I hadn't gone in and my phone was off (I would ring up later and tell them I was sick). One of the messages was from Tomomi Ishikawa posted at 18.24 on Friday. That's the time that I was coming out of the metro on my way home, a few minutes before I received her letter. A few minutes before everything changed. It said:

> Here is a Parisian enigma for you: How do you walk from
> rue du Faubourg Montmartre to the Palais Royal on a rainy
> day without getting wet? (Et in Arcadia ego.)
>
> B. X O X

Something was wrong. I got out Friday's letter and scanned through to check. And it was there, clear as day: *'By the time these pages find your hands I will have been dead for a few hours.'* These pages had found my hands on Friday at six thirty-something, and the email was sent on Friday at six twenty-four. Not possible. Tomomi Ishikawa was dead when she sent that message. That left four possibilities:

1. Tomomi Ishikawa was not dead when she sent the
   email. Maybe there had been some kind of delay and

she wasn't able to kill herself at the exact moment she had planned. Or the sword had somehow missed her vital organs and she was busily recovering in hospital.

2. Somebody else had sent it, either by Tomomi Ishikawa's explicit instruction or by the person's own volition, pretending to be Butterfly.

3. There was some kind of delay either with my email account or with hers.

4. By supernatural force Tomomi Ishikawa had sent me a message from beyond the grave.

I couldn't stop my brain racing. What if Tomomi Ishikawa was not dead? Why would she have lied to me? What if she was in trouble? Maybe there was a clue in her writing that only I could decipher, and I should go and save her or at least get help? Maybe she was trying to make a fool of me or hurt me. Perhaps she just didn't like me. I opened the curtains and looked out at the steady strings of falling water. I needed to stop my brain from thinking. Sudden and immediate sleep was one option, but I was getting bored of sleep.

I put on my shoes and coat, then took the metro to Grands Boulevards and walked up rue du Faubourg Montmartre in the pouring rain. A few hundred yards on the left I found the entrance to Passage Verdeau. I had been here before, with Tomomi Ishikawa. The grey light shone dimly through the glass-panelled ceiling. It was a sleepy and lonely place. I came out the other end, dashed across rue de la Grange Batelière and went into Passage Jouffroy. Yellow lights shone from the shops that were open, their

windows filled with ancient objects. Others were closed or unoc-
cupied. A handful of damp tourists had ducked in, sheltering from
the rain. They stared at the entrance to the waxworks museum.
They were the only other people in Tomomi Ishikawa's tiny covered streets. Back at the boulevard, I crossed and went into Passage des Panoramas. That Paris, in all its imperial grandeur, should
have a shabby selection of arcades, small and fading, is something
I love. The world of money has not yet managed to make everything fit the mould of success.

I came out at another street but there was no entrance opposite to go down. I would have to choose left or right on open-
topped streets. The rain was starting to soak through my clothes.
Galleries Vivienne (the most glamorous Parisian arcade) was the
next covered street I could think of in this direction but it was a
fair way off. How do you walk from rue du Faubourg Montmartre
to Palais Royal without getting wet? Take an umbrella, I guess.
Which reminded me that I had just passed an umbrella shop. I
walked back through the twilit street and the rain drummed heavily on the glass roof until I came to the tiny shop offering restored
vintage umbrellas and a repair service. A bell sounded as I opened
the door.

A woman with messy brown hair stood up. 'Bonjour,' she said,
as a reflex and then, 'Oh, hello.' She sounded surprised.

'Hello,' I said, unsure how she could know I spoke English.

'Hold on a second,' she said, with just the faintest of accents.
She rummaged under the counter and produced an umbrella-
shaped package and handed it to me. 'This is for you.'

I was so taken aback that I couldn't speak for a couple of seconds. 'I think you've mistaken me for someone else.'

'Oh.' She hastily pulled the umbrella-shaped package back towards her. 'I'm sorry, I thought you were Ben Constable.'

'I am Ben Constable.' I was kind of plaintive and confused.

'Your American friend said you would look through the window one rainy day and that if I spotted you I should give you this.' She held out the umbrella again and smiled.

'But I don't want an umbrella.' I didn't mean to be rude, but I seemed to have been reduced to expressing just the most basic of ideas.

'It's paid for. It's yours.'

'I don't understand. Have we met already?'

'No. She showed me a picture of you. That's how I knew what you would look like.'

She smiled at me politely and I hesitantly took the package and tore through the paper. There was a full-length wooden-handled umbrella, and a card with my name on it.

'When was she here?' I asked.

'Last week. Thursday, I think,' said the woman.

I opened the envelope and there was a sheet of notepaper with a quickly scribbled message in block capitals:

THIS IS TO KEEP YOU DRY AS YOU DASH BETWEEN
ARCADES ON YOUR WAY TO THE PALAIS ROYAL, OR ON
ANY RAINY-DAY EXCURSION YOU CARE TO TAKE. NOW,
HERE IS ANOTHER RIDDLE: WHICH TELLS THE TIME
MORE PRECISELY, A CLOCK THAT IS A MINUTE FAST, OR
ONE THAT HAS STOPPED?

Easy. The clock a minute fast never tells the right time. The stopped clock is exactly right twice a day. The clock on the wall in Butterfly's apartment was where I needed to look.

I climbed the narrow wooden stairs and knocked on Tomomi Ishikawa's door, then, without waiting, put the key in and turned it. Cat wasn't with me; that was OK. Before I could even see inside I could hear that the acoustics had changed.

The stopped clock was not on the wall. There was no note for me on the table. There was no table. There were no chairs. In the bedroom there was no chest of drawers, no mirror, there was nothing in the built-in cupboards, there was no bed. There were no plants and no pictures on the walls. There were no books on the shelves, and no shelves. The fridge was empty, but at least there was still a fridge. There was no fruit, no fruit bowl, there was no towel in the bathroom and the shower tray was dry. The apartment was completely empty. I hadn't expected that.

4

Tomomi Ishikawa's Dead

'You look like a lady,' I said, inviting myself to sit at a table with a woman drinking red wine and scribbling on loose sheets of notepaper. She was almost certainly Tomomi Ishikawa, but I couldn't be totally sure.

'Oh, hey,' she said, leaning forwards to kiss my cheeks, 'I am a lady.' It was definitely her.

'You ain't no lady,' I said, and we both laughed. 'But you're all dressed up and wearing makeup. I didn't recognise you.'

'I felt like a change.' She dismissed me, but I wasn't satisfied.

'You don't normally feel like dressing up like a lady, though. What's wrong?'

'I'm bored of being me,' she said. I felt triumphant having extracted the truth. 'I want to reinvent myself.'

'OK. But I quite liked you before,' I said. 'I mean, I like you now as well, even though I don't really know the reinvented

you yet, but I'm sure you're very nice. I'm just saying that
I thought you were very nice before. I shall miss the old
you.'

She was silent and just stared at me and I saw her eyes
were full of tears. I turned to catch the attention of the man
known affectionately to Tomomi Ishikawa as Our Waiter and
ordered a beer. She lit a cigarette.

'I don't understand,' I said. 'Why do you want to reinvent
yourself?'

She sighed. 'When I look at my life, and everything that's
happened, I want it all to not exist. I've done nothing I'm
proud of. I want to start again from scratch and be different.'

On Monday, March 19, 2007, I abandoned Tomomi Ishikawa. The
empty apartment was a merciless assault on my friendship, not a
wake-up call or a slap across the face; I was held down and beaten,
then forced to watch as something simple and precious was ripped
from my loving protection. Tomomi Ishikawa had destroyed something of mine and my only possible revenge was to forget her and
live on. On Tuesday, March 20, I got up and went to work. I didn't
think about stopped clocks or hidden mysteries. My mind no longer absently queried the whereabouts of Tomomi Ishikawa's body
or how she'd killed herself. It was over.

Curiously it didn't take a lot of effort. I worked in the day,
spent my evenings with friends and went home drunk most nights.
The spring came and went and Paris disappeared off on holiday to
the coast. My work shut down for a month and I found myself
alone and sober with nothing to do.

I was fresher in the mornings. I cooked proper meals and read
books in the afternoon, stretched out with warm air blowing in

through the open window. Cat showed up now and then. He lounged and dozed in the sun and I started doing the same, sleeping whenever I felt like it. If I had been running from something, I had caught up with myself and I started to suspect that I was happy.

Then one day in August my computer broke. I switched it on and the screen was blue and nothing I did could make it work. It wasn't the worst thing in the world. I didn't use it for much and anything important was backed up on an external hard drive, but now that it was gone I wanted it. I could have had it repaired but it was old and the keys stuck and the fan rattled. I had the money for a new one. But there was Tomomi Ishikawa's shiny laptop gathering dust, standing on its side against my bookcase. Perhaps it was the right time. Perhaps I was ready to admit the memory of Butterfly back into my life.

I lifted the lid and turned on her computer.

I made a new folder for my things and opened a new file to write in and let my fingers do the remembering.

'So, what would you like in your new life?' I asked Tomomi Ishikawa.

'Money,' she said. I was disappointed but pretended not to be.

'And do you have a surefire moneymaking scheme?'

'No, not really. I thought I could start by dressing better and doing my hair and nails to see whether it brought in some cash.'

'You mean like becoming a prostitute?'

'No, but money attracts money, so perhaps you have to act like you've got it in order for it to come to you.'

'I see,' I said. 'Maybe. But perhaps it would be good to have a plan B that involves you being slightly more proactive.'

'Like what?'

'Er, robbing a bank.' She laughed like someone who didn't find me funny but was trying to be polite. 'And bank robbery is great for reinvention because so long as you don't manage to pull off the perfect job (and with us running the show that would almost certainly be the case), the feds'll be looking for you everywhere, so you'd be obliged not to keep any of your old life. You can't go to any of your usual places or be in contact with anybody you know.'

'That sounds good,' she said with a definite lack of enthusiasm.

'The bad thing is that afterwards you'll only have me to hang out with.'

'Who says that you're not part of the past I'm trying to get rid of?'

I stopped in my tracks. I hadn't considered that I could be part of anybody's problem. And if I was, why the hell was she meeting me for a drink? I decided that she was rude.

'Fuck you.'

'Sorry,' she said.

'You didn't have to meet me. I've got better things to do than come and have you say I make you feel bad.'

'No, I'm really sorry. I didn't want to make you feel like that. I've got so many doubts at the moment. You're the only person I can tell this kind of stuff to. It just came out wrong.'

'OK,' I said, and took a big swig of my beer.

'I wouldn't normally want to rob a bank,' she said, 'but it

would be fun with you.' She was backtracking. 'What would you do with your share of the money?'

I wasn't sure whether I wanted to play anymore. 'I'd buy a boat,' I said. It's like playing word association. You don't think about the answer; you just say whatever comes out of your mouth.

'And live a life of luxury on the Riviera?'

'No, I'd be a pirate.'

'Oh, you could have an eye patch and wear a tricorne hat!'

'Don't be stupid. It's not a fancy-dress party. I'd be the laughingstock of the pirating community. This is the twenty-first century.'

'You're right,' she said. 'But I just liked the idea of you having an appropriate costume. Oh, wait wait wait . . .'

'What?'

'You'll be able to have lots of women of different nationalities.'

'What, thirty?'

'At least thirty. You'd have a woman in every port and then occasional affairs with feisty maidens on the boats that you pillage, who fall for your mean pirating ways and bad manners.'

'Do I have bad manners?'

'I'm sure you could learn some.' I couldn't help smiling. 'Sorry. I guess I'm not always very sensitive,' I said.

'What?'

'Saying that you looked like a lady.'

'Ben Constable, you are a problem because I can tell you stuff, and that's a bit like feeding my own misery.

Sometimes you just ignore me and talk about stupid things like robbing banks, which is good. My shit needs ignoring, not nourishing.'

'But you have to deal with your shit as well. I guess it's about timing.'

'I'd love to tell you all my shit sometime, but . . .'

'But then you'd have to kill me?'

'Something would have to give.'

'Maybe we should plan a bank robbery instead. Can we dig a tunnel?'

'Hey, Paris is full of tunnels,' she said. 'There might be one already there we could use.'

I stopped writing and got up and stretched, then looked in the fridge for something to snack on. I sat down, crunching on a raw carrot, and started looking through the computer. Like a big, dark magnet, the folder called 'My Dead' drew me towards it. I clicked on a folder called 'Stranger'. Inside there was a single file dated 09-11-2001. I double-clicked.

This story is a secret. You can't have it just like that. There's a time for everything. First you have to follow the clues, then you find the treasure.

I went into Butterfly's 'My Paris' folder and clicked on the file called 'Time for Everything'. It talked about a statue at Saint-Lazare made out of stopped clocks. I knew that statue. I'd seen it before. I dug out the envelope from the umbrella shop with the riddle. The first time I'd thought of the statue, but Butterfly's apartment had seemed a more probable hiding place and I had dismissed the statue as unimportant. Now I knew something was hidden there for me.

I came out through the glass-domed entrance to the metro and into the Cour de Rome. The roll-down shutters were half-closed over the archways into the station and I guessed that meant it was about to shut for the night. I passed near the statue of the suitcases, then as I came into the Cour du Havre I could see the sculpture I was looking for— about four metres tall, from its base a single finger pointed upwards made from a hundred institutional clock faces, frozen randomly to misinform train passengers and other passing traffic. The odd car pulled up at the lights and then moved on as they turned to green. I sat waiting on a bench, looking at the clocks. I didn't know what I was waiting for. And then Cat turned up.

'Hello, Cat,' I said, and he sat and looked at me for a moment and then circled the statue and stopped and rested back on his hind legs, looking up as though he thought he could jump onto the concrete plinth.

'Don't be silly, Cat. You can't jump that high.'

He jumped and managed to get his front paws onto the top, pulled himself up in one reasonably deft movement, and then sat down looking back at me. I stood up and walked over.

'I don't even know which clock to look at, Cat. There must be a hundred. And if I start climbing to the top of the statue, I'll get arrested. Besides, I'll never get up the bottom bit. I'm too old and tired and my bones ache.'

Cat looked at me, unimpressed. A few feet above his head was a clock that said twenty past three. It was tucked away with its back to the street. It didn't look like a very easy place to hide something, but as Sherlock Holmes may once have said, 'When you have eliminated the impossible, whatever remains, no matter how improbable, must be the truth.' Had I eliminated the impossible?

I looked around. There had to be something—like a wheelie bin—to stand on to make things easier. There was nothing. Fuck it. I stretched and rolled my neck. I hadn't climbed anything since childhood.

I reached up and got my fingers on the top of the plinth. I tried pulling and could get my feet off the ground.

'Oh Cat, I can't be bothered. Even if I get up, how do I get down? I can't believe that Butterfly would be capable of climbing this thing, anyway.'

Cat stood up and kissed my fingers.

'Can you at least watch to make sure nobody is coming?'

I could hear cars pulling up at the lights, but I didn't have a direct view of them so I presumed that they couldn't see me. The concrete pushed into my fingers and I pulled and got my elbows up and then a leg. *Great. What the hell do I do now?* I could feel myself slipping back and had images of falling seven feet onto my arse. I grabbed one of the clocks and it didn't fall off. I felt bad; I didn't want to damage the statue. With a big heave and some precarious balancing, I was suddenly sitting up. I raised my hand and there, stuck almost invisibly behind the three twenty clock, was a neat layer of black duct tape. I peeled it off and there was a brown envelope placed in the middle of the underside of the tape. Inside the envelope was a notebook. On the cover it said 'Stranger' and inside it was filled with blue handwriting. I put the sticky bundle in my pocket and lowered myself down, scraping the skin from my forearm and grazing my legs. I held up my hands to help Cat, but he moved to my side and jumped down on his own.

'Quick, let's get out of here,' I said, and we ran.

5

Stranger (?–2001)

It's difficult to put a date on it. It could have been the day I was born, or the day I lost my first tooth. Maybe it was the day I broke my heart. (Notice that I hold no one else responsible for this act of barbarism; I did it myself because I wanted to know what it would feel like. The curious thing is that when it happened I recognized the sensation; my heart had been broken a hundred times already.) Maybe it was the day that Daddy died, or when my best friend (who was also my nanny) died too. Maybe it was the day I lost my virginity, or who knows which of a thousand other potential candidates? But by the evening of the day of this story I had been dead a long time. My body was just an empty shell as I watched the tens of thousands, or even millions of flickering lights blown out all over the city as people felt the impact of the meaninglessness of their existence; understood that they would never change the world and that their highest hopes could be shattered, dreams and beliefs crushed and disposed of like an unwelcome insect, because life has no value in this city. If it did, the loss would be too painful and no one wants to be in pain.

And the ashes of the dead fell down on us like snow. Death was on the sidewalk and in the street, drifting up Broadway on the warm air and settling on the windowsills of Upper West Side apartment blocks, forming thick layers of dust on the roofs of cars, and in our hair as we walked aimlessly, spectators or voyeurs into intimate moments of doubt and incomprehension of the people we passed.

And now that I write it down, I realize the futility. To think that by putting it on paper I might get some kind of relief, or recognize in myself a trace of the humanity I doubt I ever had. There is no salvation in these pages, just a grim record of a curiously interesting day. It was perhaps on that day we found the justification we'd been searching for all our lives (or nonlives) for the fuckups that we are. Now there was a good excuse. We would never recover and that was acceptable, but the truth was darker, the truth was that we had never wanted to recover anyway.

By the end of the afternoon I couldn't stay inside anymore so I moved out onto the streets, leaving my footprints in the dust. I followed the Hudson, ebbing uptown, hoping I might find a world where life continued, but there was no avoiding the casualty in the stunned faces of all I passed, limping along the sidewalks of this ghost town. And I envied the dead, blowing over my head. I decided to head downtown and feed my curiosity. Anything near the water felt too exposed, so I cut inland and zigzagged down and to the east.

When I arrived at Tompkins Square Park, dusk was diluting the colors and the world was becoming flat. I sat on a bench near Avenue B and stared at nothing until a man walked by with long strides. He was unlike the rest of New York. Something didn't fit, as though this was not his day. And I would have let him go (another passing ghost) because all I wanted was a little distraction, but he looked at me as he walked by and caught my eye. It seemed that he was wandering for no other reason than to be moving. I would have liked to say something, exchange a sign of complicity, a nod of recognition, but by the time I had found the courage to speak he had moved too far ahead. I would have had to raise my voice, and in the shadows he wouldn't have been able to see my face. Besides, I didn't know what to say. So I got up and walked behind him at a distance.

The light had gone and in the shadow of the trees, flakes of orange streetlight spread out, dappling the ground. I caught an occasional glimpse of the half-moon slowly waning. And I dragged my feet a little so as not to trip or be caught out by a sudden step. He walked down to Houston and crossed over onto Clinton Street, then doglegged at Delancey, still heading south. He cut between two buildings and some trees along another street and we were on East Broadway. He never slowed and he never turned his head. I tried to make my footsteps sound unthreatening. He cut down to the tower blocks by the East River but I didn't falter in my stalking (although I closed some ground so as not to feel alone). He weaved his way left and right, disappearing and then coming back into view as I turned each corner. I kept looking over my shoulder to check where the river was, and not lose my sense of direction. He was walking in circles. I rounded the corner of one of the brown towers and he was nowhere. Gone. I didn't flinch or change my pace. I just walked straight toward the Manhattan Bridge, which was looming above me.

"Why are you following me?" he whispered, and I jumped. He was standing four feet away in a doorway, calm and curious.

"What?"

"You've been following me since Tompkins Square. What do you want?"

"Nothing," I said, and walked off toward the bridge.

For a moment he was uncertain, as though that might be the end of it. I could feel his eyes on me as I moved away. After twenty yards he called out quietly, "Wait," and I stopped and turned as he walked with feigned ease to catch me up, stopping a few yards from me to keep a respectful distance.

"Why are you walking on your own?" he asked.

"For the same reason as you," I said, and he looked briefly perplexed that I could know why he was walking.

"Where are you going now?" he asked.

"I don't know."

There was silence and I felt powerful. I turned and started walking again, but after a few steps I stopped and looked back. He hadn't moved.

"Are you coming?" I said.

He smiled and kind of skipped toward me and we walked on, but now I was leading and at every junction he watched to see which way I would choose, never voicing a preference. We headed toward city hall and then turned onto the Brooklyn

Bridge. We strolled like lovers on an evening promenade with our backs to the city. We didn't speak and neither of us turned our heads to look at Manhattan until we were well between the towers of the bridge. Then we stopped and leaned on the iron barrier and stared. We could see the dust cloud drifting in the night. The bridge felt vulnerable; I guess everybody had the same sensation. Nonetheless, there were occasional silent figures walking; some stopped and prayed, a couple of others were taking photographs. We went as far as Fulton Street Mall, but Manhattan kept calling and so we almost U-turned, doubling back on Jay Street toward the Manhattan Bridge and its caged walkway, almost back to the place he had waited for me in the doorway. We meandered without speaking, cutting left here and right there, and passed people drunk in the street and a small group breaking up a fight. I started to feel my feet aching. I'd been walking for hours. Eventually, we came to Union Square. Hundreds of people had gathered with candles.

"Let's get out of here," I said, a sickly feeling growing in my stomach. "Take me anywhere," I was saying with my body language. "I'll go wherever you go." I wasn't counting the blocks, I couldn't even remember what direction we were walking, and then we entered a building and were standing in an elevator, staring straight ahead. He took a key and opened the door to an apartment. The place was spacious and modern, well thought out, tidy; it was a man's apartment.

"Do you live alone?" I asked.

"Yes." He opened a cupboard and then slumped down on the sofa with a bottle of whiskey and two glasses.

"Can I use the bathroom?" I asked, and he pointed to a

door and then stared at the table and the whiskey. When I came back in the room, he was standing by the window, looking over the top of nearby buildings, toward the East River. He'd poured himself a generous glass and there was a similar-sized one on the table for me. I picked up the glass and stood not too close. We were high up.

"By the time the second plane hit I was on the roof, watching with everybody else in the building," I said, half spilling my mind and half making small talk. "When I looked around I could see people on all the other rooftops doing the same as me. I could hear the people next to me whispering, 'Oh my God,' over and over."

He went and slouched on the sofa. I stayed by the window.

"I was meant to meet my ex-wife in her office in the North Tower. She'd hooked me up to freelance for one of her clients. The meeting was supposed to be at nine but I told her I'd be there early so we could get a coffee. I spent ten minutes driving around, looking for somewhere to park, then gave up and went to a lot on John Street. When I came out, there were sirens and police blocking off the road. I was trying to call her on my cell, but I couldn't get the network. I waited until the first tower fell and then ran with everybody else. I couldn't get back to my car and now I can't remember what level I parked on."

"Have you heard from her?"

"She's dead, I think."

It was like a strange piece of modern theater. He walked back to the window, closer to me this time, and I didn't flinch.

"When I was out walking, it hit me."

"What did?" I asked.

"Everything I had been doing was about building a life, changing a life, starting again, turning the page. Carrying on toward this undefined goal. Pursuing my dreams."

"Yes."

"I don't think I'm going to carry on now. It seems like too much effort."

"I know what you mean. Today it all seems much clearer." He wanted to think I'd understood him, and maybe I had.

God knows how we ended up in bed. I can't plot the exact moves like chess: man's hand to woman's hip. Woman's hand takes man's hand. Check. I like to think he was the one who did the work, but I didn't make it difficult, maybe I even made sure it happened. And suddenly I wonder whether in fact it is important. I'd presumed not, but now I'm not so sure.

It was no intense or passionate experience. Our clothes peeled off listlessly, lustlessly. There was no emotion or explosive orgasms, just slow, rhythmic sex; vacuous, and wholly appropriate. We lay staring at the ceiling. And then I looked at him. I clicked my fingers in front of his open eyes and he blinked. I sat up and turned around to face him, kneeling like a geisha. I picked up a pillow and his eyes settled on me, but his expression didn't change. I pushed the pillow down onto his face, gently at first, but then harder, holding my hands firmly in place, pressing hard on his mouth and nose. He didn't move or try to resist, he just lay there still and let me suffocate him. I held on, resting my full weight over his mouth and nose. Minutes went by. Black liquid pumped through my veins and glorious darkness exploded behind my eyelids, filling me, as it does, warming and comforting.

This is the last time I do this, I thought. *We both got what we needed.*

He remembered playing hide-and-seek as a child. He was small enough to fit into the linen cupboard in his grandmother's house. He loved the smell of the dry cotton as he curled up like the cat did. It would lie there all day, happy as can be on the piles of clean sheets and towels. Only when Grandma opened the door would it raise an eyebrow, then run off before it could be dragged out by the scruff of the neck or she could say "Shoo!" Yes, he was like the cat in the linen cupboard. It was a good hiding place. It smelled good. He closed his eyes.

6

Tomomi Ishikawa's Paris

Tomomi Ishikawa and I had spoken many times about writing. We talked about plot and structure, choice of words, about pace and voice for hours into drunken evenings. But it had always been about my writing, my excitement or concern over putting words on paper, not hers. I had never considered that Tomomi Ishikawa might be a writer as well. I should have guessed from her emails, recognised it in her syntax. I felt uncomfortable that she had never felt the need to mention it. The rhythm of her words echoed in my head and my mind was racing.

Did Butterfly kill that man? Is that what I just read? Is this the factual account of what she did on September 11, 2001, or a fantasy where events bleed into one another and death seeps through the delicate barrier separating truth and construction, and into the imagination? Did Tomomi Ishikawa kill someone? It seems an important question, but it drifted downstream to be catalogued under unsolved curiosities, and my mind was already flitting to other things.

The clue to the notebook about killing a stranger had come from the writing about Saint-Lazare. The walk in the rain through the arcades came from the 'My Paris' folder as well. Maybe her computer was the starting point for all the clues in her treasure hunt. It seemed almost disappointingly easy, but the moment had come to check out the rest of the things she'd written about Paris.

And as I clicked my way through the files, Butterfly talked about streets, architects and artists. She knew where to find bars where poets had drunk and lodgings of authors I had never heard of. She had collected a museum of knowledge on Paris, unexpected histories and hiding places, the colours and smells, the way the light came down in the afternoon. Was this a guidebook? Or was this to be an education for me, who admittedly knows nothing of the city where I live and walks with eyes closed, observing little more than the thoughts in my own head?

And now I wanted to walk with her. I wanted to hear her voice drone on, telling facts that would drift in one ear and then effortlessly and completely out of the other seconds later, leaving just a memory of the sound.

Belleville/Ménilmontant

Belleville is an area in the east of Paris that has traditionally housed workers and various waves of immigrants. It was constructed on Paris's second-largest hill and stretches from the park of Buttes Chaumont in the north to Père Lachaise cemetery in the south. It was an independent town until 1860, when it was annexed by the expanding city of Paris, which took care to divide it over four arrondissements

for fear of its militant community spirit. Nonetheless it has
managed to maintain a unique sense of neighborhood
identity, and when the Commune of Paris briefly became
independent from France in 1871, the barricades of Belleville
and the incorporated neighborhood of Ménilmontant were
the last to fall against the state's reconquering army.

Despite having been adopted by artists and those
attracted to bohemian living, modern-day Belleville has thus
far resisted gentrification. It is culturally diverse with large East
Asian and North African populations and woven with narrow
cobbled streets that dip and rise and that host workshops,
bars, performance spaces, commerce, houses and gardens as
tokens of pride for its community riches and mementos of its
small-town past. The low level of many of the buildings (as
opposed to the six-story Haussmannian façades of much of
the rest of the city) is largely dictated by ground instability due
to natural subterranean waterways and consequent erosion.
Additionally, the area was heavily mined, leaving a maze of
tunnels, although, unlike the networks beneath the streets of
the Left Bank, those of Belleville have been rendered virtually
inaccessible through a program of structural reinforcement.

I thought of all the names of streets in the area that refer to water,
like rue des Cascades and rue des Rigoles. But if this was a clue, I
had no idea where to start looking. Although the next file I clicked
on seemed more likely to yield treasure.

Improbable Gardens

Paris's dense structure has left little room for private
gardens. But nature has a way of pushing through in the midst

of intense urban development and Paris has become home to a fine array of improbable green spaces. Some have been redeveloped into the infrastructure as afterthoughts, like the wonderful Jardin Atlantique on the roof of Gare Montparnasse, or the Promenade plantée (also known as the Coulée verte): a disused railway with viaducts, cuttings, and tunnels running from Bastille to the Bois de Vincennes, the length of which has been converted into a walkway with trees, shrubbery, benches, cycle paths, and even wireless Internet access. Some of the most improbable gardens are the work of individuals, like pendulous jungles dripping down buildings from balconies or window pots. There are also community gardens that sprout from vacant lots, filled with the aromas and colors of whatever fancies the residents choose to cultivate. Papilles et Papillons (Tastebuds and Butterflies) sits on terraces on Paris's steepest slope, rue Gasnier-Guy in the 20th arrondissement. Then a short walk up the hill, you reach the Jardin des Soupirs ("sighs" or "sweet nothings," depending on the translation you prefer), where there is little more satisfying than to sit and contemplate the day as the walls reflect the rose-colored light of the setting sun.

I felt slightly jealous of Butterfly for knowing these places when I did not. It was as though I had not engaged in my responsibility to explore the place I lived in, but she had learned of secret things and somehow gained value or privilege for her curious wanderings. But then Tomomi Ishikawa had had an unusual relationship with the city.

'I love Paris,' she told me once.

'Yeah, me too,' I said.

'No you don't.' Now she was accusing.

'Of course I do. I wouldn't live here if I didn't.'

'What, you love it like you want to kiss it?'

'OK, you're right. I don't love Paris after all.'

'I do,' she said. 'I want to kiss it and touch it and sometimes when nobody's looking I rub my body against it.' We both laughed raucously.

'Don't be stupid, you dirty girl, you'll scuff your clothes.'

Tomomi Ishikawa was generally funnier than I was, and generally more drunk too.

The next day I stayed in bed until eleven. After a bowl of cereal, I went on the Internet and looked at maps, trying to work out where the things Tomomi Ishikawa had talked about were, and the day drifted on as I skipped from one thought to another, allowing myself the luxury of not being in a rush for anything.

It was the second half of the afternoon by the time I got to Gambetta metro station near to the top of Père Lachaise cemetery. I wandered downhill a hundred yards and found myself at a leafy road junction, where my eye was drawn to two streets heading upwards that just disappeared as though they were on a cliff, falling away out of sight and into the sea. Surely I'd been here before, as a child maybe, or no, I was driving a car up that road, taking a shortcut. I had to remind myself that I had never had a car in Paris. This place was an image from a dream or my imagination. The right-hand of the two dream streets was rue Gasnier-Guy. I crossed at the traffic lights and walked up the hill, feeling light in my stomach as I reached the top, like driving quickly over a humpback bridge. I was almost disappointed to find just a steep decline and not a view of a hidden kingdom or some other magic. There

was a small terraced garden on the right-hand side. The sign on
the gate said 'Papilles et Papillons'. I stared through the railings for
a moment and then walked in. This was nothing like the slick
parks and manicured gardens around the city that I had come not
to notice. There was a mural on the wall and small plants with la-
bels. There was one big shrub with cones of hundreds of tiny purple flowers sticking out in all directions and two butterflies flitting
round it. I stood and watched for a second and then saw another,
no, four butterflies.

I crossed back over the road and walked up the steps that
would have once led to rue de la Cloche, the street that Tomomi
Ishikawa had said was demolished. This was the edge of her
territory. I was walking into her neighbourhood. Instead of the
old street there was another garden, new and soulless. I think it
had opened only weeks before. I guess gardens need years to mature. I carried on walking up to rue des Pyrénées and crossed,
looking out for the tiny stairway leading to Passage des Soupirs. I
went up the steps and fell in love with the narrow passage with
each of its buildings a different shape. Some modern boxy apart-
ments made from wood and older houses set back with over-
grown front gardens and other doors that opened directly onto
the street (if that's what you could call it—it was barely wide
enough for a car).

Jardin des Soupirs was on the right: long and narrow and
overshadowed by neighbouring buildings. The plants on either
side overhung the path and there were a couple of sheds with
printed memos on them that I didn't read, cupboards for storing
seeds and things, and a scarecrow. A man appeared to be repair-
ing some kind of gardening tool. He looked up at me and I smiled
as I walked between the miniature plots of flowers and herbs. I
walked past a purple wall with ivy growing up it and arrived at the

end, where a bench and some chairs waited in a small paved area. I sat down next to a pond made out of an old sink with tall, white-flowered reeds growing from it and I watched the afternoon sunlight reflect off the walls high above me. Two women approached, one of them pointing things out to the other. As they neared, the older woman knelt down and uprooted a couple of weeds. When she rose again, she smiled and said, 'Bonjour.'

'Bonjour, madame,' I said politely. 'He is magnificent your garden.'

'Thank you, but he belongs not to me. He is a community project. We are many neighbours who occupy ourselves with the garden.'

(We were speaking French.)

'Well, he truly is a marvel.' I smiled. I had nothing more to say, but she waited expectantly as though something in my tone of voice indicated that I had not yet finished. So I carried on.

'I especially love the plants in this small lake-type thing.' (The word for pond had momentarily escaped me.)

'Ah yes, they are beautiful, are they not? It is Monsieur Girault who has created this little corner. He will be delighted to know that it has so pleased you. Monsieur Girault?' She called up the garden to the man I had passed earlier. He was now ambling towards us. 'This monsieur was just praising your pond.' (I blushed, suddenly realising that I had all along known the word for pond.)

'A friend has spoken to me about your garden.' I felt shy and didn't really want to be talking to strangers. 'I am just passed by curiosity, and it makes a real pleasure. I am very happy to be come.'

'Thank you, thank you. And tell me how did your friend call itself?'

'Oh, she was an American who called herself, er, Butterfly.' Though it seemed a little informal to refer to her as Butterfly to a stranger, 'Tomomi Ishikawa' seemed more complicated than the conversation warranted.

The man frowned. 'And you are Mr . . . ?' he asked me.

'Constable. Ben Constable.'

'Philippe Girault.' He held out his hand and I shook it. 'Perhaps you would be interested to see a corner of flowers I have been tending these last few months for a friend absent. Please, follow me.'

I wasn't in the least bit interested in seeing his friend's flowers, but couldn't really refuse. I followed the man down a narrow stone path, through beds of herbs and wildflowers, to a brightly coloured patch. The man stopped.

'Here we are,' he said.

'Very good,' I said. And then, for fear of disappointing, I added. 'Really, very beautiful.'

'Perhaps I will leave you a moment to contemplate them,' he said, and stepped away, making his way back to the two women, where he spoke in a lowered voice. What was I supposed to be doing? Did they think I was some kind of travelling flower connoisseur?

Knowing nothing about plants, I was surprised at how many I could recognise. There were foxgloves and some tall daisies and snapdragons and flowers hanging from a shrub that I knew as dancing ladies. How did I know those names? After about fifteen seconds' intense contemplation, I decided to leave. I called over to the group, 'Thank you very much. Have a good rest of the day.' I waved and headed for the exit as fast as I could without seeming like I was trying to make a quick getaway.

'Wait, monsieur!' the man called after me. I stopped. And he moved hastily towards me. 'Monsieur, excuse me. I believe you have not yet finished regarding the flowers.'

'It's true?'

'Yes, look.' He held out his hand, directing me to look again at the flowers.

I looked down and stared very hard at the petals for nearly a minute. I had no idea how long would be enough to please him. Then I looked up questioningly.

'At the side of the plants is a tag saying the name of each one,' he offered.

I squatted down and looked closely at the plastic tags sticking out of the ground. The words were written in tiny letters in fading felt tip. All of them were Latin and had no more meaning to me than Martian words, but I silently mouthed them to show I was taking the whole thing seriously. One of the taller plants had a tag wrapped around the stalk. I carefully turned it so I could see the words: 'HELLO BC'.

I jumped slightly and said, 'Oh.' Then I turned the tag over and it said, 'What kind of plant would attract a butterfly?'

I looked up at the man and he was pleased with himself.

I started to speak and then stopped. 'You have seen this?' I asked.

'Yes,' said the man. I thought for a moment.

'You know Butterfly?' I said.

'Bof . . .' The man made a good-natured Gallic gesture, signalling that he had nothing to say on the matter.

'Do you know what kind of plants attract butterflies?'

'Yes, there is a plant called a buddleia. It's very common.'

'And do you have one here?' I asked.

'Sadly, no,' said the man.

'What does it look like?'

'Oh, it's a shrub with small purple flowers that make cones like this.' He showed me the size with his hands.

'Thank you,' I said. 'Thank you very much. I think I know where to find that.'

'What . . . ?' he said, and he gestured with his head to see whether I was thinking the same direction that he was (but without giving anything away if I didn't know).

'Exactly,' I said.

The man nodded at me and then turned and nodded at the women behind, who were watching the proceedings with great interest.

I walked along rue du Retrait and then went and sat on one of the low concrete bollards in Cité de l'Ermitage and lit a cigarette. This was the cobbled street where Tomomi Ishikawa and I had smoked late at night a couple of times. Then I walked down rue Ménilmontant and turned left towards a little square where there was a bar I liked.

When I left the bar it was dusk and I was a little drunk; that suited my purpose. I walked back up the hill towards Gambetta and found the dream street quite easily. When I got to 'Papilles et Papillons' I looked quickly left and right and climbed over the fence and ducked out of clear view. I took out my lighter to examine the butterfly plant with purple flowers. There was a tag on it confirming that it was definitely a buddleia, but there was no obvious clue or treasure. I scraped at the dirt in front of the base and then rummaged in my bag for something to dig with. All I could find was Butterfly's blue on/offable pen. It would do. I poked the soft earth and scraped until a few inches down I hit plastic and carefully uncovered a notebook-sized package.

7

Jay

A shadow or a movement in the corner of my eye is where Cat usually comes from. And as I closed the door to the apartment he skulked out of my peripheral vision towards me and jumped onto the work surface. I prepared food and then sat on a stool to eat and he pretended the buried package was a bird or a mouse (or whatever prey Cat likes to toy with before he kills it—probably much bigger things, like baby goats). I pushed it onto the floor and he looked at me and then down at the package. I picked it up again and opened it. There was a notebook inside and I read as I shovelled spaghetti into my mouth and Cat supervised.

> Jay Hara (1970–1998)
>
> I remembered Jay from my childhood. He was a distant relative of Komori, my nanny, and lived in Pasadena, CA, but for some reason he had come to New York for a few months when he was eight or nine. After that he was sent to Tokyo.

*Now at the age of twenty he had come back to New York
and my nanny asked me to look out for him. I was sixteen. His
real name was something Japanese that didn't sound like Jay at
all, but Jay was how he introduced himself, although my nanny
called him "Young Nephew," even to his face.*

*For the first few months, I made various efforts to see him.
He was short, skinny, and slightly uncomfortable in his gestures.
His hair was dyed light brown and his dress sense kind of
manga. He was obviously street smart but had incongruous
traits of Japanese body language and was a little camp. He
didn't fit in with the perfection-obsessed sixteen-year-old girls I
was hanging out with at the time, and neither did I particularly,
so I quickly worked out that it was easier to see him by myself. I
had presumed him to be little more than a not-unpleasant
obligation, but as he settled into New York life I was surprised to
observe that he found it easy to get along with people and he
quickly established a social scene with older artsy types who
treated him with respect, and I realized that I, as much as the
others around him, admired him. He had a dry and dark sense
of humor and in my sixteen-year-old eyes he was quite simply a
lot cooler than me. It was with slight regret that we gradually
lost contact for no particular reason.*

*Eight years later, I bumped into him in the New York Public
Library. He'd been working there since he'd arrived in New
York. I was embarrassed not to have known, but I felt genuinely
pleased to have found him again.*

*From then on we met up occasionally for coffees or
after-work drinks. He seemed to find me easier (and I guess I
had grown up a bit). He had filled out and came across as more
self-confident, yet I felt he had somehow deteriorated into*

something weaker since we had last spent time together. And as we talked I discovered he lived a cycle of an extreme manic depression, whisking him from dizzying heights to destructive lows and back again in the space of a few days. Our conversations became increasingly centered on his imagined woes, or embarrassing optimism. And so, for all the warmth of admiration I felt for him, I started to develop a taste of revulsion at his weakness.

The last couple of months of his life started with him disappearing. At first, this came as a relief from the frustration at not being able to help him. I hoped next time we spoke he would be a bit more stable and his company would be easier. But after six weeks without contact I became concerned. I called him several times, but there was no answer. So reluctantly I mentioned his disappearance to my nanny, who instructed me to go immediately to his apartment and report back to her.

He opened the door as if expecting me and turned back toward the kitchen, leaving me to let myself in and follow him through. He was unshaven, wearing powder-blue pajamas, and he smelled of alcohol. It was the first time I'd seen the apartment. It was a big, empty space and definitely not paid for on librarian wages. The décor wasn't so much minimalist as bare, as though he'd never really moved in. The living room was devoid of decoration and furnished solely with cardboard boxes along one wall and hundreds or maybe even thousands of books stacked on their sides in towers as tall as could remain balanced. There was a quilt slung on the floor and an open paperback lying spine-up next to it. I guess he had been reading before I arrived.

I sat on a foldable wooden chair at a makeshift table in the kitchen and lit a cigarette while he reheated old coffee in a pan on the stove. He looked in a cupboard to find cups, but there were none clean, so he rolled up his sleeves to wash a couple sitting in the half-full sink. His forearms were covered in neat, fine razor lines of self-harm.

"So, what's become of you, Jay?"

"Oh, you know, the usual."

"It's not usual that you disappear for six weeks," I said.

"No, I'm going through a bad patch at the moment, that's all."

"What kind of bad?" I asked.

"Oh, I don't know."

I paused for a moment, thinking. "Family?" I asked. "Work? Love? Health?"

"It doesn't matter what the subject is, Butterfly; I'll always find something. I'm infected with depression. It's a disease eating away at me and I'm going lower and lower."

"Have you been like this for a long time?"

"Years. I have ups and downs, but the ups are just a sign of how deep the lows will go to compensate and so are just as unbearable. I'm tired of this constant moving of mood; there's no rest."

"But I haven't seen you up for a long while."

"It's true. Even my ups are low these days. I'm stuck rotating in dark circles."

"What are you going to do? Have you got some kind of plan to help yourself?"

"Like what?"

"I don't know; you could go back to LA, or maybe you'd be happier in Tokyo."

"I'm just fine here, thank you."

"Or maybe you could see an analyst?"

"Not my thing, Butterfly."

"Couldn't you do exercise or take up a hobby?"

"Butterfly, shut up."

"Sorry." I stared at the floor.

"But, there's a strange thing that I've noticed."

"What?" I asked.

"I want it."

"Want what?"

"The depression. The self-hatred and doubt. The despair. The lust for death. I've become addicted to it and it's rich and delicious."

"Maybe you've actually gone mad."

"What the hell is sane, Butterfly?"

"Isn't it something to do with being able to function in a socially acceptable way and consider the value of those around you?"

"Who's to say the rest of the world isn't mad?"

"But maybe you could get help. They could give you drugs to stabilize you."

"My mother died in the asylum. Did you know that?"

"No, I didn't."

"They sent her there, my grandmother and your Komori, scheming witches, they sent her there to die, they murdered her."

That Komori could scheme was no surprise to me. But to speak badly of her was the biggest taboo. It could not be done. Jay knew this. It was as though he had insulted my religion. Nobody had ever spoken about Komori like this in front of me and I had to swallow sudden anger.

"I'm sure they sent her there for her own good," I said dryly. Perhaps Jay did have hereditary madness.

"Nobody can send me away, that's all I'm saying. I'm happy here in this sweet depression. And hopefully it will consume me alive and my body will putrefy from the inside out and I will dissolve in delightful pain, thick and sweet, and everything will become somber."

My mind raced. I was fascinated by the idea that somebody could lust for darkness; that he wanted to sustain it rather than to try to break the cycle. This rejection of the most basic value of happiness was against everything we had been programmed to believe in, yet it struck me as a fundamental reality. The rest of the world was indeed wrong and Jay was perhaps on the path to the ultimate and purest darkness. I could barely breathe. I recognized it. He was talking about something I already knew. I excused myself and told him I would return the next day.

"How is Young Nephew?"

"He's not well, Komori."

"What's wrong with him? Should we send Dr. Bastide around?"

"I'm not sure, Komori. I don't know that he needs that kind of help."

"Why? What kind of help does he need?" she asked.

"He's depressed," I said, and Komori's face stayed blank. I could never read her.

"Well, we all feel down sometimes, but you have to carry on. Life can't just stop because you don't feel happy. I have lived through war, lost my home, my country, outlived my parents, my sister, my niece and countless friends and been rejected by others. If I were to count the people I truly have left in the world, Butterfly, there would be only you. There are lots of reasons to be depressed. Life easily could have stopped, but you have to keep yourself together. Young Nephew knows this."

"It's not just that he feels bad. I don't think his depression is even linked to anything tangible. He's sick."

"Do you mean that he is mentally ill?" said Komori. "Perhaps he would be better off in the hospital."

"He said that his mother died in a hospital like that."

"It's true, may her soul have found peace. But these places are not what they were in those days."

"What days? When did she die?"

"The eighties."

"Oh my God, so recently."

"She had much difficulty, Butterfly."

"What happened?"

"She too was sick. We tried to help her. We tried to protect the family honor as she would have wished. One day I will tell you about it, Butterfly, and you will understand."

"She didn't die naturally, then."

"Dying with honor is part of nature's intention."

"Komori, I think he may want to die."

"Then he should be allowed to."

"I'm confused," I said. "The solution to sickness is surely not death. We should be looking for a way to bring him back to health."

"Nature has given us the power to make choices about our lives, and we choose dignity in death, Butterfly. That may be hard for those we leave behind, but we must support them even as they do honor to our memory of them."

"I don't really understand what you are talking about."

"I think you do, Butterfly. I think you have the gift of understanding. Death is one stage of nature's cycle. Knowing how to choose death, even in the most difficult of situations, is part of the art of living."

"So, should we leave him to suffer and then maybe die, or are you suggesting he commit seppuku?"

"I have something that I would like you to take to him," she said.

She slowly raised herself to her feet and glided to a drawer from which she drew a narrow object about a foot in length and wrapped in silk. I knew what was inside and for a second I was dizzy and my insides tingled. She passed it to me with both hands and bowed.

I went to visit Jay every day for the next two weeks, bringing him whiskey (he would accept nothing else). He always wore pajamas and always smelled of alcohol and a little of piss. His thin beard was becoming wild and his face gaunt. But somehow, through his tears, we started to laugh now and then; insane, raucous laughter. I wondered whether this was a sign of him pulling through. But he didn't want to pull through.

"I need to feel it, Butterfly. I need to go deeper." He focused and meditated on his emotional pain, nurturing his despair, but his only true worry was that he would become numb and the work he was doing would not achieve climax. I was his reality check, a way for him to gauge his descent. He was weak and trembled constantly. His hands and feet were covered in bruises and fine cuts. He'd stopped eating and as far as I was aware drank only coffee and whiskey. "I'm close, Butterfly," he told me. "I'm close."

On the last day, I went to his apartment after work. The
door was ajar (I guessed for me) and I let myself in. I could hear
him in the bathroom, muttering. I called out but he didn't
answer, so I smoked a cigarette, toying with a paper bag on the
table. It was an empty drugstore bag. I ripped the paper for the
pleasure of the sound and revealed a checkout ticket. It said:
"Double-edge SS Platinum Blades 10 Pack $4.69." Adrenaline
shot through my body and I jumped up and tried the bathroom
door. It opened and Jay was lying naked in the bathtub. From
one hand he dangled a bottle of whiskey over the side. There
were cigarette burns up his arms and on his body there were
blue marks of self-inflicted violence. But for all the shock and
nonunderstanding, he seemed to me like a holy man. He was
near to fulfillment. On the corner next to a lonely bar of soap
was the brand-new packet of old-fashioned razor blades. He
watched my eyes settle on them and said, "It's over, Butterfly. It's
over."

"What? Your beard?" I joked from nowhere.

"Ha-ha. No, it's over, Butterfly."

I paused. "Maybe you're right."

"I know I'm right."

"Not with those razor blades, though."

"Why not?"

I fetched my bag from the other room and carefully
unwrapped the silk from a ceremonial knife in a wooden
scabbard, inlaid with lighter-colored wood, gold and mother-of-
pearl. My heart raced in fear and excitement. I placed the knife
across both my hands and bowed to him. The humid air heaved
a sigh in awe.

"Thank you, Butterfly. Thank you a thousand times for

this." He lifted his hand to the knife, but he was shaking so much that he couldn't take it.

"Wait," I said. I had come equipped with a small box of diazepam. I pushed four pills out and put them in his mouth, then helped him lift the whiskey to swill them down. I should have left at that point, but I couldn't. We sat and waited as he became calm and my breathing became heavy and fast. Every inch of my skin was alert.

"Could you light me a cigarette, Butterfly?"

"Of course." I lit the cigarette and then held it to his mouth as he pulled down the smoke and then moved it away again between puffs. When he had finished, I handed him the knife again. He clasped it in one hand and tried to remove it from its scabbard, but his hands were weak and still trembled. I took it from him and swooned at the sound as it came out. My brain was blank and the silence deafening, throbbing with my heartbeat. I folded his fingers around the handle and pointed the tip of the blade to his belly.

"It might be easier if you were to sit up." My voice faltered. I didn't expect that. Something else was taking over.

"No, not through the gut, Butterfly. Please. It's too violent. I'm not a fucking samurai. The arms. You can do my arms; they don't mind the cuts."

"It's best that you do this, not me."

"Do you have any more of those pills?"

"I do, but you shouldn't have too many. They'll knock you out." Why was I still there?

"Oh please, Butterfly." Blood rushed behind my ears, filling my brain with gray noise.

I put two more pills in his mouth and poured whiskey in to help him swallow and he rested his head back, not quite calm.

"Maybe you are not ready for this, Jay." My mouth was dry.

"Oh, I am."

"There is no obligation. You don't have to do this to follow any tradition. You only do what you want to do."

"You cannot imagine how much I want this, Butterfly."

"I can't do it for you," I told him, but my fingers were tingling with hope he might let me.

He forced his eyes open and looked at me hard and then at the knife, as though willing it by psychic energy to his wrist. I clasped his fingers to make sure he had a firm grip on the knife, but his hand fell away, leaving the handle in mine. I offered up his inner arm and positioned it under the blade. My throat was aching now and my eyes began to overflow. My breathing was deep and fast. My stomach muscles were unsure whether to cramp or spasm, and my brain was bursting. He looked at me and nodded. I pushed the knife down hard and drew the blade sharp across his arm through the tendons and arteries, down to the bone. He hissed an in-breath (more from surprise than pain) and the blood flowed out of him thick and fast. I choked on the violence of my crying as it burst from me and I held myself up on my hands and knees on the floor.

"Thank you, Butterfly. Thank you a thousand times."

"This again." My words had no form as they sobbed from my mouth. Dark air filled my lungs and pain shot through my body.

He leaned his head back and watched the ceiling. I slid to the floor, sprawled out with my face down. Saliva spilled from *my mouth. In a few minutes he would be no more. No more conversations over coffee. No more loud laughter. There would be a void in his place. I wanted to stay where I was, but after a minute I forced myself, trembling, to my feet.*

"I have to go, Jay."

"Goodbye, Butterfly."

I kissed his head and my tears fell down onto him.
"Goodbye."

"Butterfly?"

"Yes?"

"Could you pass me the whiskey?"

"Yes." I picked up the bottle and lowered it onto his pocked belly (still intact). The knife fell into the water and he moved the nonbleeding arm toward the bottle so it wouldn't fall.

My crying had peaked and I could feel my body going back to normal more quickly than I would have imagined possible.

"Thank you, Butterfly. Thank you a thousand times."

"I'm going now. Goodbye, Jay." I was still crying, but I felt light and agile. Brand-new.

"Goodbye, Tomomi Ishikawa." He closed his eyes again and remembered the pretty young man with dark hair who used to come to the library every Thursday afternoon at three thirty; tall and always windswept, dressed in dark clothes. Jay would busy himself in the Rose Room, watch and anxiously wait for him. Always at three thirty on Thursdays, always at the southern end of that great reading room, and the man would take a book from his bag (always a different book, always fiction), and sit and read for an hour. Now the room was empty and the hushed sound of a hundred people reading

dissolved into a quieter silence. The sun shone in low from the west and there was just Jay and the young man. He finished his page and looked up. He recognized Jay and smiled. "I've come for you," he said. "I knew you would," said Jay. "I knew it would be you."

8

Looking Underground

Images of a knife cutting through Jay's wrist wouldn't leave my imagination and I thought of dark blood pumping out of his arm and turning light red in the bathwater. If you help someone to die because the person wants you to, is that murder? Maybe in a court of law, but it's not morally wrong, surely. Surely? Why did she have to be there? Why did she do it for him? Butterfly was a storyteller; it didn't mean that the stories were true. Her anecdotes had always been like games, exaggerated and extreme.

And so this was her treasure trail. I went back to her computer, daring myself to look further. I looked at the names in the 'My Dead' folder. Tracy, Jay, Komori, Guy Bastide, Daddy, Stranger, Ben Constable. (Ben Constable!) I stared at the screen with my mouth open. The stranger was the man on September 11. Jay was the nanny's nephew. Komori was her nanny. I guess Daddy was her father. Guy Bastide might be the same as the Dr Bastide mentioned in the notebook about Jay. I didn't know who Tracy was. I was Ben Constable. What did that mean? The others were dead, that's what I thought. I rummaged for something to write on. I didn't want to forget what Tomomi Ishikawa had said to me one time.

'I wish you were fucking dead, Ben Constable.' She was crying. Her mood had turned. I expect it had been building up for a moment, but I hadn't noticed and so only saw the explosion. 'Who the fuck do you think you are, rummaging through my life like this?'

I wasn't rummaging, we'd just been talking, drinking. She'd been telling me stuff, I can't remember what exactly. I thought about putting my arms around her, but I didn't really feel like it. I don't mind being supportive when things are tough, but I won't be the whipping boy.

'I don't know what you mean,' I said.

'I mean that I wish I didn't know you. To hate gives you too much credit.'

'I'm sorry, but I don't know what I've done and I don't want to hang out with you when you're like this,' I said.

'Go, go. I wish you would fucking go. I'll make you go, I swear. I will fucking kill you if I have to.'

I had nothing to say to that. My legs ached, telling me that it was time to leave her.

A favourite thing about Tomomi Ishikawa was that she didn't lose control when she was drunk. She didn't become intense and aggressive, or an incoherent wreck. That's why I could drink with her forever. That's what I thought.

'You don't know anything, Ben fucking Constable. You think you do, but you don't.'

'I think you should go home,' I told her.

'You think I'm a monster, don't you?'

'I think you're drunk and in a nasty mood that I don't much like.'

'I have a savage, discoloured face, and my lips are dark and swollen.'

'Stop it. Let me take you home.' I reached out my hand as a last attempt to not leave her in the street, but I wasn't feeling nice.

'If you knew me, you'd think I was a monster.'

She linked arms with me and wiped her tears on my shoulder. I shook my head and sighed.

'I don't know what's going on with you right now, but you seem pretty monstrous.'

'Like Antoinette Mason,' she said. 'You know who that is?'

'No.'

'Bertha Rochester? Jane Eyre? Emily Brontë?'

'Wuthering Heights?' I asked wearily.

'Asshole,' she sputtered, and my temper heated a degree.

'I don't know who any of your people are. You're always saying names of authors and people like you think I should know them all and I don't, and I don't care about them.'

'It's like talking to the village fucking idiot.'

'You need to start being a lot nicer to me,' I said, and she was silent and looked at the ground.

'Don't ever listen to me,' she said, still growling.

'That's not easy with you shouting abuse in my face.'

'Whatever I tell you is lies,' she said. 'None of it is true. I'm talking about stories. Do you understand?'

'Not even remotely.'

Then from nowhere she added, 'I think I'm going to have to kill myself.'

'I was going to suggest that,' I said, too bitter to be funny, but she laughed anyway. How the hell was I supposed to react?

'I love you.' Suddenly she was small and crying again.

I forced myself to feel something and tensed my arm so hers was squeezed a little where it linked at the inside of my elbow.

'You could always kill yourself another time. You know, wait for a while,' I said. 'Most of the time you're nice and I like you. There's still so much to talk about. We could go on for a long time. You shouldn't kill yourself yet.'

'I'm not feeling good, Ben Constable, and I'm a little drunk.'

'I noticed,' I said. 'If it's any consolation, I'm drunk too.'

'We'll forget about this in the morning, yes?'

'If you want.'

'I want us to forget,' she said.

And I nearly did

I printed everything I had found on Tomomi Ishikawa's computer since her death and gathered together the notebooks and letters so I had it all in one place, spread out on the floor in front of me. There were clues that I'd never followed up. There was more to find. I needed to get systematic with the 'My Paris' folder and read through the lot to know where to look next. But already there was the plant in the metro. It was more than a clue: Butterfly had specifically told me to photograph it. It was a long-overdue task.

I took the bus and watched patiently as it stopped and started through traffic at walking pace all the way to Buttes Chaumont. I got off at the southern tip of the park and hesitated, drawn through the big green gates by the trees and man-made hills rather than heading for the metro station, as though what I was about to do was scary or difficult (when in fact it was neither). Somebody once told me that the park had been a quarry and had been known for its insalubrity at some undefined point in history. I think it was the site of a massacre or mass execution. Now it was Paris's most landscaped park and arguably its most beautiful.

Eventually there was no more reason to linger. I walked down the steps into the station and took the lift to the platform.

I pulled my camera from my bag and held it up to my face, taking a couple of pictures to see whether there was enough light. The metro station in summer was unnervingly still, kept breathing only by visitors to the park too lazy to walk up from Jaurès. There were plenty of places on the train when it came, but I stood by the doors. From the window I watched the passing lights, looking for a hint of green. I tried not to blink for fear of missing it. Maybe it wouldn't be there; it might just be the product of Tomomi Ishikawa's wild imagination. The tunnel here is quite broad but seemed darker than I imagined the other lines to be. I liked the changing shape of the walls. I'd like to walk along here and explore every tiny opening and all the shadowy places. The train creaked as the track pulled it round to the right and through the glass; I could see the carriages snaking away behind me. From the corner of my eye, just feet away, I saw a flash of green, and it was gone.

There is a plant in the metro on the line 7bis between Buttes Chaumont and Bolivar; I saw it, sitting under a horizontal light, shining green in the blackness. We pulled into Bolivar and I ran back to the opposite platform to retake the same journey.

The picture that I took was blurred. Really blurred. I examined the image on the screen, hoping for a hint of green, but there was nothing but a bright horizontal streak along a dark brownish background.

Back at Buttes Chaumont for a third time, I stayed at the front of the platform so the train wouldn't yet be running at full speed by the time I passed the plant and I'd have a better chance of getting it on camera.

Now I knew where to look, I could see the plant every time I passed it. But after four times back and forth on the line I still hadn't managed to get a clear picture. The next train I took pulled out of the station and was barely round the corner of the track when it ground to a halt. The driver apologised for the delay and said we would be moving in a few seconds. The window I was looking through was directly in front of the plant. I took three pictures and felt fairly sure that I had a clear shot, judging by the image on the camera's LCD. A woman in the carriage smiled at me and eyed me up and down, then looked away. People look at each other in Paris.

At home I loaded the pictures onto Tomomi Ishikawa's computer. I deleted everything that was remotely blurred and ended up with just one photograph. I liked it. It was a good treasure. Butterfly was right. I found the idea of a plant growing in the metro amazing. It had tiny round green leaves streaming down from pale branches. It's not a beautiful plant, it's just a weed, but it's growing underground with nothing but a narrow strip light illuminating it. Can a plant survive, feeding from just a small light like that? Obviously, yes. So why aren't there more plants in the metro? It was the only one I'd ever seen and I was impressed. I loved the plant. I selected it as the background for the computer desktop.

* * *

It was two days later that I noticed what should have been obvious. Staring at me from the screen of Butterfly's computer was the plant in the metro, and behind the plant, on the brown wall, there were forms and patterns coming out of the dark: the rows of brick; painted horizontal stripes, red and white, that line every metro tunnel; and writing. It could have been graffiti, but the hand was too regular and the pale letters too small.

I opened the image in Photoshop, increased the exposure and zoomed in. I could see scruffy, hastily chalked letters, written by a girl, written by Butterfly. 'This way, Ben Constable,' the words said, and underneath was an arrow pointing to the right.

My heart leapt. There was no doubt about it. Tomomi Ishikawa had written a message for me on the wall of the tunnel. How the hell had she got into a metro tunnel? She had many fantastic ideas for activities that were less than legal, and/or dangerous, but she was all mouth. Butterfly didn't actually *do* these things. They were just ideas. But I know the shape of her letters. She wrote this. Besides, who else would have done it?

So if I'd correctly understood, I was supposed to walk into the tunnel and follow the arrow in order to find some hidden treasure. I couldn't actually go into the tunnel, of course. I was too scared and happy to admit it. It was a great idea, but I wouldn't do it in real life. I wondered what the treasure was. Another murder?

A solution came to me a couple of hours later while watching the sky shunt the clouds to the east. Well, more accurately, it was a half solution. I would go back and forwards on the metro and photograph every inch between Buttes Chaumont and Bolivar. I would take a thousand pictures and stick them all together until I could see all of the tunnel wall. Then I would scrutinise every brick and mark until I found what I was supposed to be looking for. And if it was just a picture or something interesting to look at, there would be no need for me to go into the tunnel on foot and risk my liberty and safety. Of course, it might be an envelope or something, but I would deal with that as and if the situation arose.

I spent the rest of the day going back and forth on line 7bis, taking photographs, to the feigned indifference and occasional overt curiosity of my fellow passengers. I counted the clicks of the camera and measured the spaces between the lights and any landmarks, scribbling a diagram in my notebook. It was essential that I got the whole tunnel. I worked like a zombie until eleven thirty at night, took 517 pictures, then went home. I deleted everything that was blurred or doubled up until I had two hundred or so images documenting pretty much the whole length of the wall. Then I started to build a collage on Tomomi Ishikawa's computer. A great long string of overlapping photographs.

I fell asleep in my clothes at five in the morning and woke again at eleven to carry on. And by three in the afternoon I had a single image that I could scroll along from right to left, covering the route from Buttes Chaumont to Bolivar.

Suddenly I was starving, thirsty and in desperate need of the toilet. It was as though I'd turned off my body for two days just to focus on one thing. Normally I can barely concentrate for long enough to write my own name. In the last six months I hadn't written more than six pages. I was interested to note my dedication to this laborious task. I made some quick food and had a shower.

I tidied up the kitchen, then went back and started to examine the picture. The new photo of the plant was actually better than the one I had already and I could see the writing on the wall as clear as day. I followed the arrow and I didn't have far to go. About thirty yards after the plant there was an opening, like a doorway, with steps going down and something drawn on the wall.

I zoomed in and there was an arrow on the side pointing down at forty-five degrees. Underneath it was written 'DOWN HERE, BC' in clumsy block capitals.

Fuck. She wanted me to go into the tunnel and down into some unknown subterranean world. I couldn't go into the tunnel. I would get into trouble. It seemed like a poor reason not to do something slightly adventurous, but it was true. I just couldn't imagine actually doing it. It was undoable. It was pointless to take so much risk to find something left for me by a dead person.

I stood looking southwards into the tunnel at metro Buttes Chaumont. In front of me there was a yellow sign telling me not to go past this point and blocking the route down the narrow steps. There were people on the platform waiting, too many people for me to get down the steps without anybody noticing. How do graffiti artists do it? There must be hundreds of people who go into the tunnels all the time. Why can't I? I thought that maybe I should wait until late at night when the last metro had gone. There wouldn't be any people about and it would eliminate the risk of getting run over by a train or electrocuted (presuming they turn the current off at night). There was room next to the tracks for a person to walk. It's not like London, I thought. If you were walking along the tracks in the Tube and a train came, you'd get totally squashed. Here, though, so long as you kept close to the wall, you'd have a good few inches' clearance, maybe even a foot. A train came towards me and into the station. I watched a handful of people get off and on, but even as they were filing into the lift going upwards, a new batch arrived. There was no way I could get onto the tracks. Or was I just being cowardly? And as if to prove that cowardice was the problem, Cat turned up. *Hello, Cat,* I thought. He looked into the tunnel. Then without so much as a glance in my direction, he walked under the yellow sign warning of the risk of death and headed downwards into the dark. 'Where the fuck are you going, Cat?' I asked, but he probably didn't even understand the question.

He walked a couple of metres and then smelt the ground as if he were a skilled tracker or something. *Cat, don't pretend you know what you're doing, because you don't.* He took another couple of steps and waited again, then set off walking calmly along towards the plant, a long way out of sight. *Cat, come back! Don't leave me here.* After a minute another train came. I looked up at the ceiling in as casual a manner as I could muster, then, as the train pulled away, I went back to my position staring into the tunnel and watched the back of the train disappear. *I hope Cat's all right (fucking stupid cat).* People came out of the lift and I tried to look innocent again.

As the next train pulled in, I moved back from the edge of the platform and slid down the wall so I was squatting and scowling at the ground. People passed me and another couple of trains came and went. *What if Cat doesn't come back? Do you have to wait for imaginary cats, or can you just leave them to find their own way home? I think I know the answer to that question.* And then he poked his head round the corner and looked at me. 'What?' He just looked at me and waited, then looked back into the tunnel and back at me again. 'I'm not going, Cat. I'll get caught or there'll be a horrible accident and I don't know what will happen.' He stared at me and then sat down and licked one of his paws. 'I'm not going, Cat. I can't.' A woman in a dark green uniform came down out of the lift towards me.

'Monsieur?' She asked me if I was all right and I thought about telling her that I just felt a bit faint but was fine now. I didn't want to worry her, though, or cause a fuss, so I came up with a better idea and told her I was waiting for someone. She gave me a bored look and told me to go and sit on one of the seats provided. As I stood she turned back towards the lift. I guess I'd shown up as being suspicious on some camera and she'd come to look. She looked back over her shoulder to make sure I'd actually moved, at the same time that I looked back to make sure she wasn't still watching me, which was embarrassing. I went quickly to one of the white moulded plastic seats and Cat followed at a leisurely pace. 'I can't do it, Cat. I got in trouble just for squatting on the floor, and Christ, normal people sit on the floor in the metro all the time. There are beggars who spend their whole day sitting on the floor in stations, but the moment I do, someone in uniform comes and moves me on. Imagine what would happen if I walked onto the tracks. I'm not good with authority, Cat, and I get into trouble easily. And I'm a coward. I can't do it.'

Cat got up and walked off and I waited for a minute to make sure I wouldn't catch up with him, then took the lift up out into the night.

9

Resistance

From Buttes Chaumont I trudged mindlessly up to Belleville, along rue des Pyrénées and then cut through tiny streets and stairways down to Ménilmontant. A few fat drops of rain fell on my head. I changed my route a little and ducked into a bar where I used to drink with Tomomi Ishikawa. I half expected to see her sitting alone, scribbling words for which she would offer no explanation into a notebook. She wasn't there, of course. I sat at a table in the open window with a beer and the rain picked up. I watched the pavement and let my lungs fill with the intoxicating smell of warm summer night and water that somehow crumbles the sound of voices and glasses into a comfortable drone. But despite these favourite things, I felt sorry for myself. I got out my notebook and did my own scribbling.

The last time I sat in this chair there was a bottle of wine
in front of me, two glasses and an ashtray. Tomomi Ishikawa

was sitting opposite, leaning forwards with her elbows on the table, looking serious. A long time has passed since then. Maybe a year.

'Can I tell you something cool?' she asked.

'Yep,' I said.

'At the Pantheon—'

'The Pantheon in Paris?'

'Yeah. There's a clock. It's an old clock and for a long time it didn't work.'

'You like clocks that don't work.'

Tomomi Ishikawa looked at her watch—it said twenty past three. 'I do,' she said; 'so if anything, this should be a sad tale for me, but it's not, it's cool, as you will find out, my dear Ben Constable.'

'OK.'

'OK. There was this group of intellectuals who hung out together like a secret society.'

'Is this a joke?'

'No. Listen. Their headquarters were underground in the catacombs where they would meet and watch films d'auteur, drink exceptionally fine wines and talk about art, cultural heritage, science and philosophy and how France was going to the dogs. They probably had concerts down there featuring prominent French musicians playing great French composers and that kind of thing.'

'How do you know all this?'

'Shhh, I'm making some of it up, but not all. It's a true story. They're some elite group of know-it-alls with roots going back to the Age of Reason and they get access to the

catacombs through a secret stairway in one of the schools on
the Left Bank, let's say the Sorbonne, but it's secret so I don't
know exactly.'

'What's this got to do with the Pantheon?'

'I'm getting to that.'

'OK.'

'So, one day they're moaning about modern architectural
wonders such as Le Corbusier's Villa Savoye and they drift
onto the subject of the sad disrepair of national treasures, and
somebody mentions the clock at the Pantheon that doesn't
work and they sip a 1976 Château Lafite Rothschild and tut in
disapproval. Then they have this bright idea that they should
restore the clock themselves—illegally. They don't care about
the law because they're a secret elite group and already meet
clandestinely in their secret chamber deep under the city, so
this kind of thing seems perfectly normal to them.'

'Uh-huh.'

'So they get lots of tools and go to the Pantheon at the end
of the day and hide in a secret corner that only they know
about, and wait until it's all locked up, then they go up to the
clock and set up a base where, for months on end, maybe a
year, they go at night and work painstakingly to restore the
clock to its original splendour.'

'What, really?'

'Yes.'

'Cool.'

'Anyway, when it's done they decide to write a letter to the
director of the Pantheon, telling him that the clock is now
working and giving him instructions on how to maintain it,

wind it up et cetera, but instead of being pleased, the people in charge of the Pantheon are really upset that a band of militant clock restorers could break into the place, set up a base there for a year and commit an act of such wanton vandalism without anyone noticing, and so they decide that in order to avoid a scandal they should break the clock so that nobody will ever find out. But the guerrilla clock restorers go and wind it up themselves and the next day it chimes for the first time in years and everybody looks up and notices. And the director is fired.'

'Oh,' I said, and felt sorry for the director. 'Did this happen in the sixties or something?'

'No it happened now, like last week or something. I read it in the paper.'

'What, even the bit about the 1976 Rothschild?'

'No, I added that bit for effect. But that ought to be proof enough that it happened after the sixties.'

'So what's the point?'

'The point is that they are cool and we should be members of a secret society like that. We should go underground and find out where they meet.'

'They wouldn't want us. We're not intellectuals.'

'Speak for yourself.'

'OK, I'm not an intellectual.'

'Maybe we could bring something to the group that they haven't got already?'

'Like what?'

'Fun?'

'I don't think they'd be interested in fun, and besides I'm not feeling fun today.'

*'Oh, Ben Constable, but that's perfect. They don't want fun
and you are no fun. I just know they'll let us join.'*

The man known affectionately to Tomomi Ishikawa as Our Waiter
came over to my table. His hair had grown since I'd last been here
so I couldn't completely recognise him until he spoke to me in
English (which he seemed to want to practice).

'Excuse me,' he said.

'Hi,' I replied, and smiled.

'A lady before the bar ask me to give you this.' He placed a
glass of red wine and a folded piece of notepaper on the table.

I looked up at the bar. There were various people standing in
front of it, none of whom I recognised (but that meant nothing).

'What woman?'

'The Américaine. You come here sometimes with her.'

'Where is she?'

'It was long time ago. I couldn't find the shit, but she offered a
drink of wine for you and she ask me to give the shit to you when
you arrive here.'

'The shit?'

'This shit. This. I found it now.' He pointed to the folded notepaper on the table.

'Ah,' I said, 'the sheet of paper. Eeeee. Sh*ee*t.'

'Shi-it of paper.'

'You can just say piece of paper.'

'OK.'

'How long ago?'

'A long time ago. In winter. I haven't seen her afterwards.'

'OK. Thank you. *Merci.*'

'*Il n'y a pas de quoi,*' he said, and went to clear a table of empty
glasses.

I looked at the paper.

I have something for you, BC. Go to our late-night smoking place. B. XOX

I sipped the wine and stared out of the window with my brain in a strange place somewhere between miserable, excited and cross. Maybe I should stop following Butterfly's clues. I didn't have to passively accept something that didn't make me feel good. All I had to do was stop if that's what I wanted, I snarled to myself in irritation. I knocked the wine back in one gulp, went to the bar to pay, shook hands with Our Waiter as he passed and thanked him, then left.

I trudged up rue Ménilmontant and as it got steep I felt my legs stiffen. Somebody was walking behind me so I carried on quickly, pretending I couldn't feel the burn. I turned into the little cobbled street of Cité de l'Ermitage and the footsteps followed. I turned to the left and sat on one of the concrete bollards. A man arrived, realised that it was a cul-de-sac and turned to go. He jumped when he saw me sitting there and moved quickly away. After a moment I looked back down the street to make sure he'd gone and then lit a cigarette. I wished the rain would start again, but it didn't. It was nighttime, but not late. Not twenty past three. This was the place I sometimes came with Butterfly to smoke because she loved this street. She wanted to buy a house here with a garden. I leaned back and stared at the cobblestones and the weeds in the dim light.

'What do you think, Cat?' Cat appeared and looked around and then sat down a couple of metres in front of me. Where would you hide something here? I stood up and looked around.

There were no stones or doormats to leave something under nor any earth to dig in. I ran my hand round the back of the concrete bollards that Tomomi Ishikawa and I had used as seats, and behind the smaller of the two I felt a familiar texture. Sure enough, there was a layer of carefully placed duct tape. I tried to peel it off but it had been glued (I guess the tape wouldn't stick). I looked for something in my bag to scrape it off with, but all I could find was Butterfly's blue on/offable pen. I poked through the tape and ripped out a sealable plastic bag with a brown envelope in it. On the front of the envelope was my name.

I was annoyed. This was a rubbish place to leave a clue. Anyone sitting here could have found it and it was only by chance that I went in the bar and even more by chance that Our Waiter found the 'shit' to give me.

Cat looked up at me and raised an eyebrow, but I don't think it meant anything. 'Come on,' I said. 'If we're quick, we'll make the last metro.'

> *If you are Benjamin Constable and you are reading these words, then you truly are a skilled treasure hunter. I take my chapeau off to you, sir.*
>
> *The next treasure is made of gold. My Paris and yours have overlapped at times; perhaps we came to places from different directions and with different stories. This is a drop of history, the facts of which we have disagreed upon. Do you know what I'm talking about?*
>
> *The treasures in this part of the trail are sequential, and if you choose to follow, it will carry you far away, to another of my worlds for us to explore together and me to delight in your treasure-hunting joy. I want to imagine you scrambling and*

*rummaging around for clues leading to the manyfold prize.
Some of the prize is more about me than you, but hopefully in
all of this, BC, there will be things you find beautiful and that
will give you pleasure. And if there is no pleasure (which I quite
understand that there may not be), then maybe at the very least
something may inspire you to write, notes or even a whole book.
(Not that I think you need inspiration—it's just that I miss you
and I want to leave some of my spirit here on paper with you.
Do you forgive me, Ben Constable? I don't expect you to, but I
hope there are things here that will make you smile.)*

LOVE, Butterfly. XOX

Cat got up and went to sit on the other side of the room to move
away from me and I scowled at him. I got out my notebook and a
black pen.

Dear Tomomi Ishikawa,

*There is no joy in this. You have disappeared without
explanation, leaving vague and improbable clues to bloody
and disturbing stories. Am I supposed to be entertained? Am I
supposed to laugh in shocked excitement at your destructive
adventures? Why didn't you leave something happy? Why
didn't you think that this might be confusing and upsetting?
Why do you have so little idea of how this might make me feel?
I guess you were ill and dying and weren't thinking clearly. If I
could have chosen your death, I wouldn't have done it like
this. I think I would have tried to make the end of your time
happy and comfortable. I think I would have liked to have
been there when you died, I think I would have been good at*

*that. And when you were dead, I would have liked to be able
to let you go, and for you to become a memory. Maybe I would
have kept one thing, something of yours as a souvenir, but
that's all; a tiny keepsake which I could guard preciously. I
don't want to be the inheritor of all your junk writing that
you're too vain to throw away. And it feels too precious for me
to get rid of. Damn.*

*I'm pissed off with you, Tomomi Ishikawa. You seem to
have constructed a grand scheme to waste my time and get me
into dangerous and difficult situations. I don't want to follow
your treasure trail and I don't want your spirit with me. Yeah,
and another thing, why the hell am I in your 'My Dead' folder?
Were you planning to kill me as well? Thanks. I think you
should go now.*

Ben

So, I've entered into correspondence with a dead person and I'm
being supervised by an imaginary cat. I'm not sure that this is how
I would have planned my own mental health, but hey, I still feel
fairly sane and if it wasn't for all this, I think I'd be quite happy
with my little life. I don't need great adventures. I like watching the
clouds and hearing the noises from the street. I like drinking with
friends, talking to strangers in bars. I like living in Paris and being
foreign. I don't need anything else.

My mood had changed. Writing back to Butterfly had done
something to me. I still felt bruised and embarrassed by my cowardice, but I wasn't angry anymore. I wanted to understand. I
wanted to solve the puzzle and find the treasure.

I looked at Tomomi Ishikawa's letter again. Something stood

out. *'The next treasure is made of gold. . . . This is a drop of history, the facts of which we have disagreed upon. Do you know what I'm talking about?'* Yes, I knew what she was talking about. I turned on the computer and looked in her 'My Paris' folder, scanning through the file names for something familiar, and I found it. There was a file called 'La Goutte d'Or'. I didn't read it. I didn't need to. It's the name of a neighbourhood in Paris. I know it better than Tomomi Ishikawa ever did because I used to live there. She and I did not agree on the origin of its name—her version of a golden-coloured wine produced there hundreds of years ago was more likely historically accurate. My version was probably just urban myth. I tore the reply I'd written to Butterfly from my notebook, folded it with her letter and put them in the envelope, which I placed on top of the ever-growing pile of things to do with her. Then I went to bed.

10

Treasure Hunting

The next day's lethargy was lighter of mood and I felt quite comfortable doing nothing. I was on holiday; I could do what I wanted. After breakfast I had a nap, the day passed, and despite half-serious good intentions, I didn't get out of the house until well into the evening.

I took line 2 to La Chapelle and cut through the back streets of La Goutte d'Or. Youths hung out on street corners and people scurried about their business in and out of doorways, shops and cafés. There was a smell of summer and nighttime, dry and spicy. This isn't exactly a pretty area, but it's alive and I like it.

I detoured up to rue Doudeauville, then down towards Château Rouge, where hawkers offered me sunglasses and belts until alerted to the presence of a police patrol, and street stalls laid out on car bonnets were wrapped up in cloth and swiped away in seconds. I crossed boulevard Barbès and followed rue Poulet past numerous shops for African hair products, up the lower slope of

Montmartre. At the top of the street, where rue Poulet and rue
Myrha meet, is a narrow art deco building that had recently been
converted into a bar. I sat on the terrace, ordered a beer and examined my surroundings. There was treasure here.

Before the art deco building there had been a much older one.
Hundreds of years ago there had lived an alchemist on the top
floor. He was a reclusive type who spent most of his days locked
away, calculating the transmutation of lead into gold and conduct-
ing experiments. However, later in his life he attracted attention
from locals because at eleven o'clock every day a single drop of
gold fell from the top of the building onto the pavement below.
And people would gather from early in the morning, hoping to be
the one to harvest this daily gift from the heavens, and that is the
true reason for the name of the area. La Goutte d'Or—The Drop
of Gold.

The most obvious place to hide treasure was a large plant pot
on the pavement next to me. With a halfhearted attempt to seem
normal, I adjusted my shoelace and tried to look under the pot at
the same time, but the ruse was ineffective and I spent a second
or two on my hands and knees feeling the underside of the pot on
the off chance that there was something lodged there for me to
find. I sat back as though nothing interesting had happened and
watched the street. I took Tomomi Ishikawa's blue pen from my
bag and casually plunged it into the soft earth over and over again
until it struck something remotely solid a few inches below the
surface.

Still with the hope of maintaining an air of normality, I pushed
my hand through the dirt and pulled out a sealed transparent plastic bag with an envelope inside, then smoothed the earth back
into place. On the front of the envelope was written: *'BE CARE-
FUL WHEN YOU OPEN THIS; SOMETHING MIGHT FALL*

OUT' in familiar block capitals. Wrapped in a shit of paper, bruised with blue handwriting, was a tiny drop of gold in the shape of a tear with a loop at the pointed end. It had once been part of an earring I'd found in the metro. I'd removed the rest and kept the drop and given it to Butterfly one day, and told her the story of the alchemist on rue Myrha, and she had rather ungraciously disputed the historical accuracy of my tale.

I couldn't help but smile. It was perfect Butterfly. It was a perfect treasure.

On the paper was written a single sentence in quotation marks:

> "The brown current ran swiftly out of the heart of
> darkness, bearing us down towards the sea with twice the speed
> of our upward progress; Tomomi Ishikawa's life was running
> swiftly too, ebbing, ebbing out of her heart into the sea of
> inexorable time."

I struggled to keep a straight face because I was very pleased with myself. This was a quote and I knew where it came from. I suppose it helped that the title of the book was in the writing, but I still felt clever.

Back at home I pulled my copy of *Heart of Darkness* from the shelf and flicked through the pages. I found the passage easily enough. She had of course replaced the name Kurtz with her own, like a sickening reminder of her disappearing life, ebbing, ebbing out of her heart as she prepared this whole game for my entertainment. But now I was stuck. Did I have to read the whole book to find something that would lead me down a dead-end trail to one of Butterfly's dark secrets? 'Ebbing, ebbing'—I'd read that somewhere before, and I knew where to find it scratched in blue ink on the inside cover of this very book.

> *Paris, November 2006*
>
> *A present for your dark heart. You remind me of the thoughts, ebbing, ebbing inexorably from my hands and into my brain like a twisted revelation.*
>
> *XOX*
> *Butterfly*

I had presumed the dedication nonsense. 'Ebbing, ebbing . . . into my brain.' I opened the 'My Brain' folder on her computer and clicked on a file named 'The Revelatory Vision of Saint Butterfly':

The Revelatory Vision of Saint Butterfly

Once the sun had passed below the horizon and the stain of red drained from the sky, leaving a pale wash illuminated from the streetlights below, I walked south towards a tower and the quarter of a lost generation.

And through the clouds pushed the moon, waxing regrets, heavy, falling.

From my left I heard voices from the cemetery, the calling of the dead for me to join them, sometimes in rich choral harmonies and sometimes the din, cacophonous, assaulting my ears and weighing on my spirit: Baudelaire, de Beauvoir, Beckett, Duras, Franck, Garnier, Gainsbourg, Guilmant, Larousse, Maupassant, Sartre, Sontag, wait. Wait! I'll be with you soon.

I hesitated in front of the glass façade of the station and watched the souls of the transient living come and go. About me gathered a crowd. At first I thought it coincidence, as though I had wandered into the middle of some kind of meeting, but gradually attention turned to me, with angry shouting and taunts.

I raised my hands to protect my head and wished for the ground to swallow me. What are you waiting for? Take me now. But the ground did not, and fear drove me to change my behavior.

"Stop!" I cried, and silence rolled across the square. I stretched my hands to the sides, and the people backed away. From my mouth came the words "You will not judge me," and a murmur rippled through the crowd.

Now I raised all before me, carrying them up through the station past the ticket hall and the ready-made sandwiches, the clock and the departure board, past the platforms and their high-speed trains lining up on tracks, stretching to the south and to the west, like shoots pushing up through the earth to find daylight, they reach for the ocean. "I will show you all, I will tell you everything, and you will look on in awe, enchanted by the illusion." How else could I escape them?

Higher still we went and to a garden; the island of Hesperides, an oasis in the desert mountains and a gateway across the Sargasso Sea to a new world.

The crowd watched in amazement, paralyzed by fear, but there was one who did not notice. He was distracted by the garden. "I love this place," he said.

I knew he'd come. I was right to be afraid.

"My path is chosen," I cried. "Mine is the path of the

dead. Do not judge me. Please." But he was not listening. It's not that it was of no importance, he was simply unaware. (Or was he deliberately avoiding that which he did not wish to see?)

I pointed: "Everything is written down for you to find. Look around you. It is here."

And as he looked I moved to leave quietly so as not to draw attention. Heavy clouds rolled in and the dead called out to me, come quick.

Go now, away from here. Fly from this garden across the ocean to my past and the small treasures that await you, and I will run before the storm takes me.

Shadows pushed across the moon and the wind stirred up a tempest threatening to uproot the trees and tear down the tower, and heaven will crash down, and the dead rise from their graves to bring me in, if I don't come now.

Please leave before it is too late. Wake up. Wake up and leave. Come back when the storm has blown out and the dead have gone to rest.

The garden will be fresh and green, and blossoms decorate the trees, the water from the fountains will flow, cool, through your fingers.

Bloody hell. The tower, the station, the Lost Generation and the cemetery are Montparnasse. Above the station is a garden called the Jardin Atlantique, I found it one day in winter, when I'd missed my train and had an hour and a half to wait for another. I had told Butterfly about it, enclosed by tall buildings on all sides. It is accessed either from a stairway going up from the station or from two lifts situated on the east and west adjacent streets. It's closed after dark, but I know another way in. In the centre of the garden is a steel structure called the Island of Hesperides. I checked the time and it was eleven o'clock. The metro was still running.

I took line 6 to Montparnasse and walked up through the station past the stairway leading to the garden with its locked gate at the top, and out of the east exit. I walked past the lift standing like a giant post box in the middle of the pavement and turned up past *Le Petit Journal* on the left, and the SNCF headquarters on the right. At the top of the street there is a large circus and I turned right, following the curved front of the Hotel Concorde, and onto an access road at the back of the hotel.

Cat appeared and led the way up a ramp staying close to the wall in the shadow, which seemed like a good idea. When I got to my secret entrance there were four-metre-high ornate steel gates barring my route. How had I never noticed them before? Cat squeezed through at the bottom with ease and sat down on the other side, looking out at me. 'I'll never get through there,' I said to Cat, and stood back looking higher up where the gaps were larger. I hoisted myself up the grille without too much difficulty, and with laughable ease past the spiky things to stop you climbing. There was a row of small gaps about eight feet from the floor. When I was young I had a theory that if you could get your head through a space, then you could get the rest of your body through (now on reflection I think that was a distortion of the idea that a cat's whiskers are its way of judging its width), but then I was a very skinny youth. I'm a pretty slim man as well. I barely touched the sides and I was in. 'Are we good at this, Cat, or is it just easy?'

I guessed there were cameras, but I also guessed that no one would be looking at them because they wouldn't be expecting anyone to climb through those gates. I nonetheless tried to stay in the shadows, but to get to the steel structure in the middle I had to walk across open ground. I thought about crawling commando style, but suspected it would make me more conspicuous. The Island of Hesperides is a meteorological observatory and a piece of modern art. It has four legs straddling the path and a large metal disk at the top, angled to reflect something, although I don't know what. The clouds maybe? At each corner of the structure is a device for measuring a different piece of meteorological data: rainfall, wind speed, temperature and air pressure. I hoped I wouldn't have to start randomly digging up this park because I love it, just for its improbability. I walked round the structure, looking for a more obvious hiding place. It wasn't hard to find. Facing outwards on one of the legs there was a verse in marker pen, hasty block capitals:

YET LET NO EMPTY GUST
OF PASSION FIND AN UTTERANCE IN THY LAY,
A BLAST THAT WHIRLS THE DUST
ALONG THE HOWLING STREET AND DIES AWAY;
BUT FEELINGS OF CALM POWER AND MIGHTY SWEEP,
LIKE CURRENTS JOURNEYING THROUGH THE WINDLESS DEEP.

I recognised Butterfly's handwriting. I had come out without my bag, without a pen. I read the words aloud and looked away to see whether they had stayed in my brain. They hadn't. I said the poem fifty times until the sounds left an imprint on my memory. I would have liked to hang out in the garden because that surely was the treasure, but I had to get to a pen and paper as quickly as possible.

Cat and I snuck back to the gate and climbed out, all the time repeating the poem over and over. I walked into the hotel on the corner and asked at reception to borrow a pen. I must have looked ruffled from my squeezing and climbing adventures, but if they thought I looked out of place, they didn't give any hint of it and obliged me with writing materials. What I noted wasn't terribly different from the original, and the first two lines were perfect.

But this was surely not Butterfly's voice. She had borrowed the words from somewhere. When I got home I typed them into Google in case something came up and it did. They were an extract from a text by American poet and philanthropist William Bryant, inscribed at the base of his statue in Bryant Park, New York, NY, USA.

That's a clue, I think.

PART TWO

August 20 to August 28, 2007

11

Arriving in New York

Waiting for three hours in the queue for passport control at JFK Airport was boring and kind of interesting at the same time. I pocketed one of the Department of Homeland Security US Customs and Border Protection Nonimmigrant Visa Waiver Arrival/Departure forms (with its genius questions) as a memento, or in case it came in handy as a comedy present for somebody, and they did appear to be free for the taking.

Everything in America seemed as if it belonged on television. Most people were played by actors I could nearly recognise, and the man speaking on the public address system was very probably a multiplatinum-selling hip-hop artist.

'Would passengers *Smith* and *John*son on flight BA three eighdee from London Heathrow, please go to the Briddish Airways *desk* for *information* abou cho *luggage*.'

Sadly my name was not mentioned and there was no information about my luggage, which had had ideas of its own on where to travel, without leaving so much as a forwarding address or any notion of its whereabouts.

With a two-hour flight delay, I was now a good five hours later than I'd expected. I was starting to feel uncomfortable about arriving in Manhattan in the middle of the night, not knowing where I was going to stay. I thought about trying to look for a hotel on the Internet, but the airport had a kind of middle-of-the-night feel to it with everything closed, so I got directions from the semihelpful people at the information desk.

'Where exactly do you want to go?'

'Manhattan.'

'Yeah, but where in Manhattan?'

'Er, I don't know.' I'd never been to New York before, but I had an image of the kind of place I would like and the kind of place I probably wouldn't like, but I didn't really even know if they existed (I would have liked to go to Sesame Street, for example). Someone had once told me that I'd like the East Village, but that didn't necessarily mean that I'd be happy to turn up there at three o'clock in the morning. And I didn't want to say the East Village in case I'd misunderstood and it was some kind of postapocalyptic waste ground inhabited solely by hordes of flesh-eating undead, and the people at the airport would laugh at me because I was obviously stupid.

'Well, it's a big place, and how you get there depends on where you're going.'

'How do you get to the East Village?'

'OK, you need to take the AirTrain to Howard Beach and then take the A train to Jay Street and then take the F train to, maybe, Second Avenue? Where you going in the East Village?'

'I don't know. Do you have a map?'

'I've got this Brooklyn bus map.'

'Does it show the subway?'
'I don't think so.'
'Does it show Manhattan?'
'Not really.'
'OK. Thanks.'

I took the AirTrain and stared at a sign telling me a list of things
that are forbidden in the territory of JFK Airport—including falling
asleep. When I woke up, the train was going backwards. I had got
to Howard Beach and was now heading back in the other direction. I decided to rest my eyes a little, promising myself to open
them now and then to check which station I was at.

The next time I woke I could clearly see a sign saying Howard
Beach. I stared and tried to remember why it would seem familiar.
A long beeping tone sounded, the doors closed and the train
headed off in the wrong direction again. I got off at the next stop,
which was a car park, and decided to walk to the subway; simple
enough to follow the overhead lines of the futurist AirTrain. I
walked through the car park for a few hundred yards and arrived at
the subway station.

I'd been waiting around ten minutes and had paced up and
down the platform three times before an overfriendly and oversized bum started chatting up the few people who had luggage. I
decided to hang out at one extreme end in the open air to avoid
having to talk to him, and thought this a harmless moment to
smoke my first cigarette in the eighteen hours or so since I had
checked in at Charles de Gaulle airport in France. I spotted a law
enforcement officer as he strolled over to the bum and some of his
words drifted into earshot. He had a patronising tone and didn't
want to have to tell the bum every night not to bother people. And

then he turned and continued his stroll along the platform towards me. When I felt he was appropriately near I nodded and said good evening and he said, 'Hey, you know you can't smoke that here.'

I lifted my hand and looked at it. 'It's a cigarette,' I said.

'I know what it is, and you can't smoke it here.'

'Oh, sorry,' I said. 'I thought because I was in the open air it would be fine.'

'You can't smoke anywhere on the transportation system.'

'Oh, OK,' I said. In France I'd never seen anyone get told not to smoke in the open air. I suddenly felt a long way from home and as if I didn't know the rules. I imagined putting the cigarette out on the ground and being told to pick it up, or getting thrown in the penitentiary, or deported. 'Where can I put it out?' I asked.

'You just put it on the ground there,' he said, and I thought that I could have disposed of it more appropriately. As I crushed it out I noticed other cigarette ends on the floor and judged that I had just been unlucky. 'Hey, are you English?' he asked me.

'Yes I am,' I said.

'Yeah, I recognised your accent. You just get in from London?'

'Yes,' I lied, because I thought it would make things easier than explaining that actually I lived in Paris and I hadn't been to London for years.

'You got any ID on you?'

'Yes, one moment.'

And as I rummaged for my passport he said, 'I just wanna check because if you have just arrived from London, then you don't know the law, and I'm not gonna write you a ticket because it's probably not the same there.'

'I just got here,' I assured him, and then hoped there was nothing in my passport that said that I'd actually just arrived from

Paris and not London, which would show me up to be an obvious liar. He looked at the visa-waiver form stapled to my passport.

'OK, you're lucky today because you just got here, so I'm not going to write you a ticket this time.'

'Thank you.'

'But next time I'm gonna have to write you a ticket.'

'Yes, I understand, but I won't smoke in the subway again now that I know that it's illegal.'

'It's illegal to smoke anywhere on the transportation system.'

'Yes, I won't be smoking anywhere from where one could be transported, or while being transported.'

'Look, I'm just doing my job and trying to make sure that people stick to the law. And if everyone sticks to the law, then there's no trouble and I'm a happy cop. You just got here and I'm telling you now, but I'm also saying that next time you may not be so lucky.'

'No, of course. Thank you.'

'So you just be careful.'

'I certainly will. Thank you.'

'All right, you stay out of trouble.'

'Yes, I will.'

'OK, have a nice day.'

'Yes, thank you. You too.'

It took a lot of effort, but eventually I managed to have the last word. Why did I need to have the last word? Cat would have looked at me despairingly.

When I arrived at Second Avenue it was light and I walked out of the subway station and into New York, disappointed to find that it didn't look anything like I'd expected. I thought it would be a forest of dizzyingly tall buildings, or if it wasn't all like that, then at least I'd be able to see a few dizzyingly tall buildings, or some towering district in the near distance. But the buildings around me were no taller than anything Paris had to offer. What's more, the city that never sleeps seemed to be shut down for the night. Had New York changed, or had Frank Sinatra lied?

I had no particular sense of which direction I was facing, but didn't feel worried because I guessed all the streets would have numbers and fit into an easy-to-navigate grid that any fool could understand. I guessed I was somewhere on the east side of Manhattan and I looked at the street names. I was at the intersection of East Houston Street (which I later discovered is pronounced Howston for no reason anyone could explain) and Allen Street, scuppering my idea that New York could be navigated on numbers alone. But as I had no idea where to go, this was not a real problem.

Crossing over the massive junction, Allen Street became First Avenue. The side streets acquired numbers starting from one and I walked knowing that I would check into the first reasonably priced hotel I came across. An hour later I was at Forty-Second Street. I realised I had been walking with my brain switched off—counting blocks automatically and not looking out for hotels. My tiredness made me feel sorry for myself. I could see water to my right so I headed left and New York quickly became the towering metropolis of my imagination.

Grand Central Station must surely be the most beautiful station in the world. How could anything else compete with its orangey-marble wonderfulness. I wanted to sit down. Grand Central Station offers architectural beauty, but not seating (at least not at first glance). After wandering around for ten minutes, I came to the lowest level, where there is a refreshment area with large comfortable chairs, and I sat and closed my eyes.

I found an Internet café and stumbled onto the website of a hotel that looked nice, just about affordable and in the East Village. I rang and booked myself a room. They told me I could check in at two o'clock. I went back to my email account and sent a message to Butterfly: 'I'm on the other side of the world and as tired as I have ever been in my life. I'm not really sure what I'm doing here. Where shall I go, Tomomi Ishikawa? I'm lost.'

I still had five hours to kill and felt like I was going to go mad if I wasn't tucked up in bed in the next few moments. I walked south for a while and then moved to the east a little to line myself up for where I imagined my hotel to be, and after about a hundred and twenty miles I was walking down a nice street called Avenue A which had no place on my imaginary map of Manhattan.

I eventually arrived at a big square with trees and found a bench. I sat staring at nothing, feeling the morning on my skin and wishing I had my luggage with me. Then I slid into a slightly more comfortable position, resting my head on my arm on the back of the bench, and fairly soon I was lying down with my head propped up on my elbow. My legs tucked up and my arm became a pillow and the warming air a quilt. I looked at the trees and the clouds and urged them to pass by quickly so that I could go to bed soon. It was a shame to waste precious time, but my body could do no more.

After an hour or two—who knows—I got up and staggered over to a bar with seats outside and ordered a hot chocolate. I noticed a sign on the corner saying Tompkins Square. I knew this place. Butterfly had written about it. Maybe the bench I'd just been lying on was the one where she sat on the evening of September 11, 2001, waiting for a stranger.

At ten to two I was standing at the reception desk of the hotel. An oldish man gave me a key and directed me to my room.

'I don't normally work in the day,' he confided; 'I'm the night guy.'

I tried to look interested, but I had no conversation in me and he picked up on that. I apologised, telling him I was jet-lagged, and went off to find my room. It was quite possibly the nicest cheap hotel room I'd ever stayed in, but I was too tired to care. I had a shower and went to bed.

12

On the Steps of the New York Public Library

I was too hot and woke up in a room I didn't know. My body clock couldn't tell the time, but the sun was beating directly onto the curtains. Hotel rooms may all be different, but they have something in common too, it's hard to define what, but you'd know one the moment you woke up in it.

There was a moment when I couldn't remember what was in my dream and what was in my head.

I wished I had a toothbrush and toothpaste, but they were lost with my luggage. I made a gesture towards oral hygiene with some toilet paper and went out.

I found a café I liked and ordered breakfast. I was half-asleep and muddled. Why was I here (in New York)? I was following clues, but is that reason enough to take the next flight to another continent, or am I sinking new claws into something I thought I'd let go of?

I shrugged. I could go immediately back to Paris on the

grounds that to come here was folly, or I could explore a new city, walking around, and have a break from everything.

I guessed I was near to the bottom of Manhattan, and that the southernmost point would be as good a place as any to start. So I zigzagged towards the south with shadows from the morning sun as my compass, until the buildings got so big that the sun didn't reach down to street level except at junctions. A sign pointed left to the Brooklyn Bridge, but that would have to wait for another day. As I walked past Wall Street, it seemed narrow and unimpressive below the buildings lining it. I eventually came to Battery Park and the water. I looked across to the Statue of Liberty. It was a long way off and little more than a blur to my tired eyes. I stood with my back to the water and all Manhattan before me. I stayed by the water, moving west and circling the tall buildings, and then after a while cut inland and came to Ground Zero, with its fence blocking out the world and its tall neighbours dark and shiny. On the east side was the subway station and a kind of visitor's centre with photographs of 9/11. I could see through the fence down into a great pit. On the south side there was a gateway open for lorries to come and go, leaving muddy tracks on the road. I stood and looked in. I was hungry. I didn't know what I wanted to eat, but if I carried on walking I was sure to find something.

At Washington Square my legs had had enough and I looked down at my tired feet to see mud on my trainers. Ground Zero mud. And so I walked with the dead on my feet, staring mostly at them and smelling the streets as they changed shape and size. I was on Sixth Avenue but I had no idea of a destination. Onwards, to the north. The numbers of the streets started to go up and I could feel my legs struggling to drag the weight of a thousand souls uptown with me. I cut from Sixth to Fifth Avenue along leafy West Tenth Street with its brownstone houses and broad steps leading up to wide doorways. And then, as I carried on north, buildings got higher and higher. These weren't like the oppressive dark blocks of the financial district daring doom to rain down death and misery upon them; these were older, light-coloured buildings of an outdated and maybe misplaced optimism. They went on and on.

If I'd been disappointed by how unlike my idea of New York this place had been when I'd arrived all that time ago (when was it? Only yesterday morning?), now I was in a New York so like itself it seemed like a parody, although it was curiously quiet and fresh. The taxis were yellow, but there was no honking, police cars rolled slowly and silently—the occasional and gentle whoop of a siren flicked on and off made me imagine exotic birds—and the bums seemed sober (they didn't even seem like bums—perhaps they were just people sitting). And I walked ten blocks and another ten and the buildings just kept getting taller and taller and the weight of the dead on my feet called out to me and told me to stop sometime soon, but I didn't. No time to stop. Stop when you're dead. I wonder how many miles I'd walked this morning. The Empire State Building is so tall you can't see the top (not from where I was standing anyway).

The lowest building on this part of Fifth Avenue is large and ornate with pillars and steps, guarded by lions. Butterfly must have liked this building. I walked up and stopped directly in front of it and then noticed the lettering along the front telling me that it was the New York Public Library. Yes, Butterfly loved this building. I went in through the door and joined a short queue to have my bag searched.

I walked upstairs, dragging my hand along the stone balustrade, and meandered down corridors and up more stairs. I found an enormous reading room with hundreds of people silently expanding their brains and I carried on walking. There's something about this library that I didn't understand. Where were the books? I walked down another stairway and found an empty room full of identically bound brown volumes of a catalogue for something or other. I pulled one from the shelf and opened it on the table; there were eternal entries in alphabetical order, but I couldn't understand what they referred to. I leaned my head on my hands and stared down at the page while I rested the dead on the marble floor. Time passed (probably not much, but some) and then I walked more, along, up, and down until I came back to the entrance and joined a small queue of people waiting to have their bags checked as they left. When I got outside, the sun was shining almost directly downwards onto my head. I lit a cigarette, sat on the steps and watched the people and the cars.

I don't know why I turned to look at the library again, but I did. A youngish-looking woman had just come out. Her eyes caught mine as she rummaged in her bag. I looked down at the dead on my shoes, then back at her. She came over.

'Do you have a light?' she asked, and I passed her my lighter. 'Thank you,' she said, and watched me as she lit her cigarette. I thought she might say something else, but she didn't.

'Do you know where Bryant Park is?' I asked.

Her eyes checked around and then locked back on me. 'Yes,' she said. I couldn't understand why she was staring; it wasn't unpleasant. I smiled and she released my eyes.

'It's where I'm going now,' she said. 'I'll show you.'

I stood up and she walked down a couple of steps ahead of me, hesitating as though uncertain where to go. It wasn't even a second.

'Is it far?' I said, and she looked back at me, smiling.

'No, it's near; it backs up onto the library.'

We walked slowly round the side of the building and I would have liked to talk to her, but I couldn't think of anything to say.

'Are you English?' she asked once the silence had grown uncomfortable.

'Yes.'

'Are you on vacation?'

'No. Yes. Well, kind of.'

'You don't sound sure.' She kept a straight face, somewhere between playful and not caring.

'Somebody hid something for me here and I've come to find it. Like a treasure hunt.'

'That's nice,' she said.

'In a way it's nice,' I agreed, 'but the hiding person died, so it's a bit sad as well.'

She stopped and I stopped too and she looked at me hard.

'They died?'

'Yes. She left me a treasure hunt.'

She looked at my face and then at my feet and I wished that I'd stopped to clean the dead off. Then I wished I'd changed my clothes. I wished I'd cleaned my teeth too. She started walking again.

'So, is the thing you're looking for in Bryant Park?'

'Yes.' I had become socially inept. How do conversations happen? 'Why were *you* coming to the park?' The words came out so uncomfortably I could have kicked myself.

'To have a break. I'm working in the library.'

'Are you a librarian?'

'No, I'm studying.'

We were at the top of the park.

'Do you know where the statue of William Bryant is?'

'Yeah, I think it's over there.' She pointed to a big stone thing on the terrace behind the library—a freestanding arch or dome sheltering a seated bronze figure.

'Cool.' I tried to keep the conversation going. 'What are you studying?'

But she had lost interest now. Her mind was wandering off in the other direction. 'Oh, people and food,' she said. I didn't really know what that meant. It sounded interesting. She was probably interesting.

'Well, thanks for your help.'

'So, what exactly are you looking for?' She wasn't quite ready to go.

'I don't know. I just have this clue which is the writing on the base of the statue.'

'What writing?'

'Yet let no empty gust of passion find an utterance in thy lay, a blast that whirls the dust along the howling street and dies away; but feelings of calm power and mighty sweep, like currents journeying through the windless deep,' I said, and she grinned at me.

'That's on the base of the statue?'

'I don't know, I've never seen it.'

She glanced over at the tables and chairs in the shade of the trees that were beckoning her, then back at me.

'Maybe we should go and see,' she said, and made a 'come on then' gesture with her head and started walking to where the statue was.

'I think I was word-perfect,' I said.

'I think you were.'

I ran my hand over the words carved into the plinth and looked up into the folds of Bryant's clothes and anywhere an envelope could be hidden.

'So where do you think your treasure is?'

'It might not be treasure; it might just be instructions.'

'How will you know when you've found it?'

'That's a good question.' I looked at her. 'I think it's in a brown envelope with my name on it.' I hoped she might ask me what my name was, as though perhaps she had seen such an envelope but wanted to be sure that it was mine before telling me where. She said nothing.

Emboldened by having an audience, I climbed up a couple of steps onto the plinth, pushing my hand into the only fold of cloth that looked deep enough to hide an envelope. I lost my footing and slid back down.

She put her head to one side like a curious dog and said, 'Maybe you should wait until there are less people around.'

The park was busy with summer people and lunchtime people, but no one paid any attention to me.

'It's there,' I said. 'I felt it.' I climbed up again, this time adjusting my foothold so I could better support myself while I peeled away the tape holding the envelope to the unpolished metal underside. I stepped down, looking proud, then turned away for a second to examine in private what I'd found. Large blue capital letters in ballpoint; it was almost like Butterfly's handwriting. 'Look'—I held it up to her—'my name.'

'Very Dickensian,' she said.

'What? It's not Dickensian at all,' I complained, suddenly doubting her.

She smiled as if she thought I was funny. 'Well, good luck with the rest of your search. I'm going to find a seat now and have my lunch.'

I felt frustrated not to be able to keep her attention.

'All right. Thank you for helping me.'

'It was a pleasure.'

And she walked past me towards the shade of the trees and I watched, waiting for her to turn back and wave or something. She didn't turn back.

'Aren't you even curious to know what's in the envelope?' I called after her.

'Kind of.' She stopped and looked at me and I smiled.

'Can I come and join you while you have your lunch?'

She said 'OK,' in a way that sounded as though she meant to say 'Whatever,' and shrugged her shoulders.

We went to the north side of the park and found an empty table in the shade. She pulled a tub of salad from her bag and a metal fork brought from home. 'I hope you don't mind,' she said; 'I'm going to eat.'

I said I didn't, but suddenly remembered that I too was hungry and felt jealous.

I stuck my finger in the envelope and tore it open.

'How long has it been there?' she asked.

'I don't know. Six months at least. Maybe eight.'

'Put there by a dead person?'

'She wasn't dead then.'

'It doesn't look like it's been there months.'

I looked at the envelope and it didn't look old or weathered, and neither did the tape that had stuck it to the statue. I frowned.

'Sorry,' she said.

'Don't be.' I smelt the envelope. It didn't smell of anything other than the faint smell of envelope, but then it had been tucked up well out of the way.

I pulled out a sheet of paper. On it was a photocopy, or scan, of a piece of lined paper torn from a notebook. I read the words while she ate her salad. I salivated but didn't look at her.

Leaving here and proceeding for five blocks to the east and thirty-four to the south you reach a village street. A traveler spoiled on the world's great monuments might feel disappointment compared to the wonder felt in other cities, but the special quality of this street for the man who arrives here on an August afternoon when the shadows first start to stretch along the road and from the sidewalk in front of a café a woman smoking calls to a friend across the road, "Hey" . . . is that he feels he knows this place already; that he's walked this street before with an old friend and it felt like home. At a door marked 44½ the sound of a piano draws his eyes to the top floor and he wonders what curiosity could have been left there for him.

I pushed the paper across the table to the woman. She paused her eating to read while I looked in the envelope again and pulled out a small square of paper that also had scanned writing on it.

Oh, Ben Constable,

I am so excited that you have found this. I hope it wasn't too hard. I guess you had to do some research and travel some miles. Solve the next clue. Go to the address and I recommend you take French wine or some such Franco-finery as a gift for the guardian of the treasure. Be especially charming, not that I can imagine you otherwise.

B. X O X

The writing was small and covered every available space, but the last part went all round the edge of the paper before squeezing the kisses in.

'It's in the style of a book called *Invisible Cities* by the Italian author Italo Calvino,' said the woman matter-of-factly.

'Oh,' I said, because I didn't know what she was talking about.

'I think you have to go to the East Village. East Sixth or Eighth Street depending on whether you start from Fortieth or Forty-Second.'

'OK.' I suddenly felt myself in the presence of a superior intelligence. 'You may as well see the rest of it,' I said, passing her the small square of paper.

'Your treasure hunt is cute,' she said.

'Thanks.' I looked down at my shoes and she followed my eyes. 'Dead people,' I said.

'Excuse me?'

'On my trainers. The dirt is from Ground Zero. I was there this morning and I stood at a gateway where the trucks go in and out, and when I left I had all this mud on my shoes with the ashes of thousands of dead people mixed in. I should clean it off really, but I'm carrying them round as a mark of respect.'

She looked at the dead respectfully for a second and then said, 'When did you arrive in New York?'

'I got to Manhattan yesterday at about five in the morning. But I didn't find somewhere to stay until the afternoon, then I slept until this morning, so today's my first day really.'

She was silent for a moment as if considering this. 'When did your friend die?'

'March the fifteenth.'

'Was she your girlfriend?'

'No. What makes you think she was a girl?'

'She just is. Was. Sorry. I think you said "she" at some point. It's a girl's handwriting anyway.'

'Yes, I suppose it is.' She was very pretty—the woman I was talking to. 'You seem old to be a student.'

'Thanks.'

'I mean, not old, but you're not twenty, are you?'

'I'm twenty-nine. I'm doing a doctorate, but I started late.'

'It's not really a normal time of year to be studying, August.'

'You have crazy syntax,' she said.

'It's not crazy; I'm just stupid.'

'I need to present a draft of my thesis in September.'

'Do you have a lot left to do?'

'Yes. It looks like I'm going to spend my summer in the library. What about you? What's next?'

'I don't know,' I said. 'I don't have a plan. I suppose I'll go to East Sixth or Eighth Street and see what happens. Do you want to come?'

'It's a tempting proposition, but I really need to go back and do some work. And frankly, it would be a bit strange if I just went off treasure hunting with a stranger I met on the steps of the library.'

'That's true,' I admitted. She put her lunch box back in her bag and I guessed she was going to get up and go back to the library.

Oh well. 'I think it's time I cleaned the dead off my shoes,' I said. 'Is there a toilet here?'

'You mean a restroom?' She grinned.

'Exactly.'

'It's just over there.' She pointed. We both stood up and walked to a small brick building at the edge of the park.

'I'll wait here for you,' she said.

Two minutes later I came out with clean shoes, expecting her to be gone, but she was waiting with her back to me, watching the park. We walked back round to the steps at the front of the library and the lions.

'Well, it was very nice to meet you.'

'It was nice to meet you too,' she said with a hint of fake English accent, and then, 'I hope you find what you're looking for.'

'Do you think you'd like to go for a coffee with me one day?' I asked.

'OK,' she said.

'So, how shall we do that? Shall I call you?'

'Yeah, OK. Do you have a pen?'

I dug in my bag, pulled out a notebook and Butterfly's on/offable pen and handed them to the woman. She deftly scribed her number and a name, then gave it back.

'Beatrice,' I read.

'If you give me a missed call, I'll have your number too.'

Then she shook my hand, which made me laugh. We said goodbye and she walked back up the steps into the library. I hoped she might look back at me but she didn't.

I put her number into my phone and then pressed the call button so she'd have my number. She answered on the first ring.

'Hello—Beatrice?'

'Yes?'

'It's Ben Constable, the English guy you were talking to less than a minute ago.'

'Oh yes, I remember you.'

'I was just giving you a missed call so you could have my number. You weren't supposed to answer.'

'Sorry.'

'Besides, you're in a library. You can't answer your phone in a library.'

'I stepped outside as soon as it rang.'

I turned round and she was standing by the door, looking at me. I waved and she waved back.

'You know how you wouldn't come treasure hunting with me because I'm a complete stranger you met outside a library?'

'Yes?'

'Why did you agree to have a coffee with me then? I'm still a complete stranger you met outside a library.'

'Going for a coffee is normal. Going treasure hunting with a stranger isn't.'

'What if we went for a coffee now?'

'I have to work.'

'You only had a break for about ten minutes. I don't think that's long enough.'

'It's true, it wasn't a long break.'

'Then let's go and get coffee. That's a perfectly normal thing to do.'

'. . .'

'Hello?'

'OK,' she said.

'Shall we meet in say, ten seconds at the bottom of the steps?'

'Yeah, that's good for me.'

'OK. Bye.'

'Hey,' she said.

'Oh, hi. Sorry I'm late.'

'That's OK, I've only just arrived myself,' she said. 'Where do you want to get a coffee?'

'I don't know anywhere, I'm afraid.'

She thought for a second and then said, 'Come on,' and I followed her up the road.

13

The Book in the Piano

'You answered the phone quickly,' I said.

We stopped to wait for the lights to change.

'It was an accident, I was turning my phone on; it was on silent.'

'Why were you turning your phone on going into the library?'

'I wasn't going to go in. I'd only had a ten-minute break and I've been here since nine o'clock. I was waiting for you to leave and then I was going to go and get a coffee. I only answered my phone because in a moment of stupidity I saw a foreign number and wondered who it could be.'

I laughed. She laughed.

'Shall I let you go and get coffee by yourself and call you another time?'

'No, you've completely put me off my work now. I need a break.'

We walked along Forty-Second Street and into the subway at

Grand Central, then took the 6 train down to Astor Place. I followed her out into the street.

'What do you do?' she asked. She'd resigned herself to her situation and suddenly everything seemed more relaxed.

'I work for a bank.'

'Are you a banker?' She laughed to herself as though suspecting she had made a joke for English people.

'No. I organise language lessons for bankers. I don't take it too seriously. It pays my rent while I learn how to be a writer.'

'Are you a writer?'

'I'm learning.'

'What do you write?'

'Fiction.'

'What kind of fiction?'

'Oh, I don't know. Short fiction, long fiction. Stories that I make up, or borrow from things that happen, or from things people say.'

'Have you had anything published?'

'Just a couple of short stories.'

'Do bankers take a lot of language lessons?'

'I live in France and companies there put pressure on people to be able to work in English as well as French.'

'Yes,' she said, as if she knew what I was talking about. 'There's no forty-four and a half on this street.'

'Pardon?' I was surprised that living in France didn't seem to provoke any interest.

'This is East Sixth Street.'

'I thought we were going for a coffee.'

'Oh, I thought that was a pretext to get me to come with you.'

'Well, it was, but I was going to convince you to come with me while we were drinking coffee.'

'Well, we may just be going for coffee anyway because there's no forty-four and a half here. Look, there's forty-two, forty-four and that's forty-six. Over there is forty-three and forty-five. There's no forty-four and a half.'

'I think you're right,' I said. 'What kind of number is forty-four and a half anyway?'

'People do that here.'

'Really?'

'Yep. Maybe we should check East Eighth Street while we're in the neighbourhood,' she suggested.

'May as well, while we're here.'

'Tally-ho!' she said.

I looked at her in amazement. 'Did you just say tally-ho?'

'You're very English.'

'I know. But English people don't say tally-ho.'

'Who does then?'

'No one.'

'Of course they do. It's English. It comes from your people.'

'Maybe people said it in the twenties, but it was probably already antiquated by the war.'

'Shut up, you're ruining my image of your country.'

East Eighth Street was called St Mark's Place and Beatrice said, 'Oh, of course,' like she must have been stupid not to have remembered. Number 44½ existed. It had a red door and four buzzers at the side of it.

'Which one do you think it is?'

'The top one,' she said, as though it were obvious.

'How do you know?'

'The clue said it was the top floor.'

'But what if the numbers go downwards from one and the top floor is the bottom bell?'

'Have you got some kind of specially overcomplicated brain?' she asked.

'Yes,' I said.

'Look, it's the top one. No doubt.'

I waited and looked at the button. Suddenly faced with the task of pushing it, I didn't want to. It crossed my mind to wait for Cat, but thought better of it. Then I remembered something far more important to save me from the buzzer.

'French wine. I need to take wine,' I said.

'Have you got any?'

I patted my bag as though there might have been a bottle there I'd forgotten about. 'No.'

'We need a shop,' she said.

'We need a wine merchant,' I said.

'This way.'

Ten minutes later we were standing back outside 44½ St Mark's Place with a bottle of wine in my bag. I looked at Beatrice, decided to stop being a coward and rang the bell.

There was a click and a buzzing sound. Beatrice pushed the door open and held it for me to walk through. I gave her a look that meant 'What?' and she gestured with her eyes for me to get on with it.

'Which way?' We all become stupid when we think that somebody else is better qualified than we are to make a decision, even when it's easy.

'Up.'

'Yeah.'

We wound our way to the top floor and I knocked.

A woman answered and said 'Oh, hi,' like she was expecting someone else, but gave a kind of functional smile.

'Hi,' I said. 'I'm sorry to bother you, but you may be able to help me with something.'

'Yeah?'

'It's a little bit complicated to explain but—'

'If you're selling something we could all save ourselves some time here; I'm not interested.'

'No, I'm not selling anything, I'm trying to find something which has been hidden here.'

'Are you Jehovah's Witnesses?'

'No. At least I'm not,' I said.

'I'm an atheist,' Beatrice threw in.

'Are you a Jehovah's Witness?' I asked the woman, keeping an open mind.

'I'm Jewish,' she said.

'Oh, if I was religious, I'd be Jewish,' Beatrice said, as if she'd known the answer to a question in a quiz.

And if I'd ever had a plan of how to address the difficult situation of explaining my treasure hunt to a stranger on a doorstep, it was now derailed.

'Oh wow,' I said, melting into the absurdity of the situation. 'Look at this.' I pulled the visa-waiver form I'd taken from the airport out of my pocket. 'You'll both be pleased to know that all Nazi war criminals who don't already have citizenship or a visa are required to confess upon entering the United States.' I held out the card for them to follow as I read aloud, '"Between 1933 and 1945 were (you) involved, in any way, in the persecutions associated with Nazi Germany or its allies?"'

'What is this?' asked the woman.

'It's the form that you have to fill in for US Border Control. Look at these amazing questions.' I pointed.

'"Do you have a communicable disease?"' read Beatrice.

'"Have you ever been or are you now involved in espionage or sabotage?"' said the woman dryly.

'Yes, that's me, I'm afraid,' I said. 'Sorry, I thought I'd get away with it, but now you've posed the question directly, I can't lie—I'm a spy. I guess that's my cover blown.'

The woman looked perplexed and amused at the same time.

'And look.' I knew I should shut up, but the words kept coming. '"Have you ever been arrested or convicted for an offence or crime involving moral turpitude?" What the hell is turpitude?'

'Depravity, or baseness,' said Beatrice.

'How would you know a thing like that?' I asked.

'I know a lot of things,' said Beatrice.

'Yeah, I'm pretty busy actually,' said the woman, backing into her apartment, although some kind of curiosity had stopped her from closing the door completely. 'What do you actually want?'

'Oh, I'm sorry,' I said. 'I think you may have something for me, or somebody may have given you something to pass on to me.'

'Nobody's given me anything for you.'

'Or maybe they've hidden something in your apartment.'

The woman paused, kind of amazed. 'I can assure you that nobody's hidden anything in my apartment,' she said, and she gently (maybe even reluctantly) started to close the door.

'He's got a clue telling him to come here and bring wine for you,' blurted Beatrice.

'What?'

I looked in my bag. 'Here, this is for you.' I held out the bottle and the woman looked at it and kept her hands firmly on the door.

'It's French,' Beatrice added.

'What makes you think I like French wine?'

'The clue suggested it ought to be French.'

'What clue?'

'Do you know someone called Tomomi Ishikawa?' I asked.

'Tommy who?' she said. 'I've never heard of him.'

'She's a her,' I said.

'Remind me to tell you about that name later,' said Beatrice.

I stopped and looked at her, but her expression just said 'Get on with it' so I did. 'Tomomi Ishikawa was a friend of mine,' I said. 'She died, but she left me a series of clues leading to things she'd hidden. It's a kind of treasure hunt.'

The woman scowled. 'What's this got to do with me?'

'Show her what you found in Bryant Park,' said Beatrice. I took out the envelope and handed it over.

As the woman read the clue and then the small square of paper, Beatrice and I stared hard at each other with nonverbal communication that was slightly above my level of understanding. The woman turned the papers over, looked in the envelope and frowned hard, thinking.

'You found this in Bryant Park?'

'Yeah. I know it's for me because it's got my name on the envelope.'

'Is that your name?' The woman frowned. 'It's like something from a Dickens novel.'

Beatrice choked on her laughter and the woman seemed pleased at the unanticipated success of her wit.

Now I was the one scowling. 'Of course, it's actually Hebrew,' I said, as though taking the intellectual high ground (but vaguely aware of knowing the precise origin of my name).

'Look, I really don't know if I can help you,' said the woman. 'I can't be bothered to do the math but it seems like this is the right address and I do have a piano and I love French wine. I love France in fact.'

'Oh, I live in Paris,' I said.

'I used to live there as well,' said Beatrice.

'Really?' I was stunned.

'I'll tell you about it later.'

The woman looked back and forth between us and nearly asked something, but gave up.

'Would it be possible for me to have a look at your piano?'

She shook her head in amazement. 'No. Look, there's nothing in my piano. Nobody has hidden anything for you here. I'm sorry.'

'It could have been a long time ago,' I said. 'How long have you had the piano?'

'About seven years,' said the woman. 'I bought it from a girl in the West Village, Charles Street, maybe. She was selling everything.'

Beatrice changed position as if she was uncomfortable.

'Was she a smallish girl with long, straight, dark hair and kind of ambiguously Asian features?' I asked.

'Yes.'

'Hmmm.'

'I remember her. She was funny. We talked for ages about stuff that had nothing to do with the piano; about France in fact.'

'That's my dead friend,' I said.

'I kind of really want to tell you to go away and never come back. But you've just made a normal afternoon interesting and I'm starting to want to know if you're right or not.'

I only smiled a little bit, but Beatrice grinned without restraint.

'Look, I'm expecting somebody,' said the woman. 'I thought you would be them. But hey, it's probably already early evening in

France. Maybe we should have a glass of that wine and take a quick look at the piano.'

'*Excellente idée!*' said Beatrice without a trace of an accent, and I laughed.

'I've got ten minutes maximum,' warned the woman.

I looked at Beatrice and she congratulated me telepathically for having got through the door. I let her walk first as though I were a gentleman.

'I've got a corkscrew here somewhere,' said the woman, holding out her hand for the bottle, which she opened proficiently, and then pulled three glasses from a shelf. 'Shall we go through to the other room?'

She led the way into a living room with many books and an upright piano. She placed the glasses on a low table and sat in an armchair and served the wine. Beatrice and I sat on the sofa.

'So, are you a musician?' I asked.

'I'm a piano teacher,' said the woman, 'but I play for myself as well.'

I picked up my glass. 'Cheers.' Beatrice and the woman reached for theirs.

'Mmm. Good choice,' said Beatrice.

'That's great,' said the woman sincerely.

'He bought it at the wine merchant around the corner,' said Beatrice, and I scowled at her.

'So you didn't bring it from France then.' The woman laughed and I gave Beatrice a look telling her that she'd ruined everything.

'I only found the clue an hour ago. I didn't know I needed to come equipped with wine for all occasions. Besides, my luggage was lost anyway.'

'You lost your luggage?'

'Well, the airline did,' I said. 'May I look at the piano?'

'OK,' said the woman, and came over and lifted the lid.

I played a couple of notes as though I knew what I was doing.

'I think I may need to take the panel off the front,' I said. 'Would that be all right?'

'I'm sure you'd be careful, but I'd rather I did it,' said the woman.

'That's understandable.'

She folded back the top and then lifted out the upper panel and we both peered in, then Beatrice came and joined us.

'I can't see anything,' said Beatrice.

'No.'

'The piano tuner's never mentioned finding anything. What are we looking for?'

'Probably a brown envelope.'

'Let's take the bottom panel off,' said the woman.

There was nothing in the front half of the casing.

'Behind the soundboard?' said the woman, and I was relieved because I didn't want to be the one to suggest pulling the piano out and taking the back off. 'We'll have to pull it out from the wall,' she said.

'Wait,' said Beatrice, and knelt down and pushed her hand up at the bottom of the piano, behind the light-coloured soundboard. We stepped back as she moved along the length from right to left on her hands and knees, then went back to the middle and pushed hard to get her hand right through the tiny gap. I could hear her fingers scratching around. 'Call the fire department. I'm stuck!'

'Really?'

'Nope.' And she pulled her hand out and stood up triumphant and presented me with a large unmarked brown envelope; I took it from her, sat down and opened it. Inside was a notebook. On the front was written the word 'Komori' in large letters. I finished my wine in one go and the woman and Beatrice politely took sips from theirs, watching.

I flicked through the pages of Butterfly's writing in blue pen, and then closed the book.

'Well?' said Beatrice.

'This is it.'

'Are you sure?'

I opened the book to the first page and put the clue next to it. 'It's her handwriting.'

Beatrice and the woman both leaned over. I let them look for a couple of seconds and then quickly closed the book. 'I think I should read it first,' I said. And they both stood back, suddenly conscious of seeming nosey. The woman poured more wine and I opened the book again and read a line from the first page:

> Ever since I was a child, Komori had been preparing me for her death . . .

I closed it again, put it back in the envelope and breathed out a long breath.

14

Komori

As we were leaving, the buzzer sounded and we passed a man on the stairs coming up.

Beatrice floated along the street, laughing to herself about what had just happened. 'We were funny,' she said.

I had too many thoughts to get them in any kind of order. We crossed First Avenue and carried along St Mark's Place into a café on the left. I knew this place. It's where I'd had breakfast.

We got a table near the front and didn't speak for a moment, as though there was some kind of telepathic communication going on that I didn't understand. It was nice. A waitress came over (maybe she served me this morning) and smiled as if she recognised me, which made Beatrice double take.

'We should carry on drinking now that we've started,' she said, 'otherwise we'll just get sleepy.'

I smiled. *'Bon plan.'*

'Wine?'

'Red.'

'I'll get the list,' the waitress said, and came back with a menu.

'Oh shit,' I said. 'I need to eat.'

We ordered a bottle and I ordered an entrée (which thankfully Beatrice told me is the American word for main course, otherwise I would have thought it was a starter and taken two). She ordered some olives 'to pick at'. When the wine was served and the waitress gone she said 'Ben' and I looked at her. 'That's what you're called, isn't it?'

'Yeah, Ben, Benjamin, I don't mind.'

'I know something about your friend Tomomi Ishikawa.'

'What?'

'I see her name written every day.'

'Where?'

'In my apartment.'

'How? Where? On what?'

'On an envelope that came to my address. There have been others too, but they were just junk mail so I just threw them away. This one looked as though it might be important, though, so I kept it. It sits in my kitchen on the side propped up by the pepper grinder. She used to live in my apartment.'

'Fuck!'

'There's another thing as well.'

'What?'

She took a deep breath before she spoke. 'She's my landlady.'

'Oh my God!'

'She owns the apartment where I live.'

'She owns an apartment?'

'Maybe more than one. I don't know.'

'So you know her?'

'No,' she said with determination. 'It's done through someone else, but it's her apartment.'

'That's too weird.'

'Isn't it?'

'That's just too weird. It's too much of a coincidence. Fuck.'

She looked at me wide-eyed and scrunched her mouth to the side for a second.

'Where is the apartment?' I asked.

'New York.'

'Er, yes. Where?'

'Williamsburg.' She scratched her nose.

'I've never been there.'

'It's nice.'

I considered Williamsburg's niceness for a second. My brain was saturating.

'Let's go and smoke?' I said.

When we got outside she held out a lighter and lit my cigarette before lighting her own.

'This is all too strange to be possible,' I said. 'Why didn't you tell me that you'd lived in Paris?'

'We only just met.'

'Yeah, but I told you I lived in France and you never said, "Oh that's interesting—me too," or anything.'

'It didn't seem important, or relevant. And if it's OK with you, I'll make the decisions about what I tell strangers about myself.'

'All right, of course you shouldn't tell people stuff you don't want to; I'm just surprised, that's all. And then you mentioned it like it was just a casual fact.'

'Well, it is just a casual fact, an interesting one, I admit, but I know lots of people from Paris. It doesn't get me excited anymore.'

'Yeah, but you lived in Paris and Tomomi Ishikawa is your landlady and you just met me randomly on the steps of the New York Public Library and now you just came with me to find treasure in an apartment and you just took me to the café where I had breakfast.'

'Really?' Finally something had impressed her.

'I don't know, but that seems like a hell of a lot of coincidences to me all in one afternoon.'

'It's true, that's a lot of coincidences. But coincidences are completely normal. What would be abnormal is if there were no coincidences. It would mean that there was some kind of force keeping similar things apart. Now that would be weird.'

I had to think about this for a second. 'OK, you're right,' I said. 'But I can't get over all those things. I can't decide whether I think there's something suspicious going on.'

'Don't go getting paranoid on me,' she said like somebody off the television. 'That's one thing no girl needs. You're pretty cool and funny, but you're going to have to get over the fact that we've got things in common. Normal people find that kind of thing positive.'

'But this all started because you said you needed a light.'

'So what?' Her eyes followed mine down to the lighter in her hand. 'I was looking for it in my bag when I saw you smoking. It was easier to ask you. And then you had a cute accent, and a treasure hunt, and a dead friend. That's quite an interesting combination for a midweek lunchtime.'

'OK.'

'And then you asked me to go for coffee and suddenly I was wondering if your whole story was part of an elaborate trick. It seemed too improbable to be made up, though, and you look too innocent.'

'The innocence thing's just a ruse.' My brain was still unsatisfied, but I had to stop thinking about it.

'I'm going to have to go after this wine, though,' she said. 'I still have things to do and I'm worried about getting blind drunk before it's even the end of the afternoon.'

'OK.'

'Besides, I think you want to read that notebook we found.'

We went back inside and ate the food we'd ordered and drank the wine. Beatrice was tipsy and talked a lot. She had an encyclopaedic knowledge of popular music, she'd read the same books I had and knew all Paris's best cafés and bars from Montmartre to La Butte aux Cailles. I liked her. And after five minutes and a second bottle of wine, three hours had passed and Beatrice looked at the time and said, 'Oh shit, I have to go. Can you ask for the cheque while I make a quick phone call?' Then she got up and went outside.

When she got back I'd paid.

'You paid for everything?'

'Yes.'

'Let me give you some money.'

'No, I'm getting this if that's OK.'

'OK. Thank you. It's my turn next time, though.'

'Good.'

'I really have to go, I'm afraid. Give me a call and let me know how you're getting on with your treasure hunt, and we'll get that coffee.'

'I don't actually drink coffee.'

'What?' she said with fake shock. 'You never had any intentions of getting coffee with me?'

'No, sorry.'

She leaned over and kissed my cheeks like we were French and then said, 'See ya later.'

'Bye,' I said.

I thought about staying in the café to read Butterfly's note-book, but my legs were aching from the morning's hike and my head was woozy from the wine. I wanted to be on my own so I went back to the hotel.

Keiko Sasaki (1941–1999)

One day, once upon a time in New York, a woman named Keiko Sasaki (known to me as Komori) went in a taxi to a private clinic in New Jersey where she would die.

Ever since I was a child, Komori had been preparing me for her death. She explained her will. It wasn't complicated; just about everything was for me. She told me I could sell, throw away or do whatever I wished with most things, but there were a few special objects I was instructed to distribute to people, and there were a couple of others that I had to guard preciously as keepsakes. She lived in a large apartment in the West Village. It is the apartment where I grew up and it is from here that I write, in this most improbable of gardens, surrounded by Komori's endless potted plants perched on every surface and before each window, the bathroom, kitchen, even the closets (for sprouting bulbs). As well as the flowers and shrubs there is a smallish Japanese tree (a blood willow, or Katsura tree—too large for the apartment) that Komori had potted on the day of my birth. It had been a present to her from my father. I was brought up caring for these plants—feeding and pruning and catering to their specific needs. In some respects it was quite a normal relationship between a woman and a young girl. In others it was unusual.

The precision of her will was not the only aspect of her death to be planned in detail. The other substantial part of the preparations was the death itself. Cancer was eating her from within. There were months and years of remission followed by new tumors in new organs. At times when she was so weakened by her chemotherapy I would be taken away and placed in the care of my delighted mother, then returned as soon as my nanny could stand again. But death was not to get the better of Komori. When the time came she had planned to go with dignity and (even if her judgment failed) I would assure that end. I was raised and educated for the single task of killing the person I loved the most.

Despite the innocence of my years, I knew that this was not normal and I kept it a (mortal) secret. Even now, committing it to paper seems like treachery, but somewhere is the hope that this may buy me peace.

Although appropriately vague, she first approached the subject when I was six, carefully implanting the notion that a strong person should follow strict ideals in death. It wasn't until I was nine or ten that she first mentioned that I would be involved; that when the time came, it would be important I help her die with honor, and I agreed. Komori meant to steal her own death from the hands of fate, God or whatever else could dictate her end. Her dignity was her control of all situations and it was as important to me as life itself. It still is. And thus these words are intended to go no further than the closed cover containing these pages, and yet even now, I know this is not the end of their journey; that the illusion of confession cannot work without the hope of an audience.

At times of weakness she would need assurance. "Promise

me you will, Butterfly," "Promise me you'll be here when I need
you," "Promise that you won't be afraid, that you won't back
out." And I promised.

It was five years before her death when we started to get
into specifics. She felt the inexorable draining of her life and
knew now that she couldn't recover. It was time to get
organized. "Let's make sure everything is clear while I still
have my mind," she would say. "Let's run through it again."
Komori's death was to be executed with calm precision and
without fault. Last-minute nerves or momentary loss of clarity
were not to cloud this moment of utmost importance, not least
because I didn't want to go to prison. So, like a soldier or an
assassin, I prepared, acting through every detail in my head,
training my mind to resist fear or revulsion for the task, I
learned the movements of my muscles so that even were my
head to be cut off I could still perform this one last task to
perfection, and I was not a death virgin—that would have
simply been irresponsible.

And time's elastic contracted, pulling me closer to the
moment, and I emptied my mind, concentrating as I had never
done before. My daily life became a façade, hollow actions,
running on autopilot while I meditated and rehearsed; keeping
the adrenaline down, becoming cold and rational. We come
from dust and to dust we will return, a promise is a promise
and I will do what I have prepared. Would that I could ever
refind that clarity and determination. Would that I could
reapply myself to anything else with the same dedication. But I
fear that I was born to do just one thing and now that it is done,
I am lost.

One day, once upon a time in New York, my nanny,

Komori, said goodbye to her home and her adopted Manhattan
island and went to the clinic in New Jersey where her longtime
medical advisor, Dr. Bastide, was the resident physician. She told
everybody she was going for intensive treatment, but she would
die there. That was the plan.

"We could perform a mastectomy, but it is not the cancer in
her breast that will kill her," Dr. Bastide told me in private.
"Although the surgery probably would."

I spent my days at her bedside, accompanying her
discomfort. She didn't bother with a wig now and her skin was
gray. I read to her. My father came once, and while they talked
Dr. Bastide took me to his office and explained that her organs
were shutting down one by one and that it was time to say
goodbye. I had two, maybe three days. When my father left he
nodded at me. That was our only exchange. I walked back into
the room and she told me she was feeling better

The day after, she told me that she might be strong enough
to undergo the mastectomy soon. She asked about her plants. At
shift change, a nurse came in, changed the drip and fluffed the
pillows. Then Dr. Bastide came and sat for about a quarter of an
hour, asking her questions and listening with a stethoscope.

"This is to keep you comfortable during the night," he told
her, and gave her an injection. "I'm leaving for the evening, but
I'll be in the area. Call me on my cell if you need anything,
Butterfly."

When he had shut the door we sat looking at each other
without speaking and I stroked her hand. Her skin was like
satin. Her eyes rolled back. She was old beyond her years.

"Let's get you sitting up."

"Why?" she asked.

"It's time for your medicine," I said, and took out a series of packets from my bag.

"I can't swallow very easily," she said. "They normally give me medicine through the drip." Her voice was helpless, like a child's.

"These are supplementary tablets. It's best for you to try to swallow."

"I'll try, my darling," she said, and I fought down the lump in my throat. That wasn't the plan. She wasn't supposed to call me darling.

I found the button to raise the back of the bed until she was upright and I put my arm around her to hold her steady. She weighed nothing.

"Are you ready, Komori?" I asked.

"Yes."

I popped a capsule out of its packaging and placed it on her tongue, then lifted a glass of water to her mouth. She swallowed obediently and although it caused her pain, she was quiet. I gave her two of each kind and then two more and two more. Each time there would be a pause as she gathered the strength to swallow. Sometimes her frail arm would rise up to help me tip the water.

"There are a lot," she whispered.

"Come on, nearly there. Let's take the rest."

We carried on for five minutes; each time I put a pill in her mouth it became harder to swallow.

"I expect the alstroemeria bulbs are ready for potting in the large tubs," she said.

I counted the remaining pills.

"Butterfly?"

"Yes, Komori?"

"They'll need plenty of water."

She had taken enough to kill a horse, but I wanted to make sure. After two more tablets, the water dripped back out of her mouth. She rested her head on me. I stroked the wisps of her hair and soothed her brow.

"Shhh," I said.

She stood wearing an embroidered kimono, motionless, watching. Not a child anymore, not an adult either. Before her was a green slope and from the left and the right silent figures arrived and spread out along three terraces. There were her birth parents and her brothers and sisters, and her adopted mother and aunts and uncles. In the center of the highest level was her father. He bowed formally, respectfully, but in his eyes was love and delight. "Welcome home, Keiko." The figures were now trees decorated in bright colors and a gentle breeze lifted the blossom from their branches, filling the air with a million tiny petals that rained gently down onto the terraces, onto her head, and into the palms of her hands.

I opened her mouth and found three tablets inside and then I stuck my fingers down her throat to make sure there was nothing stuck. Then I carried on sitting with my arms around her skeletal body. But this was all just functional. I was simply going through the motions of making her death pleasant. A promise is a promise and I had done what I had prepared. Emotion had no part in this. Emotion could come later or whenever. Whatever.

I lowered the head of the bed to a comfortable position, wiped the saliva from her mouth, straightened her clothes and the cover. I carefully put all the packaging back in my bag. There was nothing you couldn't buy over the counter from any drugstore, although I had done my shopping at three different stores, as any observant pharmacist would have noticed the toxic combination. I called Dr. Bastide. "Could you come, please?" I asked.

As soon as he arrived I left. Outside and out of view I lay facedown, flat, on the cold concrete. Occasional spasms pumped my chest, but I held my mind solid.

I couldn't make it all the way home. The dark growing inside me was too strong, treacle in my veins, black liquid behind my eyes. I went into a bar and drank four gins in twenty minutes and then went to another place for two more. On my empty stomach I hazed enough to make it back to Manhattan and the safety of Komori's apartment, where I could let the darkness come, and it came. It came.

15

Mr. C. Streetny

'Hello, Beatrice?'

'Yes.'

'Hi, it's Ben, you may remember me from yesterday. I'm the English guy you met on the steps of the New York Public Library.'

'Oh yes, I remember. What's up?'

'I don't know how to answer that question. In British English "What's up?" means "What's the matter?". I know in American it means "How are you?" but "Very well, thank you, and yourself?" doesn't seem to be the right response.'

'I see the problem. You could say "Nothing" and that would be like saying "Everything is tickety-boo, thank you very much".'

'Tickety-boo?'

'Yes, it's British English. It means running perfectly, or according to plan, and portrays a sense of contentedness with the current situation.'

'Uh-huh.'

'Don't tell me that you don't say tickety-boo.'

'I'm afraid I don't. I don't think anyone has for a very long time. I could be wrong.'

'Jeez, couldn't you just pretend?'

'Look, I'll try to be more British, but I'm not promising that I'll start saying tally-ho and tickety-boo.'

'Well, so long as you're making an effort, I suppose that's something.'

'Tell me,' I said, 'are you likely to have time for a coffee ever?'

'Er, yeah. When were you thinking?'

'I was thinking today, but I can do whenever you like,' I said.

'What if we meet for an aperitif at six?'

'Perfect. Where?'

'I know an interesting New York place for you. In the West Village there's a French café at the intersection of Fourth and Eleventh Streets, usually frequented by ladies in pairs discussing ladies' matters. The streets in Manhattan are supposed to run parallel and never cross; so it's an anomaly. You should try and find it without looking on a map.'

'I don't even know where the West Village is.'

'I'm sure you'll find it.'

'I hope so.'

'Well, you've got my number if you get lost.'

I wandered across the Brooklyn Bridge and lost myself in streets that felt curiously like home. I ordered fizzy water in a bar and got them to squeeze lime in it. I sat scribbling in my notebook and watching the world go by in the afternoon sun.

Who are you, Tomomi Ishikawa, and what have you done with my friend? Who else can I tell about all this? Who else would laugh? Who else would care? Don't be dead, Tomomi Ishikawa—come and hang out with me.

I don't understand the things you're giving me to read. How many people have you killed? Or do you just write stories?

Here's my question (the question that comes before 'Why?' or 'What is truth?'): What if I decide not to read what you write?

Ever since writing was invented, people have been documenting the contents of their brains, giving names to ideas, noting their dreams, and distorting their memories and making up new ones. Lifetimes of scribbling, and oceans of ink. Whole forests of trees reduced to pulp for us to collect our words. What if nobody reads them? I think we write to be read, even if we tell ourselves we don't. But the vast majority of everything written fails in its most basic purpose and has never been read by another. Where are you to read my words, Tomomi Ishikawa? Are we talking to ourselves?

Then I headed back, this time across the Manhattan Bridge, and wandered left and right through the streets until I found a place where I could see computers through the window.

I had new mail and didn't know what to think. I printed out the message and, as I paid, asked the man on the desk to point me towards the West Village. I was an hour early when I got to the French café. I ordered a beer because I was on holiday and read the email over and over.

Beatrice arrived bang on time, looking as if someone had just told her a joke.

'What's up?' she said.

'I'm very well, thank you, and yourself?'

'Oh, everything's just tickety-boo.'

'Do you want a beer?' I asked.

'Yes.' I ordered two more beers and she said, 'So what did it say in the notebook?'

I had a tiny attack of confusion. 'What notebook?' I wondered whether she was talking about my notebook, the one I write in.

'The one from the piano.'

'Oh.' It was supposed to be private. But Butterfly was dead and she had said that I could even write a book about her. I didn't suppose that it would matter. I was desperate to tell someone. I sat up straight, leaned in towards her and took a deep breath. 'It was the story of how she killed somebody.'

'She killed somebody?'

'That's what it said in the book.'

'Who?'

'Her nanny.'

'How did she kill her?'

'It's not as bad as it sounds.'

'Are there ways of killing people that aren't bad?'

'Well, this was a kind of euthanasia.'

'OK.'

I clacked my teeth together a few times, thinking. 'My head's a bit of a mess,' I said.

'Yes.' She nodded.

'I've already found two other pieces of writing where Tomomi Ishikawa talks about killing people and they all sound vaguely like acts of mercy, but it's crazy. There was no real need. The nanny was going to die anyway. The others, well, I don't know. There was just no need for any of them. They would have either died or they wouldn't. It was nothing to do with her.'

Beatrice stared at me hard to check that I wasn't joking or lying. 'Oh my God.' Then her face went white as if she'd just had bad news. 'Who were the other two people?'

My face tingled with the guilt of betrayal. 'Erm . . . a nephew of her nanny, and a stranger that she met on September 11, 2001.'

'OK,' she breathed, and her colour came back. 'So your Butterfly, my landlady, is a murderer.'

'My *Butterfly*?' I thought out loud.

'Do you really think she killed them?' asked Beatrice.

'I don't know. It doesn't make sense for her to have killed people, but she wrote it as though it was real.'

'You do realise that if she has killed three or more people and left a period of time between each one, then that officially makes her a serial killer?'

'How would you know the criteria for being a serial killer?'

She shrugged. 'My brain just collects information.'

'Evidently.' I looked at her hard. 'Why did you call her Butterfly?'

Beatrice's expression went blank and she reddened a little. 'Isn't that what she's called? I thought I heard you call her that.'

I couldn't remember calling her Butterfly in front of Beatrice, but I couldn't be sure that I hadn't.

'It's true, I call her Butterfly all the time,' I said. There was something more pressing. 'There's something else as well.'

'What?'

'Have you ever heard of anyone called Charles Streetny?'

'No.'

'Could it be the name of Tomomi Ishikawa's lawyer or something?'

'I don't know her lawyer's name. Why do you ask?'

'Look at this.' I passed her the email I'd printed out at the cyber-cafe and stepped out onto the sidewalk to smoke while she read.

To: Benjamin Constable

From: charlesstreetny15@hotmail.com

Subject: Forwarded message from Tomomi Ishikawa

Sent: 08-21-2007, 17:04 (GMT +2)

Dear Benjamin Constable,

We don't know each other, although we have both had dealings with the late Tomomi Ishikawa (also known to you as Butterfly), and on behalf of whom I take the liberty of contacting you.

Tomomi wrote various texts which she wished for me to forward to you at specifically designated moments. One such point is upon your arrival in New York.

What follows was written sometime in February 2007 in Paris. I hope it is of interest to you.

I wish you a very pleasant and productive stay in the United States.

Dear Ben Constable,

This is your official "Welcome to New York" letter. My heart jumps with excitement thinking of you wandering the streets where I grew up. I imagine I am there with you, pointing to things and telling you histories, sharing each sight and sense as you discover my city.

Right now I'm thinking of you with an oversized magnifying glass and a deerstalker hat, pacing the sidewalks, spotting details like a brilliant limey sleuth. But you must look upward, Ben Constable. Don't forget, in your determination to find hidden things, to wallow in the glory my great Gotham Town radiates in all directions.

So you found the treasure in the piano. I'm genuinely impressed. In other versions of this letter I was going to draw you to Bryant Park with rich descriptions of its beauty and past. So much of this city can be navigated by the patches of green that have punctuated my life and its urban backdrop. But you are ahead of me and you have seen the park and found the clue and the subsequent treasure, so I won't go on about it. Although I will allow myself just to point a retrospective finger at the statue of Gertrude Stein. Did you spot her seated on the terrace? Her Saturday evening salons were the center of Parisian Left Bank society during the 1920s. And it is quite the most Parisian of New York's parks, with its green tin tables and manicured avenues of trees. Oh, and the carousel and the fairy-tale view of the library and the towering skyscrapers overlooking it, lit up at night. And the fountain that I spent my youth wanting to climb in and spin around with outstretched arms, showering beneath the falling spray sparkling like jewels and splashing, as though I were a naiad, and words will never describe the lightness I would have felt, but never did . . .

I am suddenly aware of reality touching my skin and the clock on the wall telling me it is three twenty, and time is running out. I wanted to give you more clues to more treasures, but those will have to wait.

In all of this I want you to know that I'm thinking of you from my somber resting place. You are like a shard of dusty

light shining in through a crack in my wooden casing,
breathing air into me and a different sort of life.

And once again, darling Ben Constable, I am going to
leave you in the capable hands of fate and, as every time that
I sign off a letter to you these days, I shed a tear because it's
always so final. But there's more for you; there are more
letters, more clues, treasure to find, and I'm afraid there are
also episodes of my foul journal, documenting my miserable
life, that maybe you will one day put in a book, or maybe
discard and be well rid of.

Lots of love,
B. X O X

'Well, however scary a murderer she might be, the way she writes to you is sweet,' said Beatrice.

'All her letters are sad.'

'She must have liked you a lot,' said Beatrice.

'Do you think so?'

'Definitely.'

'Everything she writes takes my breath away. I feel like I need special breathing apparatus just to open an envelope or click on an email. I don't understand anything.'

'Maybe she was in love with you.'

'I don't think so. I think she loved me, though. But I'm scared she was mad.'

'I don't know. The treasure hunt, the clues, the letters. Being in love's a bit like being mad.'

'No, I'm talking dangerous mad. Psychotic. Serial killer.'

'Maybe.' She ran her hand across the top of the pages in front of her. 'Of course—it's an address.'

'I'm sorry?'

'It's an address, not a person: charlesstreetny15@hotmail .com.'

'Yes, but people make email addresses out of their names. This is from a person called Charles Streetny, or Streetny is a nickname or something.'

'It's number fifteen, Charles Street, New York. It's an address and it's two blocks from where you're sitting,' she said, then gave me a hard look as though it was unfortunate, but she had to tell me.

I stared at her, amazed. 'I feel as though every moment I spend with you the stakes get higher.'

'It's two blocks down. See the junction, not this one, the next one? It's there.'

'Shit. And the identity of Charles Streetny wasn't even what was bothering me about the email.'

'Why? What was bothering you?'

'How does he know I'm in New York?'

'Who have you told that you're here?'

'No one.'

'Nobody at all?'

'No,' I said.

'So you haven't called anyone, sent a postcard or an email?'

'I've sent one email. But the person I sent it to won't have told anyone.'

'How do you know?'

'It was to Tomomi Ishikawa.'

'When did she die again?'

'March fifteenth.'

'And she's still got an active email account?'

I felt stupid. The email I sent to Butterfly should have been returned to me.   •

'Are you sure she's dead?'

My face went all tingly.

'Every email has an identifier showing the IP address of the computer it was sent from,' she told me. 'Every computer connected to the Internet has its own address. So you can usually find out where in the world someone is when they send stuff. We could easily check, just like whoever received the one you sent to Butterfly could have seen that you were in New York.'

'When you say "we could," are you talking hypothetically, or are you some sort of hacker who can speak binary and find secret codes in emails?'

'You don't need to be a hacker. You just look at the source code and the IP address will be somewhere there. Copy and paste that address into a site that traces IP addresses, and it'll tell you at least which city it is. You might even get something more specific.'

'What do you mean, a site that traces IP addresses?'

'There are loads of them. They're not hard to find.'

'How would you know a thing like that?'

'I think what's more interesting is how most people don't know.'

'I want to do it now.'

'Well, you can't because I've only just got here. Have another beer. Then I'm going to take you and show you something interesting.'

'What?'

'A piece of New York treasure. I think your friend Butterfly would approve.'

16

Beatrice's Good Mood
Starts to Seem Strained

The gears ground, cogs spun and the world clicked forwards a notch. In a dizzying instant of motion, or lack of motion, afternoon became evening.

From somewhere behind me, Cat slinked over and smelt Beatrice's shoes, then turned his head and smelt her ankles. *Cat!* He had no shame.

'What's your thesis about?' I asked.

'Food.'

'Oh yes, you said. People and food.'

'It's about how we relate to food, from packaging and shopping to eating behaviour, rituals, tastes, that kind of thing. I'm trying to question whether food works for us as a species and whether there are alternative ways of thinking about it that might be more practical on planetary, cultural and even individual levels.'

'Is that a rehearsed line that you say whenever people ask you about it?'

'Er, kind of.'

'I'm not sure I know what it means.'

'OK, here's an example: A lot of food that we think of as being bad for our health, we consume as "treats". And then, to make us feel like we're successful, we eat treats all the time and we get these confused messages, like success equals unhealthy food. And there are loads of these strange ideas, like good food needs more packaging. Our eating habits often don't make much sense when you give them a closer look.'

'It sounds interesting.'

'It is. Complicated too. It's such a big subject. I have to narrow it down.'

'And where are you studying?'

'The New School.'

'What new school?'

'It's a school near here called the New School.'

'And is it new?'

'Er, newish.'

'Are you from New York?'

'Mostly.'

'What does that mean?'

'I've lived lots of places, most of them near to, or in New York. I went to high school not far from here. What about you? Are you from London?'

'No. I grew up in the Midlands.'

'Where's that?'

'In the middle of England.'

'I guess it's all in the name.'

'Postindustrial. Strange. I don't miss it. I grew up in a poor, multicultural neighbourhood, though, and I'm proud of that. I've got happy memories of running round in tiny terraced streets in the seventies.'

'The seventies? How old are you?'

'Thirty-eight and three-quarters.'

'You're older than I thought,' she said.

'Why, how old did you think I was?' I asked hopefully.

'Oh, maybe thirty-seven and a quarter or something,' she said, and I deflated. 'Sorry, I'm not fooled by youthful looks. Are you married or divorced or anything interesting like that?'

'No. I haven't got any of the things you should have at my age.'

'What should you have at your age?'

'Oh, you know, a house, a car, a career that you feel doesn't reflect your capabilities or interests, a wife and/or ex-wife, kids . . .'

'Yes.' She pretended to think about it. 'You haven't really lived.'

'What I'd give to be divorced.'

'You shouldn't joke about that,' she said. 'Divorce is hell.'

'All sorts of things are hell. It doesn't mean you shouldn't joke about them; all the more reason to joke about them, perhaps.'

'Hmmm. Maybe.'

'Shall we get another drink?' I said. 'Or shall we go and find your New York treasure, and maybe get something to eat?'

She smiled. 'Let's go.'

'Can we pass by 15 Charles Street on the way so I can see where it is?'

Her face hardened. 'OK,' she said, and her lack of enthusiasm caught me off guard. We set off walking and she dragged the pace, as if she was suddenly overwhelmed by tiredness.

'Are you OK?' I asked.

'Yeah,' she said. Something had changed; the light, or the atmospheric pressure, or something.

* * *

'This is 15 Charles Street,' she said.

It had a green awning stretching across the pavement towards the road. I walked up to the door and stared through the glass. There was a long entrance hall with a desk at the end and a door-man sitting behind it. He looked up. I smiled and moved back. Beatrice was leaning against the wall, watching me.

'Well?' she said.

'This is where her nanny lived,' I told her. 'And she lived here too.'

'How do you know?' Beatrice asked.

'The woman with the piano said it was Charles Street, and in Butterfly's notebook it said her nanny had an apartment in the West Village. This is it.'

Beatrice just waited and looked away down the street.

'Somebody here sent me that email,' I said.

'What makes you think that?'

'Maybe I don't think that, but it's the only thing I've got to go on.'

'It's just an address,' said Beatrice, unimpressed.

'I want to go in and ask some questions, but I don't know what to say.'

Beatrice just looked at me.

'Haven't you got any clever ideas?' I asked.

'Sorry.'

'I'm going to have to think about it and come back another time.'

We took a bus to Union Square and then the 4 train down to Brooklyn Bridge station and got off.

'Where to now?' I asked.

'Nowhere,' said Beatrice. 'We wait.'

'What for?'

'The six train.'

'Where does that go to?'

'Nowhere. This is the end of the line.'

'Huh?'

'People get off, then the train disappears in that direction'—she pointed—'and comes back on the opposite platform to head north again.'

'And so?'

'And so, if you stay on the train while it turns around and you look out the window, you see a secret place.'

'What kind of secret place?'

'There is an abandoned subway station—the original City Hall station—and if you stay on the six train while it turns around, you pass through it. It's supposed to be very beautiful.'

I felt excited, as though something magic were happening. I had images of a kind of exotic Victorian cavern mixed with something from the Arabian Nights.

The 6 train came in and we looked left and right as the people got off, then we snuck in as an announcement told everyone to leave. The doors closed and we pulled away. We pressed our faces to the window and cupped our hands round our eyes. Without warning, a world opened up with tiled arches and a barrel-vaulted ceiling, dimly lit from overhead skylights, like an underground temple running along a tightly curved platform. And it was gone.

City Hall station was an illusion, conjured into existence solely for the time we were looking at it, and then it evaporated, or was transported back to the middle of a great desert where it belonged.

'I love it' was all I could say.

Beatrice grinned at me, then pressed her face to the glass, as though there might be more.

'Again! Again!' I said.

We pulled back into Brooklyn Bridge station, the doors opened, people got on and we got off.

Beatrice's eyes were focused on nothing, and I stared at her.

'Are you sure you're all right?'

'Yeah, I'm fine,' she said, forcing some energy into her voice. 'What do you want to eat?'

'I really don't mind. You're the food specialist—take me somewhere,' I said.

'Let's go back up to Astor Place,' she said, 'there's plenty of choice around there.'

'OK.'

She glanced over her shoulder, then grabbed my arm, and we jumped back on the train we'd just got off before the doors closed.

When we came out of the subway, we passed in front of an Internet place and I asked whether we could just check my mail. Beatrice sat at the computer next to me and looked round the room.

To: Benjamin Constable

From: charlesstreetny15@hotmail.com

Subject: Another Forwarded Message

Sent: 08-22-2007 17:30 (GMT -6)

Please find a message to you from Tomomi Ishikawa, selected from several to correspond with your specific situation, which she seems to have anticipated. It was written in February 2007 in Paris.

Best wishes.

Hey, Ben Constable,

This is just a quick note with instructions for the next leg of your quest. The clue isn't particularly ingenious, but here goes. This is from the end of my secondary education (14–18 to be precise) and the location links well to the treasure. It's another confession, I'm afraid, and really ought to be removed before someone else finds it and a stink is kicked up, so you'd be doing my good name a favor (not that I deserve one), but for old times' sake could I ask? I planted the treasure like a shrub, to the right of the entrance of my old school— you may be surprised to know that I had a strict, girls-only Catholic schooling in West Midtown (you may have to do a little research). I suggest going after dark and taking something to dig with, like a spoon.

B. XO

'How do I find the IP address?' I demanded.

Beatrice took the mouse and I watched her. She was quick and precise. A menu came up and she clicked 'View source' and a new window opened. She ran her finger down the screen, scanning a page of code.

'There it is.' She pointed to a line that said 'Originating IP: 67.101.158.209.'

She copied the numbers and then opened a new window and

typed 'Locate IP address' into Google. She chose a site halfway down the results and pasted the address, then clicked a button that said 'Locate' and a map came up with an arrow pointing to New York.

'There you go,' she said. 'It was posted from here.'

'What, this place here?'

'No, from New York. It doesn't say where.'

'Let me try,' I said, and took the mouse. I clicked on the first message from Streetny and Beatrice watched over me as I copied what she had done.

I pasted the new IP address and a map came up with an arrow pointing to Paris.

'What does that mean?' I asked.

'It means that whoever Charles Streetny is, they were in Paris yesterday, and they're in New York today.'

'As though someone were following me.' The words left a bad taste in my mouth.

We found a Vietnamese restaurant Beatrice said looked nice. We ordered beers. I drank mine almost straightaway and got another. Beatrice was quiet, ignored her beer and played with her food.

'You've gone into a funny mood,' I said, because she had.

'I'm just tired. My cat woke me up too early this morning. He was standing on me and kissing my nose. I got up to feed him, but then I couldn't get back to sleep.'

'My cat does that too.'

'You have a cat?'

'Yeah. He doesn't do it because he wants feeding, though. He just bothers me to make me do things that I'd be too lazy or cowardly to do otherwise.'

'That's unusual behaviour for a cat. They don't normally have the mindset to become motivational coaches.'

'He's not like normal cats, and not strictly governed by the laws of science.'

'He's not governed by the laws of science?'

'No, because he's imaginary,' I said, and Beatrice coughed. 'But not many people know that. I don't really tell people about him.'

'You have an imaginary cat?'

'Yes. He's not really my cat, he just comes and hangs out with me sometimes.'

'Oh,' she said, and made a face as if she were trying to humour a dangerous psychopath.

'Can I ask you something completely different?' I said.

'Yes.'

'Do you know any Catholic high schools for girls in West Mid-town?'

'Why would you want to know a thing like that?' She looked at me suspiciously.

'Because Butterfly told me to go to her school to find another notebook. She said it was an all-girls Catholic school in West Mid town.'

'A notebook?'

'I think it's another murder,' I said.

She stared at me blankly for too long, weighing something up. 'It's called Saint Michael's Academy,' she said.

'You do know lots of things!'

She didn't say anything.

'What's the matter, Beatrice?'

She carried on looking. 'I feel . . . I don't know, like I'm in a bad mood.'

'Are you in a bad mood with me?'

'I am probably just tired.'

'Do you want me to take you home?'

'That's sweet. But no thanks.'

Now there was nothing to say. We stopped looking at each other and the quiet burned.

'Look, Ben,' she started again, 'your treasure hunt is making me feel uncomfortable. I don't really know who you are. You seem nice and you seem to be honest, but all those coincidences that didn't bother me yesterday . . . well, I'm bothered by them today.'

'Why?'

'The reason I know Saint Michael's Academy is because it's where I went to school. It's my school. My past.'

'Oh,' I said, my mouth gaping.

'I almost wonder whether you're playing some kind of trick on me.'

'Oh,' I said again, because no other words came to mind. 'I'm not making any of this happen. But you were at school with Butterfly.'

'She can't be the same age as me or I'd know her.'

'She'd be thirty-three now.'

'Four years older than me. I went there when I was fourteen. She would have been in twelfth grade when I was a freshman, or she might have already left. But she must know people that I know. I could ask around.'

'God, no, don't do that,' I said, panicked. 'The stuff I've told you is secret. I don't want you to know her. It wouldn't work like that.'

'What wouldn't work?'

'Knowing you. I like hanging out with you. It wouldn't be the same if you knew her.'

'I don't think you should go and look for the book.'

'Why?'

'Because it feels like this is something to do with me. There are too many coincidences.'

'Hey, now it's you being paranoid. This is all coincidence. No-body made you come over to me and ask for a light. That was your choice. I was just some random guy sitting on the steps.'

'I don't want you to go to my school.'

'Why?'

'Because of all the reasons I just said. Because I'm freaked out. This whole thing's scaring me.'

'I have to go!' I said.

'You don't have to do anything,' she said dryly.

'It's exciting, not scary. Something's unfolding and I don't know what. This is my treasure hunt. It's why I'm in America.'

Now she wouldn't look at me.

'Come and help me find the book,' I said. And then as a joke, 'I'd protect you from her.'

'I'm going now,' said Beatrice, and stood up.

'Hold on. I'll walk you to the subway.' I started to stand and fished around for my wallet.

'No, I'm paying for this,' she said. 'You can leave the tip.'

By the time we got outside, her brain had already left. She pointed. 'You go that way,' she said. 'It's at 425 West Thirty-Third just near Penn Station. I'd take a cab if I were you.'

'Can I drop you somewhere?'

'I'm going a different way.'

'OK. Can we meet again sometime?' I asked.

'I don't know,' she said.

'All right.'

'Look, call me,' she said. 'Not tomorrow. Call me another day.'

'OK,' I said.

She kissed my cheeks and left me standing in the street, watching her. It would have been nice if she'd turned back to let me know that everything was all right, but she didn't.

17

Tracy

I tried not to play through the conversation I'd just had with Beatrice; trying not to change the things I said, or to be more dynamic and convincing, trying not to consider that I might have been insensitive. I was cross with her for not wanting me to look for this book. I wanted her to be excited. I wanted her to be like she was yesterday.

The street seemed well lit and exposed but there was nobody in view. Just the occasional car. Black railings with points on top ran along the front of the school. I could have jumped over, but I didn't need to. On either side of the entrance was a large ceramic plant pot with a shrub in it. Sticking my hands between the bars, I could easily reach the pot. I pulled out Tomomi Ishikawa's blue pen and squatted down. A streetlight cast my shadow over where I was working. It would have cast the same shadow while Butterfly was planting her treasure. I started piercing pilot holes in the hope that what I was looking for was not too deep. The earth was hard and hadn't been disturbed anytime recently. Butterfly had once been here doing exactly the same thing as I was. The only thing that separated us was time. I thought of her, small and delicate, digging by herself in the night, touching the space that was touching my skin now, smelling the street and the dry earth, infringing on my personal space as if her memory were being projected inside me, like claustrophobia.

I tipped the pot and carefully pulled out the whole plant, roots, earth and everything. There was a small package in the bottom, wrapped in several layers of polythene and sealed with duct tape. I pushed the plant back into the pot and made sure it didn't look as though it had been disturbed in any way. I took the bundle, headed to the subway and found a route back to the hotel that was surely far more complicated than necessary. I unpicked a notebook from the dusty plastic. It was old and had got damp at some point, but it was dry now.

Tracy Wyatt (1966–1997)

Every story has a beginning and this is mine. With any luck this book will rot away, or be found by future archaeologists long after my death. Perhaps it will be discovered and discarded without attracting interest. But I take the precaution of changing the names of those concerned, not to protect the innocent, but to save my sorry ass should someone ever pay attention to these words.

When I was seventeen, I had a hopeless crush on one of my high school teachers. He was new and young and serious looking with glasses. He had an air of being preoccupied with higher pursuits than daily matters that concerned the rest of us. He was soft-spoken and delicate. One might have expected him to be a target for ridicule, but his effortless superiority and aloofness caught our imagination and we loved him for it (although perhaps none more so than I).

For the sake of this text, the teacher's name was Mr. Wyatt, although we called him Tracy and he made no objection. He taught English with a passion that was frankly lost on us all, but my weeks revolved around his classes, or absentminded anticipation of them. I would frequently wait at the end to ask questions, and my homework assignments were completed with previously unknown vigor.

Life outside school had started to flow in turbulent currents. My parents were all but absent in their respective worlds. The adolescent turmoil of doubt and isolation was augmented by the pact I had with my nanny, laying the foundations for her death. With my friends I maintained a brave face. I was slightly on the badder side of predictably naughty. But I was an outsider, and in solitude I plunged to new depths, wading through murky pools, considering—and confusing—love and loss (themes that have since dominated my reflections). I can only hope one day to be swept along in clearer waters.

Despite the metaphorical apples left for him at the end of every class, and other such advances on my part, Tracy behaved with admirable propriety. Underlining his wish not to encourage my attentions, he was considerably more jovial with other students. He did, however, seem to enjoy my creative writing and encouraged me to show him any extracurricular work should I so wish, which I did on several occasions. He took the time to go through my writing and offer gentle but constructive criticism of my efforts. And little by little I managed to gain his confidence and he became more relaxed in my presence.

As I approached my eighteenth birthday, I snagged on the
blissful delusion that Tracy had held me at a distance because I
was a minor and that soon, when I was an adult with voting
rights, we would become an alpha couple to the admiration of
my fellow students. In my imagination they had already guessed
and had overcome their envy to wish me nothing but the best.

During one of our frequent class tangents (this time on
astrological references in literature), I managed to learn that his
birthday was just a week away. He would be twenty-six. I told
the other girls that I would organize a gift and everybody
contributed a dollar. I made up the rest from my own money. I
bought him black cashmere underwear for $140, wrapped
lovingly, a card inserted with the legend "Dearest Tracy, you're
the best. I love you. X." There was another card as well for
everybody to sign. But I knew he would recognize my
handwriting and I knew that he would think of me every time he
put on those exquisite shorts.

As it was I who had gone to the trouble to organize
everything, it was only right that I should make the presentation.
He opened the packet before the class to his obvious discomfort.
And I found it so endearing. He thanked us all and moved
quickly back to Harper Lee. From then on he avoided all
one-on-one contact with me. I interpreted this not only as an
admission of our complicity, but as a firm reminder that should
the school authorities ever become aware of our love, he would
lose his job, and thus our evolving relationship must take form
off campus, away from the curious gaze of the world. So I
followed him.

He rode a bicycle, which made the task more difficult, but by
waiting ever farther ahead I managed to learn of an address to

which he was a regular caller. Two weeks later, I conspired to bump into him outside the door. I waited, made up and perfumed, the anticipation burning me. He appeared around the corner and I jumped from my hiding place and ran straight to him.

"Oh, hello, Tracy." I feigned surprise, of course.

"What the fuck are you doing here?" His head shot around for fear that somebody might see.

"Oh, I was just . . ." I had barely started my rehearsed lines when he exploded.

"Fuck you. Don't ever come around here again. This is fucking off-limits, OK?" He made like he was going to slap me and I flinched, shocked, my eyes full of tears.

"But I was just at the bookshop on . . ." I pointed, and my voice cracked.

"Get. The fuck. Out of here. Now, Butterfly. Don't ever fucking follow me again. Got it? Go!"

I stood there dumbstruck.

He pressed a buzzer. "I'll see you in school tomorrow," he said, then a woman's voice said, "Yes?"

"It's me," he said. The door clicked and he went in.

I ran home weeping hysterically and locked myself in my room until Komori drew me out with soup and sympathy.

I received good grades from my studies with Tracy. The heartbreak ripped at me for months, not soothed by having been so public with my foiled intentions. For a long time after, it seemed his death would be the only way I would ever heal from the relentless humiliation of his rejection.

Five years later, I had become a self-confident young woman, and perhaps for the only time in my life, I was happy. I worked as an assistant at a small but well-reputed publisher of poetry and experimental fiction. It was my first job after graduation and one of my responsibilities was filtering the submissions, that is, reading the beginning of all the manuscripts sent to see if they fit our tight criteria. Anything of remote interest was passed on to an editor; most, however, were returned with a standard note of refusal.

One winter's morning while opening the mail I found, quite unexpectedly, the manuscript of a novel written and submitted by Tracy. By this time the pain of his rejection was all but forgotten, and the renewed thought of him and his dramatic overreaction provoked an embarrassed smile. I took the book home to devour that evening.

His writing was disappointingly keen to please. The narrative, however, caught my attention. It was the story of a male teacher, entering into a relationship with an adolescent girl. It wasn't Lolita by any means, but one could imagine from where he may have taken courage to document such a damning fantasy. My heart raced as I read his version of the cashmere underwear incident and I dreaded being exposed, but as the tale unfolded I recognized not myself in its pages, but another; a rather plain girl (I shall call her Jane), even younger than I, but she was a real person and I knew her. According to the story, Tracy developed a sexual relationship with her that lasted several years.

I wondered whether this could be true. It seemed the only way to be sure was to hear it from the horse's mouth. I found Jane's mom in the phone book and told her I was an old friend. She was reluctant to give any information but wanted to be polite. She said Jane was at a college upstate and mentioned *the name of a reputable establishment for the education of young women. She was thinner than I remembered and she was shy and broken. When I told her about Tracy's book she looked at the ground. She confessed that they had had an affair, starting when she was fourteen, and which had only finished a few months before. The story she told was of being groomed and seduced by Tracy and then bound by a pact of secrecy, although she blamed herself for everything. I promised her that I would see to it that Tracy would never publish the work. She begged me not to turn him over to the authorities and I promised her that I had a much simpler way to resolve the problem.*

Death was something I thought about a lot. I had never killed anybody, but I regularly toyed with the idea, pushing my understanding of moral limits, testing the boundaries in the hope of finding space for Komori's death. It was absolutely necessary that I adopt this thinking. It was part of my preparation, my education, and so I regressed into a state of mind where individuals lose their value, and fantasy is fueled by fiction, shame and jealousy.

I had a plan, made easier with the certainty that I would never follow it to its conclusion. I would instead play a game of chicken with fate and see how close I could get. With the manuscript came a letter and at the top of the letter an address. It was not the same as the one I had gone to five years previously. I left work early on Friday evening and waited on the other side of the road, opposite his door, in the cold. He eventually arrived, walking briskly with his collar up and head down. I skipped across the street and literally bumped into him, knocking his briefcase to the ground. This may seem

*exactly like my last attempt to fake a surprise encounter, but
this was infinitely more refined, more audacious, less subtle
and carried out with ultimate confidence. The result was
joyfully effective. He quickly apologized for his clumsiness and
then recognized me. And it was he who insisted that we go
immediately to get a drink and warm up lest we catch a chill
talking in the street.*

*We were wholly unremarkable in a bar full of after-work
drinkers. We found a corner table and I spied myself in the
mirror, overly made up (a gesture toward disguise) and with the
naïve confidence of inexperience. He smelled of winter and
cleaned his steamed glasses, then drank with a thirst. His hands
were slightly too soft looking and boyish, but, with nicotine-
stained fingers, unsettled. He was nervous. I guess he always
had been.*

*When I answered his question about where I worked he
could hardly contain himself and told me about his book.
(Curiously, he lied about the plot.) I assured him that I would
look for it and make sure it got into the hands of an editor.*

*As the warmth of the bar worked into his bones and the
alcohol his blood, Tracy relaxed. We took to talking about
many things, including his continued work at the school and
how he felt it was leading him nowhere. We laughed at the
underwear incident, and without any encouragement he
apologized for the day I followed him, with no hint of
accusation in his voice. I could see that he was more drunk
than I was.*

*Now was the time to get out. I'd had my fun, I'd taken my
dare respectably far, there was no need to continue. I would
leave and write to him in the next week. I would tell him that*

if his manuscript ever saw the light of day, I would testify to make sure he was imprisoned for statutory rape. But some memory of old affection kept me where I was. Or maybe in this game of chicken I had plenty of dare left in me. I could go much further than this. After two more drinks he was blind drunk and slurring, and I was well on my way. I suggested we go and eat and he took care of the rest. As we staggered out into the street, he said he was too cold and asked whether I minded passing by his place so that he could put on another layer. I followed him up the stairs to his apartment. It was a sad one-room affair with a separate kitchen and bathroom. The sofa was a bed and hadn't been put away. The walls were lined with books.

Having shut the door behind us, he pushed me lightly against the wall and kissed me. It could almost have been romantic; it could almost have been my teenage fantasy. But there was a slight aggression as he rubbed his crotch against my hip that reminded me why I was there; how far would I take this? There was something perverse and victimlike about him, something cruel as well; it all added up to a sense of disgust in my gut. He had his hands under my clothes and was pushing me toward his bed. He undid my skirt with unexpected dexterity.

I pushed him back forcefully. It wasn't my strength that stopped him, but the look on my face. This was the point where I chickened out. It was over. And then he started crying.

I stood amazed as he wallowed in inconsolable self-pity. "I deserve to die," he slurred and sputtered. "I deserve to die for what I have done."

I wondered for a second whether he had somehow known

why I was there. I really was about to leave, but he'd hooked me
back. Challenged my cowardice, and I found my second wind. I
can go further. I should go further. "Don't be too hard on
yourself," I taunted him, testing the water. I could definitely go a
little bit further.

"When you read the book you'll know," he said.

"I know already," I said, and pulled him up. "I know
everything." Power raced through my veins. I put my arms
around him and kissed his neck. "I know everything," I said.

"I deserve to die," he teased.

I pulled the straight pin from my hair and lined it up an
inch and a half behind his ear, where the vertebral column enters
the skull. I had sharpened the end to a point earlier that day. All
that stood between his life and its end was tender tissue and my
nerve. I kissed his neck and he wept.

For those who have never killed, the sanctity of human life
must seem like an impenetrable fortress protecting us all. There
is something immature about finding the will to commit murder.
The decision to pass from fantasy to the action of killing is brutal
and dehumanizing, it's the logic of an undeveloped mind. I held
my breath and jumped.

In a small burst of violent movement, the hairpin sank into
his neck and his body turned to heavy liquid and ran through
my arms to the floor. I yelped in panic. He watched me,
paralyzed, like the dreams where you can see everything but you
control nothing. A sense of calm and acceptance overtook him.
There was something simple and almost pure in the warmth and
goodwill he felt toward the girl standing over him in panty hose,
her skirt on the floor next to her. He wished her everything, he
wished her well in everything. He was able to relax and clear his

mind and now he was sitting in a large, dimly lit room with a wooden floor and several light-colored canvases on the walls, and words came through the silence to his head; a song or a poem. They were so beautiful. It was a shame not to be able to write them down.

I couldn't breathe. I squealed, holding back a full-blown scream. I called to him, but he didn't move; maybe he was faking it to scare me. I shook him but there was nothing. I felt the blood leave my head and a dizzying nausea overcome me. I rushed to the bathroom and vomited.

When I got back he was still there. A minute before he'd been standing, crying. A minute before he'd been alive. My hand had traveled such a short distance. There was so little separating then and now. And now he would never stand up again, never speak. Never ride his bicycle.

I couldn't stop myself from crying. I'd never heard myself sobbing like that. It sounded put on, but there was no one there to witness my dramatics. And as I cried I dragged my thoughts together. I retrieved my hairpin and dark blood spilled from him, diffusing on the floor, expanding gently like an opening flower, deep and red. I heaved streams of tears as I scrubbed the toilet to get rid of all traces of my vomit, then I wiped all the surfaces. There was nothing more I could do. I left, pulling the door closed behind me. I went home to sleep and cried in my dreams. When I woke I was an adult. I carried more weight, but I was stronger; my performance enhanced. Having taken life, you either crumble with the pain of understanding the gravity of your actions, or you can turn the page and move on. But never can you escape the new truth, that life is not protected by God or the easily perverted laws of man; our existence, so tenuous, is protected by nothing more than a thin layer of choice, like tissue paper. Death is present in us all.

I mailed the manuscript back to Tracy's address with a standard letter of rejection.

18

Yogurt and the East Village Gardening Association

The next day my luggage arrived, but that was small comfort. I woke up feeling irritated and stared meanly at the ceiling for a long time, then I turned on the television and watched until boredom drove me back to the ceiling. I considered that I missed Butterfly, but that was just confusion, like thinking you want to sleep when in fact you are thirsty. Nothing made sense. Not only was Tomomi Ishikawa dead, but she had tarnished my memory of her and now I couldn't even miss her. I thought of phoning Beatrice, but she didn't want me to, so I wrote her a text message that I promptly deleted. Then Cat slinked along the fire escape and jumped in through the open window with hesitant precision. He carefully chose a place on the bed and settled down. 'Things are a bit crazy here,' I told him, and went back to sleep, heavy and unnecessary. When I woke he was gone.

* * *

It was four in the afternoon. I showered, shaved and put on clean clothes, which felt good. But I had to keep blocking out thoughts about Butterfly and her dead. I went out and ate in a pizzeria, then afterwards found a bar with an outside table, sat down and wrote and drank pints of beer. My legs told me I should get up and walk somewhere. I wandered until I found a Japanese restaurant on Avenue A. I ate sushi to my heart's content and drank a small pitcher of sake. On the way back to the hotel I went down the steps of a basement bar, wrote some more in my notebook and drank two pints. That was my day.

At eight the next morning I got up with a thick head and drank as much water as would fit in my stomach. I had barely fallen back to sleep when I got a text message from Beatrice saying, 'Are you up yet?' I wondered whether it had been sent to me in error and thought of ignoring it, but wrote back, 'Kind of. How you?'

'Better 2day. What bout U?'

'Arsey.'

'What the hell does that mean? Wanna meet up this afternoon? I could come 2 yo hood. How bout we get coffee @ your breakfast place?'

'Arsey /ˈaːs iː/ colloquialism. UK. adj. grumpy. From Anglo-Saxon arse meaning bottom. Breakfast place sounds cool. What time?'

'Ha-ha. 2 o'clock.'

'OK. See you later.'

I went back to sleep.

On my way to meet Beatrice I checked my email. Streetny had got slack and didn't even bother with a formal introduction.

To: Benjamin Constable
From: charlesstreetny15@hotmail.com
Subject: From Tomomi Ishikawa
Sent: 08-23-2007 12:49 (GMT -6)

Ben Constable,

You must be building up a horrific picture of me. I sometimes wonder if it was fair to choose you to bear the grim secrets of my past. I really couldn't say what you've done to deserve it. I could almost stop now and leave you in peace, but there would be things unfinished. I feel I should follow this through and tell you everything.

But not today.

Today's prize is about simple New York pleasures. I was going to bury it in a favorite green place, but suddenly suspected you might need a break, so there are no clues or need for digging equipment today. New York has hundreds of tiny gardens that people have converted from vacant lots—more than Paris, I think. One such spot that has played a significant role in my past, as a place to pull up a few weeds and read a book or two, is the community garden on the corner of Sixth Street and Avenue B. I was never a member myself as I didn't live in the right neighborhood, but I was fortunate enough to have a fond acquaintance with an old lady called Iris who is chairperson of the East Village Gardening Association and very trustingly let me tend her plot on numerous occasions when she was out of town or just for fun. As well as for its lush trees and plants, it is notable for a work of art in the form of a sixty-foot wooden tower decorated with abandoned toys. If you go one afternoon, you will almost certainly find Iris, as she spends them all there. I should mention that she has had a tracheotomy and, despite much training with one of those vibrating machines, cannot speak, so don't ask her too many questions. Tell her your name is Benjamin Constable and that you are a friend of Tomomi Ishikawa and she will give you something.

Suddenly I am tired and pity myself. I fear you will hate me. My reflection is beastly with fearful blackened features; a savage face. I do love you, Ben Constable. I'm sorry if I've made you sad.

Butterfly

I checked the IP address. It had been sent from New York about three hours previously. I printed the message and took it with me. By the time I got to the café, I was twenty minutes late and felt bad, but Beatrice was in an easy mood and smiley, sitting on the terrace, wearing big sunglasses.

'Hey, what's up?' she said.

'Very well, thank you, and yourself?' I said. 'Sorry I'm late.'

'No problem. Hey, I'm sorry for the other day.' She sipped at a clear drink through a straw. 'I was feeling no good.'

'That's all right.'

'Today it's you, though,' she said.

'I'm not sure how much fun I am.'

'Oh well, you can't be fun every day. Have a drink.'

'I'm wondering if I should just go back to Paris now.'

'Have you done as much as you want about Butterfly?'

'I don't know.'

'Do you want to be on your own? I've always got stuff to do. I don't mind.'

'No, I'd like to hang out with you. I have a thing I'd like to do, though. It's near here, I think.'

I handed her the printed-out message from Streetny and she scanned through it in a couple of seconds.

'It's a cute place,' she said. 'I think you should have a break from this crazy stuff, though. Once you've got your thing, I suggest we go to Central Park. It's pretty, nothing to do with Butterfly and very New York. Every visitor should see it at least once.'

'Sounds good.' I smiled. 'Should I get a drink or shall we just go?'

'Get a drink,' she said, and then looked me up and down. 'Hey—your luggage arrived.'

'Yep.' I smiled.

'You look kind of fresher.'

'Thanks, you're not so bad yourself.'

On the way to the garden at Sixth Street and Avenue B, we crossed Tompkins Square Park.

'Did you find the treasure at my school?' asked Beatrice as though she'd been building up her courage.

'Yeah, it was pretty easy.'

'Was it another dead person?'

'Yep.' I didn't mean to be so blunt.

'Was it something to do with me?'

'You weren't mentioned. It was her old English teacher.'

'OK. When was this?' She was calm, but she was bothered too.

'I think it was 1997.'

'OK.'

'There was a girl mentioned,' I said, 'younger than Butterfly, called Jane. Do you know a Jane? Apparently she was plain looking and had an affair with the teacher—before the murder, of course.'

'Of course.' She didn't speak for a while and eventually it made me turn and look at her. She smiled from behind her big sunglasses. 'Maybe I should read it,' she said.

I felt hesitant about showing it to her, but I'd brought it with me. I must have imagined letting her read it because there was no other reason to have it in my bag.

'One of the teachers from my school went missing shortly after I left. I don't want to be pushy or anything, but like I told you last time, your treasure hunt is slightly too close to my life for comfort. I'd like to read it, please. I'd feel better knowing that I was just a walk-on character in your story and not some key player.'

'OK,' I said. I took the book out of my bag and handed it to her.

'You brought it with you?' she said.

'Yes.'

Beatrice put the book away, and with it any wavering of her improved humour.

We found the entrance to the garden and sure enough it was lush and shady with trees and plants, more mature than the community gardens I'd seen in Paris. The whole thing was overshadowed by the slightly sinister sixty-foot wooden tower with abandoned dolls and other toys hanging from it.

'Is that to ward off children?' I asked Beatrice in a lowered voice.

'Excuse me?' Beatrice ignored me and was addressing a woman squatted down, turning the earth between the flowers on one of the tiny plots. 'We're looking for Iris. Do you know if she's here?'

I was shocked. This was my treasure hunt. I didn't want Beatrice to take over.

'Iris Gunther?' asked the woman. 'Yes, she's just over there.' We both looked to see whether the old lady she was pointing at could be our Iris. 'Iris,' called out the woman. 'There're some people here for you.'

Iris was tall and beautiful with white hair in a bun and dressed entirely in white. She had a high-necked blouse (presumably covering a hole where her larynx had once been) and a shawl across her shoulders attached at the front by a brooch in the form of a butterfly.

I put out my hand to stop Beatrice from speaking, but she was just staring in amazement.

'My name is Benjamin Constable'—I held out my hand—'and this is my friend Beatrice.' Iris placed a pair of secateurs in the pocket of her skirt and then took off her gardening gloves with care. She smiled and shook my hand and then Beatrice's. 'I am a friend of Tomomi Ishikawa's. She said that you had something for me.'

She smiled and nodded, then from her other pocket drew a notepad and held up a page with the words 'I'm afraid I am unable to speak; I have no voice' scribbled with the effortless perfection of another age.

'I know.' I smiled. 'Butterfly told me.'

She looked blank and I said, 'Tomomi Ishikawa.' She smiled and nodded.

She motioned with her eyes and her hand that we should follow her. It was slightly childish, as though reducing her language to gestures had rendered her innocent. She led us to a small rectangle of carpet laid out to protect her knees while working on a plot overflowing with flowers in pots and growing from the tended earth, and a buddleia with cones of violet blossom. Next to the carpet was an old leather bag with tools around it: a pair of kitchen scissors, a hand fork and a trowel. From the bag she pulled an envelope and handed it to me.

'Thank you.' I beamed.

There was no wad of paper, no notebook, but something three-dimensional and well wrapped. We were all silent for a few fat seconds. I looked at Beatrice, kind of surprised she hadn't spoken. She was watching the woman intently but stopped briefly to catch my eye. We all shook hands again and I had to almost drag Beatrice away. I turned again and waved as we walked through the gate.

'Oh my God, I love her,' said Beatrice.

I tore the end off the envelope and we peered in. I offered it to Beatrice for her to dip in her hand, but she pulled away in theatrical fear, so I did it myself. There was a bundle of bubble wrap held together with an elastic band. Inside were two metal spoons, three one-dollar bills and a small square of yellow paper like a Post-it note with no sticky.

The note said:

> Here is a complete guide to eating exceptional yogurt (if you took a girl, you would impress her): Go to deli on Elizabeth Street between Bleecker and Houston, buy blueberry yogurt, go to Albert's Garden on East Second Street, eat yogurts with spoons provided, sit on bench and bask in the simplicity of this little-known treasure.
>
> B. X O X O X

I passed the yellow paper to Beatrice, she looked at it, then turned it over to check there was nothing on the other side.

'What makes her think you'd be with a girl?'

'I don't know.'

'Do you know a lot of girls?'

'Some,' I said.

'Let's not go,' said Beatrice.

'Why?' I asked.

'We said we were going to go to Central Park. I know a place where we can get amazing yoghurt in Midtown.'

'But the yoghurt might not be the treasure. Somebody at the deli might give me something.'

'Poison probably. Let's not go, Ben. Come on. You're a big boy. You don't have to do everything your dead Butterfly tells you.'

I didn't say anything.

'You said you wanted a break from her. Even she said you should have a break. I don't actually want anything more to do with your treasure hunt. Come on. Let's do something else.'

I smiled.

We took the F train from Second Avenue station, where I had arrived in Manhattan four days earlier. At Forty-Second Street Beatrice grabbed my arm.

'Quick, let's get off,' she said, so we did. 'It's a beautiful day and there are hundreds of things to see. We should walk. I'll be your tour guide today.'

And so we strolled up Fifth Avenue talking, and every now and then she would point things out. 'Look, here's a French bookshop'; 'This is Rockefeller Center'; 'Just down there is the Seagram Building—it's got a restaurant that commissioned the big paintings by Mark Rothko that are in your Tate Museum in London.'

When we got to the park we walked round the edge of the zoo and looked over the fence. Then we climbed up a rocky mound to a pagoda, where we sat and smoked a cigarette. The skyline to the south was like a drawing of a towering city through trees; to the north the park disappeared into the haze of eternity.

'Are you going to write a book about Butterfly?' Beatrice asked.

'No, because then it would have to have murders and suicides and miserable stuff. I don't want to write about that sort of thing. It is a bit like a novel, though. Maybe one day I'll write it.' I pulled out my notebook and flicked through the pages in front of Beatrice. 'I've already started making notes.'

She leaned over and looked. 'Wow, you have crazy handwriting.'

'Thanks.'

'If you're going to write about Butterfly, though, you should finish your treasure hunt.'

'I know.' I nodded.

'The thing is, if you really think that she's killed people, maybe you should go to the police.'

'I know that too.'

'And there's something else that we haven't really said, but you must think, even if you're not totally sure, and I think it too.'

This made my heart beat fast and I felt uncomfortable, but I didn't flinch. 'What?'

'You think Butterfly's not dead.'

'Talking to you always makes things just a little bit more complicated.'

'But it's true, isn't it?' she said. 'It must have crossed your mind.'

'I can't answer that question. I can't think about it.'

'Why? You're getting regular emails from her. She knows where you are and what you're doing. She even knows who you're with. This isn't normal behaviour for a dead person.'

'Being dead isn't something you just make up to entertain your friends. If I start questioning everything, I'll go insane. She's dead. She has to be. Otherwise it means there is some crazy conspiracy and suddenly I feel like I've got clinical paranoia. I'm scared of going mad. There's stuff here that I don't understand, but that's OK. I don't have to understand everything.'

'What's your dating situation?'

I looked at her, unsure whether this was a subject change or a twist in the conversation we were in the middle of. 'I'm only interested in women who are unavailable or uninterested,' I said flippantly.

'Look, I hope you won't get mad at me for asking this . . . '

'Go on.'

'Do you think you might just be a little bit in love with Butterfly?'

I sighed. 'It's a fair question. But no.'

'You sound sure of yourself.'

'I know the answer because I've thought about it already. It's clear in my head. Besides, she's dead and she was a serial killer.'

'I know your treasure hunt is kind of sad for you, and even distressing, but there's also something very romantic about it. It's a cute story. She's spent so much time thinking of you and preparing an adventure for you. It's a massive compliment, and what's more, you want to write a book about her. That's a massive compliment too.'

'I do love her, just not in the kissing way.'

'What, you've never felt attracted to her physically?'

'It's not that she's unattractive, it was just never about that with me and Butterfly. It happens. People sometimes do think others are wonderful without wanting to jump into bed with them.'

'Yeah.' Beatrice wasn't totally convinced.

'What about you?' I asked.

'What about me what?'

'What's your dating situation?'

'I'm unavailable.'

'That makes sense,' I said.

'Hey, if it was a movie, who'd play you?'

'Will Smith,' I said off the top of my head, as though it were a decision I had made a long time ago.

'He's nothing like you.'

'It'll be a challenging role for him. I think he could do with a challenging role.'

'I think Gary Oldman would be better. Or John Malkovich.'

'No, you're too literal. And they're too old. Anyway, it's not that kind of film.'

Beatrice laughed.

'Films are never like books,' I said. 'You may as well have a surprising cast.'

'Shall I show you where to get amazing yoghurt?' asked Beatrice. 'Or would you prefer ice cream?'

'Ice cream,' I said, to prove I was independently minded.

'Come on then,' she said. 'Tally-ho!'

19

Guy Bastide

To: Benjamin Constable
From: charlesstreetny15@hotmail.com
Subject: A Clue
Sent: 08-25-07 09:13 (GMT -6)

Darling Ben Constable,

So, you are adjusting to the rhythms, shapes and smells of New York, and you have wandered some of the streets of my history. Now I would like to take you to another spot that you have passed a couple of times already, perhaps without noticing (although it is a joy to behold and of significance in both my life and that of the city).

There is a clock that sits atop the tower of a redbrick and white-granite castle that could have been whisked directly from southern Germany to the heart of Greenwich Village, where it marks the hour with an inharmonic chime. It was in fact the neo-Gothic folly of architects Frederick Clark Withers and Calvert Vaux. The whole delightful edifice was constructed in 1883 on the site of the former Jefferson Market, and for years was reputed to be one of the most beautiful buildings in the United States. Its official title was the Third Judicial District Courthouse, but by the second half of the twentieth century it had fallen into disuse, symbolized by the hands of the clock, which for many years had been marking the hour ceaselessly as twenty minutes past three.

Quite apart from its constant presence throughout my childhood as the landmark overshadowing the garden where I first dirtied my hands for the benefit of the community, and a place for books and reading, it had particular relevance in the life of the woman who raised me.

Late in 1959, Yutaka Sasaki from Sumitomo Bank, his wife, Kimiko, and their eighteen-year-old daughter, Keiko, attended a cocktail party at 51 Fifth Avenue. Keiko clearly remembered a woman saying to the portly cigar-smoking mayor, Robert F. Wagner Jr., "What we would really like for Christmas is to get the clock of Jefferson Courthouse working again," thus starting the campaign that led to the building's restoration and transformation into its current incarnation as Jefferson Market Library. The clock eventually chimed for the first time in decades on March 15, 1964, just as Keiko Sasaki was leaving the doctors with news of a shadow on her abdomen, thus marking the beginning of the end of her life. Damn that clock, she thought. If it could just have waited at twenty past three, then I would be able to live happily ever after.

It is a curiously invigorating pleasure to be writing to you,

Ben Constable, and how I would love to dally further. (Did you know that the shortest correspondence ever was between Victor Hugo and his editor? On the publication of *Les Misérables,* Hugo sent a telegram with just a question mark. His editor replied with a single exclamation mark.) But once again it is the point that draws me from my endless parentheses and crashing back to reality. And because it is a clue to a foul treasure (read "fowl" if you will), it is to be found in the section on domestic birds of a library close to my heart (can you guess which?) in an unlikely book by a man (or possibly a woman) named Wright.

But for now, my dear, once again I am sad to be leaving you for a moment, while you find the next installment of my gruesome memoir. Until we meet again . . .

B (is for X X X M X X X U X X X R X X X D X X X E X X X R X X X ! ! !)

Jefferson Market Library was every bit as Tomomi Ishikawa had described. And I had indeed passed it already without taking note, proof if any were needed of my lack of observation for even the most notable sights.

I had never seen Cat in a library before and it seemed to suit him well. However, his knowledge of the Dewey decimal system was poor, and when I asked him to lead the way to the section on domestic fowl, he looked at me blankly and sat down and started to lick his front right paw. I felt rather embarrassed to ask a librarian, but it seemed the only option.

Wright's Book of Poultry (636.522) was a hefty tome about chickens, which had not, in my judgement, been removed from the shelf for many years. There was nothing inserted next to either of the covers (front or back), but two-thirds of the way through there was half an inch of pages glued together. A few of the sheets at the beginning and end of this bunch were whole, but it was clear that ones at the interior had had their centres cut out, leaving a secret (or not so secret, but at least not visible) compartment. Cat watched with interest. I pulled out Butterfly's on/offable pen (more out of habit than need) and punctured a small hole at the top right-hand corner of the cavity, dragging down to leave a fairly neat cut and inflicting the least damage possible on the already abused work of Wright. Inside was a smallish brown envelope and within was the tiniest of all the notebooks thus far associated with this trail. I returned *Wright's Book of Poultry* to its Dewey-decimally designated position and Cat and I got out and walked round the corner to the French café at the intersection of Eleventh and Fourth Streets, where I had met Beatrice. I drank a bottled beer as I read.

Dr. Guy Bastide MD (1944–2000)

This is the story of a murder.

To this day I believe that I had little choice but to kill Dr. Bastide. And that lack of choice might in some way have justified my actions, but it couldn't push aside my desire to punish him. Worse than that, I know I would never have considered killing anyone, out of need or vengeance, had I not already had several experiences of that most exquisite and violent of delicacies. The pitiful truth is that I was looking for an excuse to do it again. And so I drifted into premeditation and, ultimately, execution. There is no mitigation, only motivation, and the motive is not good enough.

My father had followed his best friend from childhood across the globe from Manchuria, where they were born during the Japanese occupation, back to postwar Japan, then to California and eventually to New York. That his best friend should be a woman was unusual, that he should find excuses to live wherever in the world she went was more so, but for those who know him, it was further proof of his ingenuity and perhaps neediness. My father had no siblings and found all the community he could wish for in this fraternal relationship. That was the nature of their bond.

Komori decided not to mention to my father that she was dying. Besides, she wasn't dying quickly. It could take five, ten or even fifteen years. Nobody knew. It wasn't until much later, when a sudden gastric disorder scared her, that she confessed everything. Daddy was devastated. He sought the best medical advice and sent her for the most high-tech scans and every test imaginable. She saw consultants until she could no more, then alternative practitioners were sent to her, but the only person whose advice she felt comfortable following was a young, calm and fairly conventional Dr. Guy Bastide.

Bastide's ancestors were French but had come to New York via Quebec two generations previously. Although he spoke no French, he was delighted to correct anybody on the pronunciation of his name (Ghee Basteed) and was known for his good humor and gentle manner.

He worked with the terminally sick. He had no miracle cures and no specialist techniques. As a doctor he was pragmatic, taking one problem at a time and dealing with it in the most appropriate manner statistics-based science would

allow. There was something solidly reassuring about his method.
And in this way he kept Komori alive.

Several months after her death he called me. He spent a
long time finding out how I was before coming to the delicate
point of some unsettled fees that were not covered by the
insurance. I was embarrassed and apologetic and said I would
look into how to settle the matter.

Her estate didn't contain a stock of cash. Komori had left
little more than her apartment. I tried to contact my father, but
he was absent (as ever) and wouldn't return my calls. I hoped
that I might be able to get a bank loan to cover the debt. But first
things first, I needed to know how much was owed and whether I
might be able to negotiate terms of payment.

After a few days spent procrastinating, I left a message for
Bastide and he called me back later that afternoon. He suggested
coming to the apartment to explain everything and I agreed.

His manner was as careful as always.

"As you have experienced, Butterfly, accompanying people
through a terminal pathology is incredibly consuming. This is
something I had discussed in depth with Keiko. It is not just the
practical responsibilities, but the profound emotional strain."

"Of course," I said, although I had no idea what he was
talking about.

"The clinic and staff are funded in a number of different
ways. The lion's share of our resources come directly from
insurance companies. There are certain state subsidies as well,
which though small are a great help. There are also a couple of
charities and foundations who offer aid, but sadly we are also
obliged to ask that patients make a donation, solely in line with

their means. In order to ensure the continuity of service, we stipulate this contribution as a condition of treatment."

"And you discussed this with Keiko?"

"Yes, on several occasions."

I flushed. "I'm afraid Keiko didn't have any means. She has been supported by my father for all the years of her sickness. I . . . I . . ." I didn't want him to interrupt. "I could . . . if you would tell me how much of a donation you would like, I'd find the money and pay you, Doctor."

"Thank you, Butterfly. That is truly a great kindness, especially at this difficult time. I'm ashamed to have to even come to you with this matter. I wish that I had the means to simply offer all the support I could, as a friend. And I do consider that over the years Keiko and I became good friends."

"Yes, Doctor. It was my impression too that you were a friend of the family." I remembered the times when he had been there during the evening or eaten with us. "I have a very real problem of limited income, though, Doctor. I am still trying to contact my father to ask if he would help me. I was wondering if there was any way that I could pay you in installments— perhaps over a year, or even two. How much do you think would be an appropriate amount?"

"Oh, I don't think there's any need to get your father involved."

I understood this to mean that we were not talking the kind of money that would be inaccessible to a young graduate. "I'm very surprised, though, because Komori never spoke of this and she was so organized in every other respect of her death," I said.

"She was an incredible lady. Yes, she did in fact explain her financial situation to me with just that same attention to detail *we have both admired. I understand that you were to inherit this apartment.*"

"*The apartment?*" I had to check to make sure I wasn't about to overreact but I had a sudden suspicion that this kind-talking friend of the family was setting me up to extort money. I hardened. "*What do you want, Doctor?*"

"*The donation that I talked about with Keiko.*"

"*I think I would like to see an invoice or a contract or something.*"

"*Butterfly, please, I think you misunderstand the situation.*"

"*Sadly, Doctor, I think I have understood that you are trying to extract money and without legally binding documentation showing monies owed. If you thought you might be able to abuse your position to manipulate a poor bereaved girl out of her inheritance, you are gravely mistaken. I will pay nothing. I think you should leave now, Dr. Bastide.*"

"*Butterfly, this is not at all the case. Keiko spoke for many years about making a donation from equity she had tied up in this apartment. You dishonor her name not to even listen to her wishes.*"

"*What did she wish?*"

"*To make a donation.*"

"*You're a liar. She would have told me.*"

"*I think this may be the problem, Butterfly. It seems she told you and me different things.*"

"*I'd like you to leave now, Doctor. I'm not going to sell the only thing I have left of my nanny to give you part of the money.*"

"*Oh, I don't want part of it, Butterfly. I want it all.*"

"*Get out before I call the police.*"

"*Calm down. We can sort this out without any stress. Breathe deeply. Calm. That's good. You know you can't call the police. Don't forget, I signed the death certificate.*"

"*But you said . . .*"

"*You murdered her, Butterfly.*"

"*That's not fair. You said it had to be somebody else who did it. Nobody from the clinic.*"

"*That's correct.*"

"*You were complicit. You told me what to give her. You told me how to do it.*" I was panicking now.

"*I don't know what you're talking about. My suspicion is that you gave her a lethal combination of products, which can be purchased at any drugstore. No doctor, even one who believed in the morality of assisted suicide—which I do not—would prescribe such a crude and painful method to end a life.*"

"*It wasn't painful.*" Tears were streaming down my face.

"*You effectively disengaged her means to express pain. That doesn't mean she could not feel it.*"

"*That's a lie. They were fucking painkillers.*"

He held his arms out to me, and despite myself, I crumbled into his chest, sobbing. "*It's OK,*" he said. "*It's OK.*" He gently stroked my head and rubbed my back.

I had an idea.

I slid my arms inside his jacket and held him, my fingers almost imperceptibly caressing the small of his back. I felt his hands spread a little wider, moving slowly. I could smell his pheromones. I pulled away, wiped my eyes and straightened myself out.

"*I misjudged you,*" I told him. "*Don't think I am going to do this out of willingness. Don't imagine for one moment that you*" convinced me or that I was gullible enough to fall for your lies. I will cooperate with you for the simple reason that you have access to incriminating information on me."

"I'm glad you understand."

"I'm not going to sign all I have directly over to you, though, Doctor. I'm going to try and negotiate. I'd like to make you the kind of offer that will assure you never feel the need to take this further. But I want something for myself."

"Butterfly, there really is nothing to negotiate."

"You may be right, but I'm a clever girl. This apartment is worth more than its market value to my father. Much more. I may be able to convince him to buy it from me and then, although I will hate you for the rest of my life and I will find a way to destroy you, you will get your donation in full without any trouble, and I will get to keep the change and not be destitute."

"I'm not sure that your father has the means to buy this apartment again, Butterfly. He's already bought it once."

"Neither am I. Let me contact him. Meet me tomorrow for dinner and we will settle this. I swear on Komori's memory."

"Dinner?"

"Don't get excited. I never want you to set foot in this apartment again, that's all."

The trouble with information blackmail is that it can just go on and on. The doctor was a clever man and he would always be able to find ways to take money from me for the rest of my life. There would be no end to my donations, of that I was certain.

The next day I got dressed up and spent some time putting on makeup. "You were right about my father," I told him. "He'd have to sell his own house and probably then some as well. The apartment is worth a lot to him, but it's money he hasn't got."

"OK," said Bastide. "So we need to organize you signing the apartment over to me. I can get that sorted."

"Look, Doctor, we're both involved in this. We can sell the apartment and share the money."

"I'm sorry, Butterfly, but that can't happen."

"But you don't understand. I'll have nothing."

"Don't be so ridiculous. You have parents who are not in poverty, you have a job. Frankly, your poor-little-spoiled-middle-class-girl idea of 'nothing' is an insult to the millions who have neither food nor shelter."

"Fuck you, Doctor. That apartment was left to me. I looked after Komori all my life. And at her end it was me who took all the risk. Please, let me keep something."

"No."

"Oh God . . . I can't believe I'm going to say this: I'll let you have sex with me. Please."

"No."

"Please, Doctor. I mean it."

"Butterfly, I'm not going to turn into some sort of abuser in pushing you to humiliation and prostitution."

"Doctor, you're already an abuser. I'm twenty-six. I live in New York. I have boyfriends, I have sex with people. What's one more fuck? You're not the most unattractive person in the world. It wouldn't be torture, Doctor. Just let me keep something."

"What?"

"Half."

"With all due respect, Butterfly, your sexual favors are not worth half the value of Keiko's apartment. I like you, Butterfly.

And, you know, I would actually very much like to make love to you. I'll give you ten thousand."

"Don't ever imagine that it would be making love. It would be a fuck, that's all. But I need more than that."

"How much?"

"Fifty."

"No."

"OK, Doctor. I'm tired. I don't know what to suggest. I'll have sex with you for a month. I'll fuck you as though I love you. You can call me Mommy while I suck your cock if you like. I'll belong to you for thirty days. You get the apartment and I get fifty thousand dollars and I will hate you until I die. But it'll be over and we'll never talk about this again."

He looked at me. I met his stare hopefully, with none of the venom of my words. "You got a deal," he said.

I grinned like it was the best news in the world.

"I'll get the check," he said. "Then I could drop you off at my new apartment."

"That sounds like a good idea," I said.

One thing I definitely didn't want was Guy Bastide anywhere near my apartment again. I stupidly hadn't expected to have to come up with a sexual down payment right away. I wasn't ready. I thought I would have more time to get organized.

Bastide had a shiny black Mercedes that fortunately he had parked on the street and not in some high-security parking lot. We drove off and my brain was racing. After two or three blocks I said, "I don't feel like going home yet. What if we went for a drive?"

He looked at me and I smiled back, trying to look shy but fuckable.

"Where do you want to drive to?" he said.

"I don't know. The ocean. Let's go someplace where there's nothing but ocean."

"OK," said Bastide, and patted my leg. I stroked his hand, trying to hide my disgust.

We drove out through Queens toward Long Beach and then beyond, heading along the coast for what seemed like an eternity. My heart was pounding double time, desperate for a plan. Somewhere around Jones Beach we crossed a bridge and pulled off the road onto sandy scrub. I wondered who was in more danger. I looked around for ideas. Nothing in front of me but a stainless steel ballpoint pen in the opening below the radio. I pushed my feet forward and looked at my shoes: highish broad-heeled sandals. He reached for my knee and ran his hand up my skirt, gently massaging my thigh as we rolled slowly over the scrub until we were facing the angry waves of the Atlantic and he stopped the engine. I unstrapped myself and let him watch as I went into my bag and took out a condom. I leaned over and kissed his chest, and as I did so picked up the pen from beneath the radio. I ran my hand down to his belt and undid it. He held his hand to the back of my neck, trying to encourage my head down toward his crotch. I ignored him and started unbuttoning his shirt, running my hands over his chest. I hitched up my skirt and straddled him, squashed up against the steering wheel. He let go of me for a second and moved the seat back. His hands were all over my body. I took my top off and moved my left hand, the pen still concealed, up his chest and pushed him backward, fumbling for the electric buttons to recline the chair still further. I leaned forward and kissed his neck and moved around his head and kissed his brow so my breasts were in his *face. He reached his hands up for them, but I gently pushed him back and raised myself so I was sitting with my left hand over his chest. With my right I removed a sandal. I pointed the pen at his heart and he looked at it confused as I circled for a second, finding the space between the ribs to the side of the sternum. I brought the heel of my shoe down on the end of the pen with all my strength. He would have screamed but it was muffled as he tried to force his body to function. He pushed me back, but the steering wheel held me firmly in place. I hammered down again and again. His arms flailed, trying to strangle me, trying to grab my hands. He punched my face, but I felt nothing and hammered away, pummeling my fingers, but hitting the pen as well and it sank in, clicking on and off with each blow. In a last throe of violence he nearly managed to lift me off him, but I held on tight, pulling at the pen to try to get it back. It suddenly came free, unplugging the hole in his heart, and blood burst out as he collapsed backward, twitching a little.*

And then there was Jesus. Jesus? "Come and sit, Guy Bastide," said the Christ. "Who—me?" Jesus looked around the room. "Can you see anyone else called Guy Bastide?" "No, my Lord." "Come and sit." Jesus handed him a cup and poured wine from an earthenware jug, then lifted his own cup and they both drank the exquisite liquid. "It's good," said the doctor. "It's my blood," said Jesus. "It's taken you a long time to understand, but everything can be good if you choose it to be," he said. And Guy Bastide had to agree.

I moved back to my seat and closed my eyes, my body throbbing. I was covered in blood. Tears and snot began to trickle down my stinging face, but I felt strong like a goddess. I put my shoe back on and opened the glove box. There was a handgun, which surprised me. I left it there and looked around. On the back parcel shelf was a box of tissues. I reached over and grabbed them, cleaning my face and wiping as much of the blood from me as I could. I got out of the car and checked myself over for any blood I had missed, then put my top back on. I leaned in, turned the key in the ignition and then walked around to his side of the car with the tissues in my hand. I opened his door and lowered all the windows. Next I went around the car, wiping any surface I thought I might have touched. I gathered all the used tissues around his body. It took me a couple of minutes to find the lever that opened the fuel cap, then stuffed some tissues into the gas tank. I found a cigarette lighter in my bag, then put the car in drive and released the brake. The car rolled forward and I walked along easily next to it and lit the tissues around Bastide, then the tissues sticking out of the gas tank. The car bumped along in the direction of West Africa and down onto the loose sand, where it stopped with one of the back wheels spinning freely. I wanted it to roll into the sea or at least far enough down the beach for the sea to cover it when the tide came up. Then I remembered it was on fire and ran back. Seconds later, it burst into flames.

I walked back over the bridge we had come by and turned back to see the tips of flames through the dark. The car was burning well. I turned into the back streets as soon as I could and scurried left and right. I wondered how long it would take me to walk to anywhere there was public transport. It took five and a half hours to get home, unnoticed and elated. I scrubbed myself in the shower. My left hand was grazed and bruised where I had battered it trying to get the pen through his heart, my cheek was swollen and blue and there was a cut under my eye, but nothing serious, it would be normal in a week or so. The uncomfortable feeling wherever he had touched me lasted for months.

Bastide made the morning edition of the paper, which was faster than I'd expected, but that didn't shake me. The story did, though. It said he was found by the police in a burning car. He had been stabbed but was still alive. He died shortly afterward in the ambulance. Another surprise was that he was survived by a wife and three children. I'd never heard about his family. I wondered whether he had been able to talk. I'd find out soon enough. I spent the next two weeks waiting fatefully for the police to come and arrest me, but they never did.

20

McCarthy Square

'Want to get a beer?' I texted.

'We meet in café @ 11th & 4th?'

'Already there with beer and Cat.'

'Wow, that's weird. Always coincidences. Me there in 20.'

Beatrice arrived, kissed my cheeks, ordered a beer, then sat down opposite me.

'So, what have you been up to apart from drinking with your cat?'

'I went to Jefferson Market Library and there was a book that was hollowed out, and in it there was another murder.'

'Are you joking?'

'No. Streetny sent me there to find it.'

'I suppose I shouldn't be surprised about death in a library. *Et in Arcadia ego.*'

'I've heard that before, but I don't know what it means.'

'Even in Arcadia am I. "I" being death that goes, not only everywhere else, but to Arcadia as well.'

'Is that something to do with covered shopping streets?'

'No, Arcadia in Greece, stupid. The word "arcade" for covered shopping streets comes from the Latin word for arch.'

'Do you know everything?'

'I'm not sure. Maybe.'

'Anyway, the story's pretty distressing and I wonder if I'm just being instructed to go round collecting all Butterfly's imprudently abandoned writing because she can't. Did you read the notebook I gave you about the teacher?'

'Oh, yes. Here. I brought it back for you.' She dug it out of her bag.

'So what did you think?'

'It wasn't about me.' She wasn't saying much.

'That's the only thing you think?'

'I don't think it's a true story.'

'But what kind of an idiot would write themselves into a piece of fiction, saying that they murdered people?' I asked.

'I don't know the answer to that,' she said.

'No, neither do I.'

We both thought about it for a second as if there might be more to say, but nothing came out. Perhaps it's best not to talk about it.

'Can I read what you found?' she asked.

'Sure.' I passed the latest notebook over to her and she read while I looked out the window.

'Sorry, this is rude,' she said. 'I shouldn't read it now.'

'I don't mind,' I said truthfully. 'I'd like your opinion.'

So she read the story of Guy Bastide and made uncomfortable facial expressions every now and then.

'What do you think?' I asked.

'It's very crazy.'

'I don't believe it anymore,' I said. 'Something's changed. Like you said, they're not true stories.'

'I think you're right. You shouldn't be thinking of this as a trail of murders. It's a trail of writing.' Beatrice was thoughtful.

'Like some violent fantasy,' I said.

I showed her the email leading to Jefferson Market Library.

'She really does like you a lot,' she said.

'I guess so.'

'Maybe she's obsessed with you.'

'I find it unnerving that you talk about her in the present tense.'

'Well, you know my opinion on that,' she said. 'Anyway, where's your cat?'

I looked under the table and about the place. 'I don't know,' I said. 'He might have gone.'

'This morning I had to spend ten minutes getting cat hair off my clothes and I thought of you.'

'Oh God, yes. Cat's kind of longish-haired. It gets everywhere.'

'Is he called Cat?'

'Yes.'

'How unimaginative,' she said casually, and I felt slightly injured.

'He's not my cat; he's just a cat. It wasn't my job to give him a name,' I said defensively, 'but I had to call him something.'

'Has anyone else ever seen him?'

'I hope not. That would make them mind-readers and nothing would be private. It would be like walking around the streets naked. Very natural, a little cold and uncomfortably exposed.'

After two beers we wandered out into the street without thinking where to go.

I suddenly felt tired and hungry. 'Do you want to get something to eat?'

'Yeah, we could do.'

'Do you know somewhere we can get sushi?'

Beatrice smiled. 'Yeah, come with me.'

After a few minutes we came to a tiny Japanese restaurant and ordered maki, sushi and sashimi and drank bottled beers.

'Maki always reminds me of small trees and the French Resistance,' I said.

'Why?'

'Because traditionally French deserters and the Resistance ran off into this kind of low forest called the maquis, because it was very thick and no one could find them and so running off into the *maquis* became a euphemism or a metonym for joining the Resistance.'

'What do you mean low? Low like broccoli? Low like bonsai?'

'No, about three metres tall. Maybe four. I don't know; I've never been into the *maquis*. It's very dangerous because you can get lost and it's probably full of wild boars. It's like a jungle with short trees.'

'Short trees, but taller than broccoli.'

'Yes.'

'Good. I was having trouble imagining people running off and getting lost among the broccoli. Where do you find these forests?'

'In the south of France. Perhaps near Avignon. I saw them from the train once. They were like an ocean.'

Beatrice considered this for a second.

'I want to go back to 15 Charles Street,' I said.

Beatrice's expression didn't change. 'Pardon?'

'I want to go back to 15 Charles Street, New York. I want to talk to that man.'

'What man?'

'The doorman. Do you want to come with me? I think you exert good influence and a kind of positive preposterousness on any conversation you participate in. It makes it somehow less strange than if I'm by myself.'

'I can't, I'm afraid. I have to go home.'

'You never stay out very long.'

'It's a New York thing. No appointment lasts more than two hours. You're lucky, sometimes we've hung out for as much as four because I lost track of time.'

'People only do things in two-hour blocks?'

'Well, not officially, but it's my impression. It would be very easy to hang out with you for longer, but I can't.'

'Why not?'

'I've got other priorities.'

'OK,' I said.

When we got outside, Beatrice kissed my cheeks.

'Let's call each other tomorrow and you can tell me how you got on,' she said.

'All right. Which way are you heading?'

'That way.' She pointed to the buildings on the other side of the street, indicating northeast. 'I'm getting the J train. Charles Street is in that direction.' She pointed to the west.

I wondered whether it took self-control for her not to look back, or if it just happened naturally.

* * *

When I walked into the lobby of 15 Charles Street the doorman looked up.

'How you doing?' he said.

'Hi. You may be able to help me. I'm trying to find some information about somebody who used to live in this building. Have you worked here long?'

'What name is it?' he said, not answering my question.

'Sasaki.'

'Oh yes, Miss Sasaki'—his tone became softer and he shifted in his seat—'she passed away a few years back now.'

'Yes, I know.' I didn't want to go too far into the realms of dishonesty, but I tried to look as though this were a matter of personal regret to me in the hope it might make him more willing to help. 'Could you tell me who lives in the apartment now?'

'I'm afraid I can't give you that information without authorisation, sir.'

'Yes, of course. Tell me, did you know the girl who Miss Sasaki used to look after, Tomomi Ishikawa?'

'Oh yes, I know Butterfly. Is that who you're looking for?'

'Yes, she's a friend of mine. I've kind of lost her.'

'Maybe she wanted to be lost, in which case I don't know if it's my place to give you any information.'

'Oh, she definitely wanted to be lost. But she's in contact with me as well. She keeps sending me things.'

'Things?'

'Well—letters, emails, pieces of writing.'

'Maybe you should ask her where she is then.'

'All I have is this address. I don't know how to contact her.'

'Well, if she sends you emails, all you have to do is press the reply button.'

'It's not that simple, though. She's dead.'

'Dead?'

'A few months ago.'

'Aw Jeez, that's terrible.'

'She was a good friend of mine. She left me some stuff, letters and things she wrote before she died, and somebody keeps sending them to me. I think it might have something to do with whoever lives here.'

'I'm sorry, mister, but I can't help you.'

'No, don't worry, I think you already have. One more thing,' I said.

'Yeah?'

'Miss Sasaki had a lot of plants. Do you know what happened to them?'

The doorman smiled. 'Butterfly gave most of them away to people in the neighbourhood. Every time she came down she had some potted flowers she was trying to get rid of. I took one for my mother; she's in a home now.'

'There was a small tree—do you know what happened to that?'

'I've got an idea, but I'm not sure. Just around the corner to the right, there's a cleaners shop, the guy there's called Chan. He knows everybody around here. He knew Miss Butterfly. If anybody can tell you what happened to the plants, it's him. He lent her a trolley for her to get the last ones out. Go and ask Chan.' He looked at his watch. 'He should still be there.'

In the cleaners, a small Asian man greeted me with a broad smile.

'Hello, I'm looking for someone called Chan.'

'I'm Chan,' he said. 'What can I do for you?'

'My name is Ben Constable. I'm a friend of somebody you know. A girl who used to live just round the corner called Butterfly.'

He looked at me, pretending to scan his memory, while weighing me up.

'Ah, Butterfly Ishikawa; she was Japanese.'

'Exactly.'

'So what do you want from me?'

'She told me that you lent her a trolley to carry all the plants when she moved out from her apartment.'

'Yeah'—he nodded over to a four-wheeled trolley at the back of the shop—'that's it.'

'I'm curious to know what happened to the plants. Where did she take them?'

'Butterfly was a very crazy girl, you know?'

'Yes.'

'She tried to give as many away as possible, but it was difficult to find good homes for them at nighttime. I took three, but there were too many.'

'So what happened to the rest?'

'She planted them.'

'Where?'

He hesitated, then pointed outside. 'There,' he said. In the middle of the road there was a triangular road island with a flagpole and a flowerbed overflowing with plants and a small red tree. 'It was my suggestion,' Chan said. 'There was nothing there before, just dirt. I thought it would be nice to look at from my shop, and it might bring people in.'

I felt short of breath. 'Wow,' I said. 'I think that's all I wanted to know.'

'OK, no problem. Hey, what's Butterfly doing now?'

'Oh, she lives in Paris.' I took the spur-of-the-moment decision to stop telling people that she was dead because it simply
wasn't my responsibility. Besides, she still wrote to me on a daily
basis.

'In France?'

'Yeah.'

'Very nice.'

'Yes, it's a nice place. Thank you again. Bye.'

'You tell her Chan says hi.'

I walked round to the other side of the traffic island and
crouched down to look at the plants. The tree was only a couple of
metres in height and had red heart-shaped leaves draped from the
branches. This was Keiko Sasaki's tree. She had potted it the day
Tomomi Ishikawa was born.

I rummaged in my bag and pulled out a pen. Fuck. I turned it
round in my hand, examining it in the street light. Surely you can't
stab somebody in the heart with a pen! I called Cat and he walked
towards me down the road from the direction of Jefferson Market
Library.

'Will you keep me company, Cat?'

He sniffed the tree and then walked a couple of feet away and
sat like a lookout on the corner.

I broke the earth with the pen and scratched the mud away.
Cat got up and looked around and I carried on digging. Then he
came over and nudged me. He wanted me to look at something. I
could see into Chan's shop and there was a woman talking to him.
He passed some clothes on a hanger over the counter and the
woman walked out. I lowered my head so it didn't look like I was
watching, but she wasn't looking at me anyway. She walked off in
the direction I'd come from without turning back. My eyes were
tired and blurry and I couldn't make her out in the light. She

looked like someone I could have known, but then anybody could be somebody I know and I wouldn't recognise them.

'It's all right, Cat; I don't think she was interested in us.'

Cat looked at me and I glanced back up the road at the woman walking away. I carried on scraping away at the ground. I struggled between the roots, but managed to dig a hole of about eighteen inches and a little bit underneath the tree. And then I struck plastic. I knew it. I *knew* it. The tree was important, I knew it would be. It took me a further five minutes to wrench the package out. Carefully sealed within polythene and duct tape was a notebook. I pushed the earth back into the hole and tried to brush my hands clean.

As I walked away, Chan leaned out of the door and called, 'You people are crazy,' laughing at me.

'She left something for me under the tree.'

Chan looked curious. 'What is it?'

'I don't know yet.'

'Well, I hope it was worth all that digging.'

'Yeah, I hope so too.'

'You wanna wash your hands? You look like you could use a clean-up.'

'Yeah, thanks.'

Chan showed me to a sink and while I scratched away at the ground-in dirt on my fingers I said, 'I wonder how she managed to get the tree all the way from her apartment and plant it here? It's bigger than she is.'

'She had help,' said Chan, and winked.

I grinned at him. I wanted to thank him for helping her, but it was none of my business.

'So you saw her bury that?' I asked, nodding at the package.

'Yes.'

'And you never wondered what it was?'

'I asked her what it was.'

'What did she say?'

'She said it was a present for someone important. I guess that's you.'

'But she didn't even know me then.'

'OK. Perhaps you better put it back.'

I looked at him and thought for a moment. 'Did you never think to go and dig it up?'

'No. It wasn't for me.'

'But weren't you curious to know what it is?'

'Yes.'

'It's a notebook filled with her writing. It's like a story or a journal.'

'How do you know?'

'Because it's for me. Look.' I tore through the plastic and pulled out the notebook and I handed it to Chan. He flicked through the pages in awe and then started reading. I made an involuntary noise and he looked at me.

'It might be kind of private,' I said apologetically. 'It's about her father.'

He shut the book quickly. 'I'm sorry. It's none of my business.'

'No, that's fine. I just wanted to show you what it was, so you'd know it was for me.'

'That's OK. I know it's for you. I wouldn't have let you dig it up if I didn't think it was.'

I was impressed.

'Hey,' he said, as if he was about to change the subject, 'do you know the girl who lives there now?'

'Lives where?'

'In Butterfly's apartment.'

'No.'

'Oh, I saw you looking at her when she walked out. I thought you might know her, that's all.'

'I don't know anyone in New York.'

'Well, if you're a friend of Butterfly's, you know me.'

21
Daddy

Takeo Ishikawa (1942–2001)

Before he died, Daddy went a bit mad. I hadn't seen or heard from him in a few years. I tried to contact him after Komori died, but he never got back to me. My mother told me he had moved out to the desert in California, and that he had become a recluse. Then in the spring of 2001, he called me out of the blue. He told me he would like to see me and I agreed to visit.

I took the plane to Las Vegas and hired a car. I drove northwest into the Mojave Desert, and across the state line into California, to a town called Death Valley Junction, population twenty (although I only saw one). There was a hotel and I booked a room under a made-up name, then wandered around until sunset. The only other functioning building was a theater

called the Amargosa Opera House. It gave weekly shows written
and performed by its owner, an old woman who painted the
interior with murals of an audience so that she would never
have to play to an empty house.

The next morning I followed the directions I'd been given
and drove for an hour or so, pulling off the highway and up a
dusty track. The house was visible from below: a modernist glass
block from the 1960s perched high above me among the rocks.

The track arrived at the back, where there was an empty
space for cars, although none were on show. From this side, the
building had white walls jutting out to form shaded enclosures
and a ramp that led up to the roof. Daddy appeared from a
shadowed doorway. He was older than I remembered, his skin
gray and hanging from his face. His hair, also gray, hadn't been
cut for a few months, although he had made an effort to shave
and groom himself. He reached out his arms and smiled
pathetically. I made a kissing noise close to his cheek and held
stonelike as he hugged me.

The house was open-plan and unexpectedly cool, its floor-
to-ceiling glass looking out over the rocks and desert for endless
miles. The furnishings were 1960s modernist design pieces. I
guess they were chosen by a professional. Daddy would never
have gone to the effort to acquire taste, good or bad.

"Nice place," I said.

"Thank you. It belonged to an architect, I don't remember
his name."

"Why do you live here?" I asked.

"I feel safe."

"Safe from what?"

"Everything."

The first hour or so was uncomfortable. He asked me how my mother was and he inquired about my job. I tried to tell him as much as I could, trying to fill time and hoping we would stumble on something of genuine interest to us both to make it a successful visit. But he had an agenda.

"I'm pleased you did so well at college."

"College was years ago, Daddy," I said.

"I know, I just never had the opportunity to tell you how proud I am of you."

"Thanks."

"I have never thought about your future or your happiness, Butterfly. I have always tried to keep myself separate from your life. Yet as I get older I am starting to understand how wrong I have been about so many things. I wanted to say sorry. I wanted the chance to explain."

"That's OK. I turned out all right in the end."

"Well, we learn to survive in all kinds of conditions, and you have truly flourished despite the wrong that has been done to you. That is a wonderful thing. But however wrong a parent can be, it is always innocent of intention. You do know that, don't you? I never consciously wanted bad for you."

I'd traveled three thousand miles to come and see him. It was obvious he had stuff to get off his chest, but it didn't mean that I wanted to hear it. Maybe he had found God or something. It wasn't my problem, but I let him talk. Maybe I would learn something, and I could always tell him to shut up if it got too intense. Or I could leave and be as angry as I wanted.

"I'm sure you did your best," I told him, but even as the words came out I knew that I didn't believe them.

"It's true, I was trying to do my best. But it was the best for Keiko. And I guess in a way the best for me. I never took your feelings into account."

"Don't talk about Komori, please."

"But she's part of the explanation."

"You just disposed of her like she had no value to you."

"That's not true, Butterfly," he said. "I loved her."

"Oh, so that's why you abandoned her. Your life must be full of love."

"No, you don't understand. I was in love with her and she was in love with me. We have always been in love, since we were children. We were lovers. Nothing in the world existed outside what we shared."

"Wait, wait. What you're saying doesn't make any sense. You and Komori were lovers?"

"Yes."

"I don't understand. You grew up together. Your families were best friends. You went everywhere together. If you were in love, why weren't you a proper couple?"

"It couldn't happen like that, I'm afraid."

"Huh? There was nothing to stop you having your dream life together. Why did you abandon her? You married Mom and had me. You abandoned Mom, you abandoned me. You're one shit lover, father, husband, everything."

"We couldn't be together."

"Why, what stopped you?"

"As you know we were both born in Manchuria, which was a territory in northeast China that Japan had annexed in the thirties."

"Yes."

"As the war came to an end, the families of businesspeople and the administration grew closer to each other. There was little food and the Russians were coming. Chinese families were dying of starvation. We were all hoping to be repatriated, but we were at war and nobody knew when there would be the time or resources to get us back to Japan, so we waited to see whether we would die or be saved."

"So?"

"One day, the army told us that the women and children would be leaving immediately. We had to leave only with the things we could carry. We knew those who stayed behind would probably be killed or taken prisoner by the Russians. Chinese families who had cooperated with the Japanese risked exclusion at best; starvation or execution were more likely. The Sasaki family were close to their Chinese servants. They didn't want to leave without them. But there was no choice. There were no resources to protect the Chinese. So the Sasaki family made a deal with the servant family and took their daughter, passing her as their own. She was given a Japanese name, a Japanese identity and came back with us."

"I didn't know Komori was adopted. You're talking about Komori, aren't you?"

"Yes. Do you understand now? Keiko was Chinese."

"Hold on, are you telling me that the reason you couldn't marry her was that she was Chinese?"

"It wasn't just that."

"What, that she was a servant girl?"

"We were from two different cultures."

"What the hell difference does that make? Anyway, her culture was Japanese! Everything about her was Japanese. She *was brought up in a Japanese family. Besides, you lived in America. The land of the free where anything is possible."*

"There was social pressure. Sadly, the people of my parents' generation didn't even regard the Chinese as human."

"The Sasakis did. They adopted Komori. They brought her up as their own."

"They were unusual. Others weren't so kind. They didn't expect her to be a real Japanese lady. People thought she would be a secretary, or a nurse, or a mistress."

"Fuck. So you just went along with that. You were the brilliant boy who could do anything, go anywhere. If love was so important to you, why wouldn't you go against the culture of your parents?"

"I did. I followed her family to California and then to New York. The Sasakis went back to Japan and Keiko and I stayed. We had run away. We had freed ourselves from history."

"This whole story stinks like shit. It sounds like you're just making excuses for your lack of commitment, for wanting to own her, while you fuck around and marry a respectable Japanese girl, but never do the right thing by your mistress. Never make her your equal. And then when she was dying you abandoned her."

"I couldn't be with her."

"Of course you could."

"I couldn't, Butterfly. I wasn't able to watch her die. It was draining the life from me. I would have died too. The pain was unbearable. Putting distance between us was the only way I could survive."

"So she loved you and existed for you while you gave her nothing when she needed it most, for fear that you would suffer?"

"It sounds stupid, but that was the reality."

"Oh my God, that's pathetic."

"I know."

"That's like having a flower that makes your life wonderful, but refusing to water it because you're afraid there will be none left for yourself. So the flower dies and you are miserable. Your life has been ruined by your own selfishness."

I turned to the door and walked out into the yard. He came out as far as the front step but wouldn't go farther. "Wait," he said. "Are you going?"

"I don't know. I need a couple of minutes on my own."

"You should wear a hat to protect your head from the sun." He stretched out a hand as if he might be able to touch me from where he stood, but he couldn't. I remembered him coming to collect me from ballet, waiting in the street. And I remembered him watching from the car as I walked into school. I remembered him watching through the railings of the community garden as I weeded, dug and planted, always a barrier between us. But it was too late to change that now.

I walked farther up behind the house and out of sight, making loud crunching noises with my feet so any rattlers could get out of my way. And on this lunar landscape I learned something about silence that I had never known existed. The tiniest sounds, my shoes on the ground, my breathing, my heartbeat dissolved in the sun, never making it far enough to bounce back or to be absorbed by the porous dust. They just evaporated into the air around me.

A thousand generations can pass in the blink of an eye and civilizations rise and fall (like time-lapse photography) in the time that the desert takes just one breath. Life and death are meaningless. God doesn't cry at the loss of every living creature; if he did, the desert would be flooded with his tears. God has not even noticed us as he shuffles the tectonic plates, watching the mountains ripple up and crumble down. And I am nothing. Nothing.

I found him sitting motionless in a large armchair. Waiting for me to come back in again, I guess.

"And so you gave her a job as my babysitter and she ended up with a standing befitting to her class."

"She wasn't your babysitter, Butterfly."

"Isn't that what komori means? You weren't there, neither was Mom. She brought me up, alone, with no help from either of you."

"Sit down, my darling."

"I'm not your darling."

"Sit down, I need to tell you something. I need to explain and it's not easy."

I sat and waited while he tried to get his thoughts in some sort of order.

"Keiko wanted a child. Her condition made becoming pregnant an impossibility. There was nothing I could do to ease her suffering. So I gave her the only thing I had that could improve her life. You were my present to her. You belonged to her."

I started to cry. "Was I just something to be given away? Didn't I have any value?"

"I'm sorry."

"But Daddy, what about me as a person?"

"You were the most precious thing in the world. But I'm not

trying to justify myself. I'm just trying to explain, and to apologize for not being in your life, to say sorry for not sharing the love that I felt. I only hope you can understand that all this came from a good place, from a wish to help somebody I cared for deeply. And I am proud that you have grown beyond anything that was planned for you into a full and rounded young woman. You were right. You have turned out all right, and I am so proud to have a daughter like you. I'm so happy to find you after all this time."

"But why? How could you have a child and not wish to give her the best possible life?"

"Keiko needed somebody. But nobody could have survived watching her die unless they were educated in a different way. You were brought up to do something that I didn't know how to. You were brought up to live with loss that none of the rest of us could accept. You would be harder, stronger than us. You would be able to survive where we could not."

"And what makes you think that I can? What makes you think that I am not injured by the pain and even more so by the fact that you planned it, that I was given away at birth in order to deal with shit you couldn't handle. What about my mother? Why did she accept to just be a walking womb for your little death servant."

"She was young. It was difficult for her, but she understood."

"Why were you even having children with other women if you were so fucking in love with Komori?"

"I told you. I had you in order that Keiko could have a child. I know this can't be easy for you, Butterfly. But I wanted you to understand why."

"Thanks. That's put my mind completely at rest. Have you

*got anything to drink here?" I stood up and moved toward the
kitchen.*

*"Yes. There are a few bottles in the cupboard on the left. Let
me help—" He made to stand but I cut him off.*

*"Stay where you are. I can make a drink." I breathed deep,
calming myself down and finding my cool. "Do you want one?"*

"No, thank you. It's a little early for me."

*"Well, after this I'm going to leave and never come back.
You'll never see me again. So, if you ever want to have a drink
with your precious daughter, now's the time. I'm having a gin
and soda. Sure I can't tempt you?"*

"OK. I'll have a gin and soda too."

*I looked back to where he was sitting. There were tears
rolling down his face.*

*I picked up my bag and as I prepared the drinks I pulled out
three packets of pills—medication you can buy over the counter
at any drugstore. I'd brought them with me. The idea was
already in my head. I may not have planned to kill him, but I'd
made provision should the need arise. I broke three capsules into
his gin and made sure they were fully dissolved. I had the
obscene confidence (or complacency) of the experienced. All he
had to do was turn around. He would have seen me, but he just
sat still.*

*"Here you are." I handed him a glass and sat down with
my own.*

"Thank you," he said.

"Cheers." I raised my glass.

"Yes, to your good health." He took a sip. "It's very bitter."

*"Yes," I said. "There's a funny aftertaste in your gin. It's
drinkable, though, and I don't fancy whiskey."*

We sat in silence, sipping our drinks and smoking.

"I feel like shit, Daddy. I never really felt the warmth of family love, but now I feel nothing. Just a pawn in your twisted plot, because you were too racist to be with the woman you loved and too scared to face death. It's the singularly most natural thing, the most common experience in our existence."

"You were brought up to understand death. For the rest of us it is painful beyond comprehension."

"What makes you think you are so special? What makes you imagine that you feel more pain than me? I don't know you. I don't understand who you are or what your values are, if you have any."

"I don't know what my values are either. Maybe fear of pain, and self-loathing. At least I haven't passed them on to you. For the first time, I can see that you are a real person. I imagine that you value people and their feelings. That you value art and beauty. I imagine that you want good, and that you have understood that the world is bigger than just your ego. You are different to me. If I have done nothing else, at least I have not passed on my pathological fear of life." His voice was starting to slow down like an unwinding musical box.

"We may be more alike than you think. Have you ever killed anybody, Daddy?"

"No. Thank God. That's at least one crime I haven't committed."

"I killed her, you know? Komori. I gave her an overdose."

"I didn't know how you did it, but it was always the plan that you would be there to end her life if need be."

"Oh fuck, it just keeps getting worse."

"Butterfly. I love you," he said even slower. "Do you know what love is?"

"No. I'm not sure that it even exists."

"That's a shame. I hope you find out one day. I hope you learn what a wonderful thing love is."

"Well, that's a beautiful sentiment. But I think we're just animals, trying to save our asses or our species. We are big piles of self-obsessed meat with lust for physical pleasure and chemical impulses driving us to procreate. Hormones provoking emotions that incline us to protect our young. Jealous need of possession. That's what I think love is. We think we are higher beings, but we're just running around constrained by our animal bodies and superstition. It's all chemical."

"Maybe you're right," he said.

"That's how it seems."

"Do you think this is the first real conversation we've ever had?"

"Maybe."

And so, strangely, a few minutes before his death, my father and I made some kind of contact, and I don't think I could have asked for more.

I searched through the kitchen cupboards and found some candles. In an enclosure at the back of the house was a collection of propane canisters. I dragged one inside and opened the valve.

"Are you still awake, Daddy?" I asked.

"Mmmm." His head was slumped to the side. I lit all the candles and stood them up well out of reach on a table. Then I kissed his head.

"Goodbye, Daddy. I'm going."

I got in the car and drove.

From nowhere a torrent of rain fell and the sun shone through, illuminating each drop. Takeo knocked on the door of the house, trying to stay dry. He was a boy. A woman answered. "I can't let you in," she said, "an angry fox came looking for you. You have offended the foxes. Go to where they live and ask their forgiveness." "But I don't know where they live," he cried. "On days like this there are rainbows," she said. "Foxes live under the rainbows." And so he walked down through a meadow full of flowers and a bright arc filled the sky ahead. He could smell the rain and ground and flowers of every color. So many beautiful flowers.

The house was still in sight. I stopped and got out of the car and stared. All I could see was a reflection in the distance under the rippling heat and then it burst into flames. My stomach spasmed and I choked, tears pouring freely for a second. A low rumbling sound rolled across the dust toward me and a plume of smoke mushroomed up, marking the position. I wiped my face on my top and my body filled with energy like warm liquid flowing over me. A car pulled up and the window lowered. An overweight suntanned couple asked me whether I knew what it was.

"I've no idea," I said. "I was just standing here and it went up."

Then there was a second, much bigger explosion and the couple let out a gasp. "Pass me the video camera, Jan."

I wished them good day and left before I ended up on tape.

22

Unfinished Things and a Goodbye

I knew Streetny would have something to say about all this, but when I checked my email the next morning he was more formal than he had been of late.

To: Benjamin Constable
From: charlesstreetny15@hotmail.com
Subject: Impressed
Sent: 08-27-07 07:21 (GMT -6)

Dear Mr. Constable,

   It appears that you are ahead of the instructions Miss Ishikawa has left for you. The clue for the treasure under the Katsura tree in McCarthy Square had not even been given. One can only imagine that she would be very impressed at your treasure-hunting skills. Congratulations on your determination and intuition.

There is something for you at the Chelsea Hotel. The clue to its position is: Low trees somewhere high up.

Low like broccoli.

Good luck.

Mr. C. Streetny.

'He knew about our conversation in the Japanese restaurant.'

'Yes.' Beatrice was seething but trying to hold it in.

'And he signed it Mr C Streetny; that's a street. I'm the only person in the world stupid enough to think that it would be a name. He knows about me. He knows what I do, when I do it, and now he knows what I think. He knows all the things about me that only you know.'

Beatrice measured a couple of heavy breaths. 'She's got somebody listening to everything you say.'

'She?'

'Butterfly.'

I looked all around me. I really looked, for a minute or more, but I couldn't see anyone.

'Butterfly's dead,' I said. 'Somebody is sending me things from her and that person is you, or has something to do with you.'

She bit her lip. 'It's not me, I swear. None of this is what it seems.'

'What is it then? I think you should explain some stuff.'

'I can't, Ben.' She leaned forwards, looking straight in my eyes. Hers were wet with tears, but she kept control. 'It's not coming from me,' she said; 'I'm not doing this. But it's all there for you to work out. You just have to open your eyes.'

'Work what out?'

She shut her mouth and looked at me as if she would say no more. Maybe she was telling the truth and she wasn't doing any of this, but it was to do with her and she knew what was going on. My stare was accusing. She was uncomfortable. I'd come back to this later. I tried to breathe for a moment and let her welling tears subside.

'Where's the Chelsea Hotel?' I asked nicely.

'Chelsea.' She sniffed and wiped her eyes with a napkin.

'Is it well-known or something?'

'You haven't heard of the Chelsea Hotel?'

'No, sorry.'

'That surprises me.'

'Why?'

'It's famous. It's a hotel for artists and musicians. I guess it's been there since the late sixties and it hasn't really changed since. Lots of famous people have lived there.'

'Like who?'

'Oh, I don't know. Bob Dylan. Janis Joplin. Probably Hendrix for all I know. Sid Vicious died there.'

'Will you show me where it is?'

Beatrice sighed. 'OK.'

'You sound like you're just saying OK, but you don't really want to.'

'I think it'll be easier if I go with you.'

I didn't argue.

Beatrice was no longer a random stranger; she'd just admitted it, although what she was I had no idea. My understanding of everything was about to change and it made me feel sick. I didn't show it, though, because Beatrice looked sicker than me. She was quiet as she led the way to the Chelsea Hotel. She didn't look for landmarks, check street names or house numbers. She knew this place well. I should have guessed.

The walls of the foyer were crowded with colourful paintings. A horse's head stared at me unnervingly and a figure on a swing hung above my head.

'Most of these were given in lieu of unpaid rent,' Beatrice informed me casually.

We walked past a man behind the reception desk who smiled and said hello and we turned left and waited for the lift.

'Where are we going?' I asked.

'Shhh,' said Beatrice. When we were in the lift and the doors closed she said, 'To the roof.'

We got out on the tenth floor and climbed some stairs to a door with a sign clearly stating that it was alarmed and that there was no public admittance.

'We're not allowed up here,' said Beatrice, pushing the door.

'Won't the alarm go off?'

'There isn't an alarm.'

'How do you know?'

'I know someone who stays here sometimes.' Her voice was soft and measured.

'Does the guy on reception know you?'

'He recognises me.'

'Why are you pissed off?' I asked.

'Because I feel like I'm being manipulated.'

'Yes,' I said. 'By who?'

'By whoever is sending you up here.'

'Butterfly?'

'I thought you said she was dead.' There was a hint of bitterness in her mocking.

'She is.'

'How did she think you were going to find your way to the roof without me?'

'I'm not totally incapable of doing things by myself.'

'You wouldn't have even known there was a roof to come to if it wasn't for me.'

The roof was divided up by changes of level, chimneys, ducts and vents, and a water tower. Parts of it were separated into little gardens and parts were just bare. The view was of a different New York. I could see down onto the roofs of lower buildings and was on the same level as the raised turrets of water towers perched on the buildings in every direction. There were brown-coloured tower blocks like the ones by the Manhattan Bridge, and grey-white towers (among them the Empire State Building) stretching towards the sky above me. New York was suddenly more three-dimensional from here. Taller, dirtier, older, newer.

'I need to find a small tree.'

'You'd better look around then.'

'I don't want to go into the garden bits. I might not be allowed.'

'You're not allowed up here anyway. I'd look around for a small tree if I were you. It's not hard to find.'

'You know where it is!' I accused.

'I think so.'

'Show me.'

'No. You have to find it.'

'I don't want to.'

'Mmmm. That's rebellious.' Now she was sneering.

'Show me.'

'No.'

'Let's go,' I said.

She stared at me. 'What, really?'

'Yep.'

'And I thought I was in a bad mood. Why won't you look for it?'

'Because you know where it is. I don't feel like playing anymore. There's too much stuff in front of my eyes I haven't asked about, stuff that I've let go of for the sake of playing the game, or to not upset you. But I'm not playing anymore; I'm being played with. I've become the toy, not the playmate. You said you were pissed off because you felt manipulated, but the questions I haven't asked are for you. There are things I don't know that you do and you're not telling me. There's something else. It's you playing the game; it's you doing the manipulating and I don't know why.'

'I can't explain. I didn't mean to mess with you. I promise you, I'm being manipulated too.' Her voice was soft and strained. 'I was happy being your helper. It's been fun. You're fun. Now I have been made a part of it against my will. I don't like that. It puts me in an awkward situation and now I have to lie and not tell you stuff, just to make sure your adventure goes according to plan.'

'Whose plan?'

'Your friend—Butterfly.'

'Butterfly's dead.'

'You keep saying that, but there are lots of things that suggest otherwise. You're supposed to be the one who can understand clues.'

'What lies? And what stuff haven't you told me?'

Beatrice walked over to me and kissed my cheek. Just once.

'Come on. I'll show you the small tree.'

'What was the kiss for?'

'Because I'm sorry.'

Beatrice led me round a chimney stack and down some wooden steps into a little garden and the light reflected green for a second on the leaves of climbing plants. Then she pointed down to a bonsai in a pot resting on two bricks on the ground.

'Low like broccoli,' she said, and I thought that I would like to kiss her. Kiss her mouth. But I didn't.

I crouched down and looked at the tree. It was pretty. I hoped I wasn't going to have to uproot it in order to find what I was looking for. I lifted the pot and between the two bricks was a tin. An old-fashioned tin for boiled sweets. I prised the lid off and inside was a sheet of lined A4 paper folded into a small square with a large 3-D letter *B* drawn on it, and what looked like two boiled sweets, hand wrapped in see-through plastic. The note said:

There's just one more thing for you, Ben Constable; one last treasure and it's very precious. You'll find it underneath a tree that nurtures young butterflies before they are grown, on a patch of green where I have lingered with many a book, and got my hands dirty weeding and planting. The space next to Jefferson Market Library was the nearest patch of green to where I lived and the closest thing I ever had to a garden of my own. The sweets are adapted from a recipe my nanny taught me: bitter toffee almonds, I call them. I made them myself. Hope you like them. There is of course so, so, so much more to say, to find, to do. I have loved losing myself in the streets of Gotham Town with you. It's such a treat to be able to show someone the places of your past. I wish I could have seen the streets where you grew up. But time has run out and we have

gone from parenthesis to parenthesis and the opening clause is
still unresolved . . .

Butterfly.
X X X G X X X O X X X O X X X D X X X B X X X Y X X X E
X X X.

I turned it over, looking for more, a PS or a last parenthetical note.
There was nothing. Suddenly I thought I would burst into tears. It
all seemed to be coming to an end too quickly. I passed it to Beatrice when I'd finished. She read it, folded it up and handed it back
to me and I put it in the tin.

'The bitch,' said Beatrice, and I laughed louder than I would
have expected.

'Do you really think so?'

'God knows. I just wanted to say it.'

'Want a homemade sweet?' I held out the tin.

'No. I wouldn't eat anything with a name like that. Especially
coming from your friend Butterfly.'

'Do you think she'd try to kill me?'

'I don't know anything. In fact the more I think about it, the
more I think you definitely shouldn't eat that shit.'

I tapped my finger on the lid of the tin, thinking, then put it in
my bag.

'Shall we go?' I asked.

'Don't you want to look at the view from this great and historic
building? As an artist it's part of your cultural heritage.'

'No thank you.'

'OK.'

We walked down through the nonalarmed door and Beatrice

said, 'Even so, we ought to take the stairs so you can get a feel for this place.'

'OK,' I said. The stairway was white and had a kind of pop art mobile hanging from the skylight, dangling into the empty space that the stairs wound themselves around, and there was an occasional painting on the wall—more like an art gallery than a foyer. We plodded down the stairs without speaking. Beatrice said goodbye to the man on reception. I didn't even look at him so I don't know what expression he wore, seeing us come down five minutes after having gone up.

'Where to now?' said Beatrice.

'The West Village again.'

'It's a pity. There's so much of New York that you haven't seen. You've really been running around the same corners since you got here.'

'Well, I got from Battery Park to Central Park, from West Thirty-Third Street to Brooklyn. And I've only been here a week.'

'It feels much longer,' she said. 'Did you ever get a map?'

'No.'

She was silent with the weight of unsaid things and we walked down Sixth Avenue, and I was silent with the weight of unasked questions.

I led the way through the gate into the little garden next to Jefferson Market Library. Cat was lying on the grass and Beatrice and I went and sat on a bench next to him and I looked around.

'Can you see any butterflies?'

'No, but young butterflies don't live on the same things grownup ones do.'

'Really?'

'Come on, think about it. What are young butterflies?'

'Caterpillars!'

'And what do caterpillars eat?'

'Lettuce?'

'Isn't that slugs?'

'Oh, yeah.'

'The only thing I know that's a great host for caterpillars is pussy willow, like that one there.' She pointed to a small willow tree.

'You actually do know everything, don't you?'

'Yes. I'm afraid so.'

'Well, you can call me a coward for not digging underneath that tree in broad daylight, but I'm going to wait until it's dark.'

'Sounds like a good plan to me,' she said.

'Tell me something.'

'Yes?'

'How do you pay your rent?'

'With difficulty. I had some money saved, but that's all gone. I need an income quick.'

'No, I mean how do you do it? What happens? What actions do you make to get the rent to your landlady?'

'I write a cheque,' she said bluntly.

'Where do you send it?'

'To an address in Chelsea.'

'Near the hotel?'

'Yes,' she said.

'Who do you make it payable to?'

'Butterfly.'

'Tomomi Ishikawa?'

'Yep.'

'Whose name do you write on the envelope?'

'Her mother's.'

'Do you know her mother?' I asked.

'Yes,' she said, and I could feel it all unfolding.

Cat looked at me and I thought for a moment.

'Will you take me to meet her?'

'I'll give you her number. You can call her.'

'I think you should come with me,' I said.

'No. I don't think I should.'

'What does it matter?'

'I think we should leave things as they are,' said Beatrice.

'I'm going to ask her questions. She might tell me stuff. Even if she doesn't, that will tell me stuff.'

'I don't want to be there.'

'Take me.'

'Why?'

'I don't know,' I said. 'It'll make things easier. I'm shy.'

'You don't seem shy to me.'

'Sometimes I am, sometimes I'm not. You've been withholding stuff, you said so yourself. I'd like to see you faced with something true. I'm grateful for all your help, but I think you owe it to me to come to Butterfly's mother's.'

'Owe it to you? Yeah, I think you got me confused with someone else. I don't owe you anything. Quite frankly, I'm not even sure why I'm still here.'

She was right. She could get up and leave and I'd never hear from her again. She looked capable of it.

'I'm sorry,' I said. 'But I still think you should come. I can't make you. It'll have to be your choice.'

She looked hard for a second, as though she was deciding whether to spit at me or just get up and leave.

'I'll take you tomorrow. Come on.'

'Come on what?'

'Come on, I'm taking you for a drink,' she said.

'Why?'

'To say goodbye.'

'I don't understand.'

'Because I don't think you'll want to know me after tomorrow.' She stared at me hard, with no expression on her face, and I stared back.

'I'm going to take you to a new place. There's an area near here called the Meatpacking District. It's very weird and industrial and it smells of raw meat. It's also very now.'

'Like me,' I said.

She kind of laughed without smiling. 'We're going to sit down and have a beer and we're going to talk about some other stuff. You can tell me about England and what it's like growing up as a limey colonialist and I'll tell you about childhood holidays in Pennsylvania, or we can compare notes on France or something, and we can laugh and say stupid things and then we're going to say goodbye, I'm going to go home and you can come back and get your last treasure.'

I stared at her. I didn't know what to think. I guessed I'd offended her at some point. I should never have thought about kissing her. She was probably psychic.

We got up and left and Cat watched us. He seemed happy enough. *See you later, Cat.*

The gate to the garden was padlocked when I got back. Feeling bold with beer, I walked round to the back corner of the library on Tenth Street, had a quick look in both directions, climbed over the fence and walked directly to the willow tree. Cat came and sat down next to me. I cursed myself for still having nothing to dig with but a stainless steel pen. I pushed it down into the earth a few times in the vain hope that I might be able to locate what I was looking for without digging an opencast mine. How deep would a child bury something?

I started carefully digging round the roots so as not to cause any stress or alarm to the tree. It was like an archaeological dig, but after a few minutes I was scraping with my fingers, pulling at chinks of earth, stabbing the ground to get deeper. And there, enmeshed in the roots, was a plastic container, a small Tupperware-type thing. I pulled it out and pushed the earth back, carefully patting it down. I don't think I'd damaged it. Cat and I went and found a shadowy spot and sat down. I took out the sweets from the Chelsea Hotel and smelled one. 'I don't like almonds, Cat. Do you want one?' Cat ignored them so I put them back in my pocket and opened the treasure chest. On the top, covering the rest of the contents, was a shit of paper with child's handwriting on it.

Time Capsyul

(Not to be opned til the yer 2000)

Mach 15th 1980

My name is Tomomi Ishikawa but pople corl me Butterfly. I live in a big citee called New Yorc wich is one of the bigist sitees on aer planit wich is coled Eath. I go to elimntree school and then I woud like to go to colij. I like reading and riting and dansing. Wen I gro up I would like to be a techer. My favrit bilding is Jefoosn Marcit Libree becus it has an unyooshul stile for the west vilige wich is neer the hudson river in the Unitid Stats of America. The werld trade senter is the talist bilding in New Yorc. Jimee Carta is the presidunt of awer cuntree.

Underneath the letter were three black-and-white photographs showing a small child with long, straight, black hair in the garden where I was sitting. In one she was on her own, looking up at the camera, in another she was sitting on a bench with a woman, and in another she was squatted down over a flowerbed, concentrating intently on the trowel in her hand. There was a postcard of the Eiffel Tower with nothing written on the back, a marble, a ribbon, an antique-looking subway ticket, and (rather disturbingly) the head of a Barbie doll with much of its hair cut off. I laughed out loud and Cat looked around, slightly alarmed.

I put everything back in its plastic container and lay back on the grass and closed my eyes. I dreamed that Butterfly was standing over me or maybe it was Beatrice. She bent down and kissed my head and scratched Cat behind his ears, which he liked (that's how I know it was a dream).

23

In Which Some Unsaid Things Are Said

When I got back to the hotel I didn't have my keys. I searched my pockets and my bag over and over, but they really weren't there. I thought about going back to the community garden, but at this time of night it felt a very long way to go to not be sure of finding them, so eventually I conceded to ringing the bell and disturbing the Night Guy.

The Night Guy smiled when he saw me through the glass.

'Ah, I have your keys. You should tell your girlfriend that she was lucky, I don't normally let people up into rooms like that. Next time you want somebody to come and get something for you, you should call at least. Anyway, it was no problem this time, it was obvious she knew you and we did try calling, but your cell wasn't on.'

'Thank you,' I said, and wondered why I wasn't asking questions and kicking up a stink.

'Oh, and the manager told me to ask you if you knew when you would be checking out yet.'

'That's a good question. I was thinking about maybe the day after tomorrow. Could I confirm that tomorrow?'

'No problem, sir.'

As I climbed the stairs, I got my phone out of my bag. It was off. When I put it back on it had plenty of battery. There was no reason for it to be off, but phones do that sometimes. In the room everything was normal except that all of Butterfly's journals were gone. They'd been in a pile on the bedside table. I climbed into bed fully clothed and stared at the ceiling for a long time.

The next day I met Beatrice in a dimly lit Spanish restaurant called El Quijote, just underneath the Chelsea Hotel, and we sat at the bar drinking bottled beer and staring straight ahead without really speaking much.

'I know it's a stupid question, but I don't suppose you came to my hotel last night before I got back, did you?'

'No. Why?'

'Somebody did.'

'Who?'

'I don't know. A girl.' I played with my beer bottle. 'I do hope there's an interesting twist to this story. I feel like I know where it's going, but I'd prefer a surprise. I'm getting this kind of sinking feeling of inevitability. And I've got travel sadness as well which means I'm leaving soon.'

'What's travel sadness?'

'It's the sad feeling you get before you make a long journey. Don't you get that?'

'I don't know.'

'Hey, there *is* something you don't know!'

'So, what are you going to do if it all comes to the end you're expecting?'

'Contemplate getting very annoyed. Ask a lot of questions

while keeping my cool and come to the irritating conclusion that in life, unlike fiction, you rarely get all the answers you need, and that there probably won't be any satisfactory resolution to all this, and I won't understand why. And I'll go home and be frustrated. And for a few months it'll all come back into my head unexpectedly, like Cat does, and I'll think, "If only I could understand why," and then gradually it won't be so important anymore, and it will just become an interesting story I tell whilst lingering in bed with a favourite lover, or who knows, maybe I will write it down one day. Not yet, though. I think I need to let it get some distance.'

'Well, Ben, I may know some things that you don't, and you're going to find out about them because I'm going to explain everything to you later on today—I didn't want to, but I've given it a lot of thought and I'm going to do it—but what I can tell you now is that I don't know the end of the story. Maybe I ought to be able to guess, but I can't. It could be a surprise, or it could be obvious. Either way, I don't know.'

'It's interesting how we choose to define endings.'

'This sounds like the beginning of an intellectual conversation.'

'Stories don't normally carry on until everyone is dead, which would be nice and clearly defined. We arrive at a moment and then we just say "the end", but that doesn't mean that nothing else interesting happened; it just means we stopped telling the story. Maybe this one should finish now.'

'What, before we get to the dénouement?'

'But what if that doesn't happen? Or the explanation's a disappointment?'

'Jeez! Stop thinking about how disappointing everything might turn out and get on with it.'

She was right. 'Come on then,' I said, and jumped off my stool.

We finished our beers and I followed Beatrice out of the restaurant and in through the door of the Chelsea Hotel. We smiled and said hello to the man on reception on our way to the lifts and Beatrice pressed the button for the sixth floor.

We stood on opposite sides of the lift with our hands behind our backs, leaning against the walls, and looked at each other in the mirror and kind of smiled.

'You were here yesterday,' I said.

'Yeah.'

'I mean before you came with me.'

'Yeah.'

The doors opened.

'Can I just check, we're going to see Butterfly's mum, right?'

'Right. She's expecting us.' Beatrice led the way down a white-marble-floored corridor and knocked on one of the doors. It opened and a Japanese woman, younger than I expected, looked at us and smiled.

'Hello, Beatrice, how are you? And you must be Ben.' She shook my hand. 'My name is Nanako. I'm Butterfly's mother.'

'I'm very pleased to meet you.'

'Do come in. Would you like a coffee? Oh, you're British, I expect you drink tea. I have some Earl Grey if you'd prefer.'

'A glass of water will be fine for me,' I said.

'I'd love a coffee,' said Beatrice. 'Thank you.'

'Please, sit down.'

Beatrice and I sat. The air smelt deliciously of linseed oil and, much like the reception of the hotel, the walls were lined with paintings. There was an easel with a large canvas on it. On one side there were stacks of canvas-covered frames with bold abstract designs leaning against the wall. The room was homely, but with the sense of belonging to another age. Perhaps the early 1970s.

'So, apparently you're a writer, Ben?' said Butterfly's mother.

'Well, I do some writing.'

'How delightful. Beatrice tells me that you wanted to meet me. Are you doing research for a book about my daughter?'

'I don't know. Maybe. I was trying to find out some things about her.'

'Well, ask me anything you'd like. I don't know if I'll have all the answers, but I'll try.'

'Why was she called Butterfly?'

'It was a nickname given to her by her nanny when she was born. Such a tragic name. I never liked it. The name I chose for her was Tomomi, which means beautiful friend, but everyone called her Butterfly and eventually so did I.'

'Did you mind her spending so much time with a nanny?'

'To be honest, at first I was glad that Keiko was there to help me. I was very depressed after Butterfly's birth and I was young and felt terribly ashamed not to be radiating joy at the birth of my new child. Later I tried to get more time with Butterfly, but her father kept me away. I was very angry but I didn't know what to do. I didn't know how to get my daughter back. Did you know that Keiko, the woman who looked after Butterfly, was terminally sick?'

'Yes.'

'After a while they explained to me that Butterfly was all she had and that I couldn't take her away from a dying woman. After several years I managed to negotiate an access agreement where I was guaranteed to see her once a week, but she never stayed with me.'

'Oh my God, that's terrible.'

'Don't feel too sorry for me. They looked after me and gave me a lot of things. They gave me a life, culture and an education, but all that was payment for taking my child. Now I paint and I earn my living. It's taken me many years but I have a very good quality of life and I am starting to get to know Butterfly as an adult, although that only really started when she went to France.'

I scrunched up my face with a question that just came into my head. 'When *did* she move to France?'

'Oh, a while ago. I don't remember exactly. It must have been just after September eleventh, 2001, because I was worried about her flying.'

'I'm starting to realise that there were a lot of things I never knew about Butterfly,' I said. 'I feel sad that it's only now that I'm starting to piece it all together.'

'Oh dear, you're talking about her in the past tense. Have you fallen out?'

'No, not at all.' I flushed.

Did Nanako not know that Butterfly was dead? Or was Beatrice right and Tomomi Ishikawa was still alive? Tomomi Ishikawa told me she was dead. Why would she lie? Why would she cause so much hurt? I looked at Beatrice and she scowled at me, shaking her head. I knew that what I was about to say was wrong, but it came out anyway.

'We didn't see each other much at the end,' I said. 'I think there was still a lot of good feeling between us. She left me some of her diaries, which I've been reading, but it's good to be able to meet you and have you fill in some of the gaps.'

'I feel as though I've missed something important. What's the end? I don't understand. What's finished?'

Beatrice coughed. 'Ben is under the impression that Butterfly is dead. It's not entirely his fault.'

So Beatrice knew for certain that Tomomi Ishikawa was alive. I guess she always had done. She had tried to tell me lots of times.

Nanako was shocked and looked from Beatrice to me and

back again. Beatrice's face said not to take me seriously, as if I were either deluded or deranged. We both looked at Beatrice.

'Butterfly told him she was dead and he's totally incapable of believing otherwise. So he ignores the obvious signs that it's not the case.'

'Well, unless she died in the last hour or so, she's definitely still alive.'

'She was here?' I asked.

'Yes.'

'What—an hour ago?'

'Let me see . . . it must be about that, yes.'

'I'm so sorry to have come out with such disturbing rubbish,' I said.

'I don't understand,' said Nanako, looking lost. 'She told me that she'd come to New York to see you.'

'Well, she may well have seen me, but I didn't see her.' I couldn't help staring hatred at Beatrice.

'Oh dear, I can't begin to think what could be going on.'

And then the phone rang and we all stopped like musical statues. Nanako answered, she was clearly disturbed, and I wanted to apologise profusely and get out of there as fast as possible. Beatrice sat back in her chair and sighed, tears welling up in her eyes. I could see her keeping her breathing slow. Deep, steady breaths, full of self-control. I stopped hating her and looked at the walls. Then I came back to reality and the sound of Nanako's voice.

'There's someone here who might like to speak to you,' she said into the handset, and then gave it to me.

'Hello?' I said.

There was ambient noise of a busy space and a single heavy breath. Maybe it was a sigh. Then I could hear the voice of a famous rapper over a public address system in the background. It said, 'Would passengers Smith and Johnson on flight BA380 to London Heathrow please make your way to boarding gate . . . ' and then the line went dead.

I stared at the floor. I stared really hard.

'It was Butterfly,' I said, and looked from Beatrice to Nanako. 'It was Butterfly, wasn't it?'

'Yes,' said Nanako.

'She's in New York.'

'She's at the airport. She's flying back to Paris.'

'She's really not dead.'

'No. She's not dead.'

'Who lives at 15 Charles Street?'

Beatrice put up her hand. 'That's me.'

My mobile phone made two double beeps in my bag and vibrated. I looked at the screen and it said: '1 message reçu'. It was from Butterfly (US).

> I'm sorry, Ben. It wasn't supposed to be like this. Beatrice fucked up. Ask her what she really has to do with all this. I'm sorry. Butterfly. X O X

I stood up and took Butterfly's mother's hand in mine and said, 'I've been incredibly stupid. I came here to try and find out things about Butterfly. I should have just asked her.' Out of nowhere I felt cold and dynamic, but I was polite and sincere to Nanako. 'I would have liked to have met you under different circumstances. Hopefully we'll have another opportunity sometime. Right now, I'm afraid I need to leave. You must think me terribly rude. Thank you for your help. For what it's worth, you really did help me. I'm sorry to crash in like a hurricane and then go. I really am pleased to have met you.'

'I don't really know what's going on. I think Butterfly's upset you. I doubt very much that it was her intention. She spoke about you many times. I think she is very fond of you.'

'Thank you, that's very kind of you to say. Thank you for your time. Come on, Beatrice, we have something to do.'

When we were in the lift Beatrice asked, 'What do we have to do?'

I managed a smile. 'Go get a big drink, and maybe if I can stop feeling mad at you, you might do some explaining. It'll be the dénouement. And then I guess that will be the end of the story.'

'I'll do some explaining. Where do you want to go for a drink?'

'Wherever. Not here, though. And not in the West Village either. Somewhere new, please.'

'OK.'

Walking down the street towards the east, I took Beatrice's hand. I don't know why. She was watching the paving slabs pass by under her feet.

When we were both sitting at a table with large vodka and tonics, I started.

'Why did you take me to Butterfly's mother's?'

'If you remember, I didn't actually want to. You insisted.'

'You could have just told me that you knew for certain Butterfly was alive. You could have told me what was going on.'

'I'd promised not to.'

'What does that mean?'

'I was in a no-win situation. I did a favour for a friend to help make something exciting, to help create an adventure for somebody special. And for that to work I had to make some things up. I promised not to say certain things as well. And then I got drawn in, and it all got weirder and weirder and the pressure on me changed to new proportions and suddenly I was hemmed in from all angles, or I was messing things up for everyone, including me. I think I'd better start from the beginning.'

'That sounds good.'

'OK. Butterfly asked me to do her a favour . . .'

'So you know Butterfly?'

'She befriended me when I was at college. She was nice, like an older sister. I thought meeting somebody who'd gone to the same school as me was a coincidence, but now I guess it wasn't.'

'Why not?'

'Uh, because while I was at school a certain teacher started paying me a lot of attention.'

'Oh God. So you're Jane.'

'I'm Beatrice. Butterfly imagines everybody in her life to be characters from books, although she makes up her own twisted stories for them.'

'Did she kill him?'

'I don't know.'

'Is he dead?'

'I really don't know. I lost contact with him. He disappeared.'

'Did he write a book about you?'

'That's what Butterfly told me.'

'What, and nobody asked any questions? There were no police or anything?'

'There were police; a nice lady cop. She asked me questions. They offered me counselling, but they never told me what happened and I never asked. They said it was all over, that the case was closed, but they never told me what happened.'

'Oh my God. So you've been part of all of this.'

'I didn't want to be; I tried not to be. Let me explain. It's complicated.'

'OK.'

'Butterfly came and found me when I was at college and told me that a teacher had written a book about me. I was scared as hell that my past was going to be exposed and she told me that she could make sure the book never saw the light of day, but she needed my help and I agreed. And that was the end of it until the police came and I answered all the questions like she had told me . . .'

'Butterfly told you?'

'Kind of. I was like a child still. And after that we saw each other occasionally and we had these crazy big drunken talks. It felt like she was the only person in the world who had any idea about who I was. She became my new best person in the world. She was like my big sister, my hero. She was a god. I loved her. And I don't know how it happened, but one day in 2001 we decided to move to Paris, and like two weeks later we were there. We shared an apartment for a year, then we started to get our own lives and saw less and less of each other, but we still hung out for coffees and the occasional drunken evening. I was even at a party at her apartment that you were at. We talked.'

'What? You and me?'

'Not for long. You arrived really late and I was leaving. But I remember you. I thought you would recognise me when you saw me here, but Butterfly assured me that you wouldn't be able to because I would be out of context and you've got some kind of affliction where you can't recognise people.'

'Prosopagnosia.'

'That's it.'

'I like to think of it as a superpower rather than an affliction, but I can't believe I met you in Paris.'

'You were drunk. We only spoke for a minute. I was leaving and you said something to me. I don't remember what, but we laughed. I remember thinking you were funny. I was almost tempted to stay and find out who you were.'

'I still don't get how Butterfly could be so sure that I wouldn't recognise you.'

'It seems strange to me, but she said that I'd changed my hair and that so long as I didn't tell you that I knew you, there wouldn't be a problem. And she was right for a bit. But I'm getting ahead of myself. At first she just asked me if I would hide something for her as part of a treasure hunt that she was making for a special friend. And she told me who it was and I remembered you. Then she said it actually might be really cool if I could hang out with you a bit (if I was willing) and perhaps give you some pointers on New York and then she got this idea that I could actually be part of the adventure. Now I wasn't too hot on this because, firstly, I thought you'd recognise me straightaway, and secondly, it felt a bit weird. I wasn't sure what she was asking me to do. But she kind of assured me that she just wanted me to entertain you for a day or so until she arrived, but that for the surprise to work it was absolutely imperative that I never mention that I know her. I didn't actually agree to it. I agreed to hide the treasure. It was the note on the statue at Bryant Park, and that was all. I was going to the library to work anyway. Butterfly emailed me these scanned notes she'd written and I cut them out and put them in an envelope and it was me that wrote your name.'

'Ohhhhh!'

'So I hid the note in the morning and when I came out at

lunchtime you were there on the step. I hadn't known when you were going to turn up because I'd wriggled out of that part of the conversation with Butterfly, but there you were and it really was a coincidence. You see? They do happen—it wasn't all lies. Anyway, I asked you for a light and you didn't seem to have any idea who I was and I was excited and kind of scared. I thought I was going to be busted at any moment, but I wanted to watch you find the treasure. I felt involved and you were nice and funny and I couldn't get away from you—I mean, I didn't want to. I was interested in your treasure hunt and totally disturbed that you told me Butterfly was dead. Then there was the fact that you seemed to want to hang out with me. It made it all a little too irresistible. I didn't want you to think that Butterfly was dead, though. It didn't seem right. But to say that I knew her meant that you would know that I had lied to you from the get-go, and I would have done the exact thing Butterfly asked me not to do. So I dropped hints. I was trying to make you find out for yourself so I wouldn't feel bad. I owe Butterfly an incredible debt. She rents me this enormous apartment for way under market value because I'm her friend, and right now I'm really short of cash and she offered to give me a break on some rent if I helped her. But that was later.'

'So, can I just check: you don't live in Williamsburg?'

'That was a lie, I'm afraid. Well, I have lived in Williamsburg, but it was a long time ago. And Butterfly used to live in Williamsburg as well when I first got to know her. I was improvising. I needed an address quickly of an apartment that Butterfly could own and I could rent. That's the first thing that came into my head.'

'So you live at 15 Charles Street?'

'Yes.'

'In the apartment that Butterfly lived in with her nanny?'

'Yes.'

'And that apartment belongs to Butterfly now and you rent it from her?'

'That's right.'

'So you're Charles Streetny?'

'No, that's Butterfly. Or at least I think it's Butterfly.'

'Right.'

'So, let me carry on. I went with you to find the book in the piano and it didn't seem fair to me to see that you were actually genuinely upset about Butterfly when she wasn't dead, and I kind of resented her lying to you. I was a bit drunk and I thought I'd just harmlessly put you on her trail a little bit. After all, the next day she'd be there and I wouldn't have anything more to do with this adventure. And then I went home and I couldn't help thinking that I'd had a crazy day and I can't remember the last time I'd had so much fun. And then Butterfly rang. She wanted to know every-thing and I told her (except that I'd told you she was my landlady). And it was becoming a tangled web.'

'Wow, you're a great liar.'

'Thanks. I like to think of it as acting. Anyway, that's when she offered to give me a break on some of the rent if I carried on the game. And I really didn't want to and it was really tempting at the same time because I'd had such a good day and Butterfly asked me to show you some New York things and I thought of the lost subway station, and the money would be more than useful and I was still a little drunk and I said yes.'

'So basically Butterfly paid you to be my friend in New York.'

'You've got to understand that I wanted to.'

'But she bought you.'

'In a way.'

'Carry on.'

'Well, the next day I wasn't drunk and you told me that Butterfly had killed somebody and I was a bit alarmed. I was making excuses for her and trying to have as much fun as I did the day before, but you were a bit distressed and understandably so, and it was getting more and more complicated because you wanted me to take you to my own house . . .'

'What?'

'Fifteen Charles Street.'

'OK, yes, of course.'

'Anyway, so now I was in a bad mood and then you wanted me to take you to my old school to find another murder and I panicked because I suddenly thought my past was about to come spilling out.'

'Yes, but you don't think Butterfly really killed that guy, do you?'

'What the hell do I know? I've spent the whole of my adult life getting over what happened in high school, trying to be normal and trying to forget about what happened with Butterfly.'

'Why, what did happen with Butterfly? How did you help her?'

'It was just talk. I didn't do anything and neither did Butterfly. The guy just disappeared.'

'But you said you helped her.'

'No, she asked for my help, but we didn't do anything. It was like we were making up a story. Nothing happened.'

My brain froze. I was on delicate ground and I should back away, but Beatrice was lying about the teacher. Now that she'd pointed it out it was easy to spot.

'And then I read the notebook and it was all OK.'

'How can it be OK that she wrote that she killed your ex-boyfriend?'

'Because it's not true and it was a good story. I would have loved to kill him myself. It was my fantasy.'

She carried on and I stared, trying to get some distance from what she had just said. 'And so I started to sabotage your ideas of Butterfly because I don't think it's fair that you thought so highly of her when she was lying to you, even if it is for the sake of an adventure. And I really did feel like your treasure hunt was too close to my life. Ever since college I have been trying to move on from that past and everything about your treasure hunt seemed to be related to me. I decided I wanted out and I told Butterfly. She was really cool with me and said she understood, and it caught me off guard. I agreed to meet you the next day, but you had gone to Jefferson Market Library and you were up to your third murder and I was starting to feel stupid and like I was being used.'

'By then it was my fifth murder. There were two in Paris as well.'

'Of course, you told me. The other thing is that now I felt like I had some obligation to you because I'd helped make all this mess. And I was wondering if Butterfly was kind of blackmailing me. I didn't know what to do. When I was hanging out with you it was nice. When I wasn't I wanted to run away and never see anybody I know again. I kept saying to myself: next time I won't reply to that text message, or I won't answer the phone, and then when it came I felt like it would be nice to hang out. And I was in a shit position and you too; you believe everything everybody says to you. And I didn't want you to feel stupid because I think you're not stupid and that you don't deserve it. And that was the day when I couldn't go to the cleaners next to my house because you were digging outside. I waited for ages and then I put my hair up and sneaked in, hoping you wouldn't notice me and thinking that even if you did you wouldn't recognise me because I was out of context.'

'Cat saw you. I didn't know it was you. I just had a funny feeling, though, but I didn't know what it was.'

'And then I decided I was going to confess everything to you and that, without directly betraying Butterfly, I was going to betray her and then maybe she'd ask for all the rent and the whole thing was turning out to be very expensive, but it was time to put a stop to it all.'

'I'll get these drinks.'

'It's not about the drinks. Listen, I went to see Butterfly, who was staying at her mother's, and we went up onto the roof to talk in private and to have a cigarette, and I told her I wasn't playing anymore and she said she was really sorry to have upset me, and she wouldn't ask me to do anything else, and that she was really grateful for my help, and that I wouldn't owe her rent for this month as agreed. And then I realised that I was looking at a bonsai tree and I laughed and I told her about the low trees in France. She asked me if I was going to see you again and I said that I would like to have a chance to say goodbye, and I went to see you and she had dragged me back into the whole game with the fucking bonsai clue. She wouldn't let me get away. It was like she was trying to fuck me up. I wondered if she was jealous of me hanging out with you.'

'God. That would be strange.'

'Well, I was really pissed. I'm sorry. It was nothing to do with you. So I took you to her mother's. That was just out of spite for Butterfly, and because you wouldn't let me not go, and it was so that she could tell you that Butterfly wasn't dead and then I wouldn't have betrayed anyone's trust, sort of. So that was that and here we are. I think I've told you everything.'

'God,' I said.

Beatrice touched her eyes behind her sunglasses.

'Well, even if it was all a setup, I really enjoyed your company,' I said. 'You're clever and funny. I couldn't have hung out with just anyone.'

'I really liked hanging out with you. I just wanted to be able to stop it all and start again in a more normal way.'

'But you never wanted me to hit on you, though,' I said bravely.

'You didn't hit on me.'

'That's true.'

'Look, it was fun knowing that there was this slightly flirtatious thing going on. And I'm fascinated by you and your crazy story, but you were dragging me into a past I'm trying to grow out of. I don't want to live anymore in that dark world that Butterfly inhabits, that you are obsessed with.'

'I'm not obsessed with it,' I said.

'Well, it's dominated your life for months,' she said. 'I can't carry on being in Butterfly's stories. I'm going to leave her apartment. I've already told her. I want to get better, and you're part of something that I don't want.'

'So that's why you always went home early.'

'I just didn't want to get drunk with you. You're trouble. Nice trouble, but too dangerous for me.'

'You said you were unavailable.'

'Well, it seemed nicer than saying I wasn't interested—easier to explain. You're great in so many ways, but you were on the wrong treasure hunt and I don't think that's ever going to change.'

'OK,' I said, thinking too quickly, 'did you kill that teacher?'

'No.'

'But there's more to that story, though, isn't there?'

'I'm never going to tell you. I'm never going to think about it.

It doesn't exist anymore. You can keep Butterfly and her stories, but I'm not part of it.'

'OK.'

'Are you annoyed at me?' she asked.

'I was when we were at Butterfly's mum's. Then I didn't know what you were, but I was thinking that you were a bad person.'

'I know. I thought I was going to explode in tears.'

'I watched. I'm sorry I was cross.'

'Cross? I was almost forgetting that you were English and then you go and say something like "I was so terribly cross".'

'I wish I could meet you in completely different circumstances.'

'Oh, that reminds me, there's one other thing I didn't tell you.'

'Oh Jesus. Does it have to be now?'

'It's not bad, I just couldn't tell you before because I needed to escape from you, like I explained, so I omitted to mention that I'm coming to Paris in two weeks for a short break before the new semester starts. I wanted to see some old friends. Anyway, I wondered if I came, if you'd want to get a coffee or a drink sometime.'

'I'd like that.'

'Well, I'll call you when I'm there.'

And then we just sat for a while, breathing. I couldn't see what was going on with Beatrice's eyes behind her shades. She put her arms on the table and leaned in towards me and said, 'I still don't want to get drunk with you. And I still think I might cry.'

'Are you going now?'

'Yeah.' She stood up and got out her purse.

'No, I really am getting these drinks,' I said.

'Well I'll get the next round.'

'OK.'

And then she came over and kissed both my cheeks like we

were French people and she said, 'Nice to meet you, Benjamin Constable, with your imaginary cat who I never did see.'

'He saw you.'

'Did he like me?'

'I don't know. He can't talk.' And Beatrice laughed and I said, 'I liked meeting you too, Beatrice. I half feel that I want to thank you. I really appreciate everything you've done for me, but to say the word seems kind of wrong.'

'Thank you's not the right thing to say.'

'No.'

And Beatrice smiled and walked away and I watched her, waiting for her to look back, but Beatrice doesn't do looking back.

I went to an Internet café and there was no new mail. I booked myself on a flight for Paris the next day and telephoned the hotel to confirm that I would be checking out early in the morning. I found an Italian restaurant and ate seafood linguini and drank a bottle of wine myself like a boozy old man. I wondered how much money I'd spent in the last nine days. I must have seriously eaten into my overdraft.

Everything was OK. Somehow I was a winner. I'd done what I set out to do (whatever that was). I wandered out into the street and walked. I thought about Beatrice and I wondered what it would be like to meet her in Paris. Maybe it would be lighter without all the treasure-hunt limitations. I would never ask her about the dead teacher thing.

And then I thought about Butterfly. I walked into Grand Central Station and it was quiet as the evening was coming to an end and I walked along Forty-Second Street. I sat down on the steps of the New York Public Library and smoked a cigarette and then walked round the north side of the library and into the park. I walked past the statue where I found the clue and along the south side to the carousel, wrapped up in tarpaulin, shadowy and still. I walked round and looked towards the fountain.

In real life we don't get the answers we need. If Butterfly were here, I wouldn't even ask her.

I sat down on a bench facing the carousel. I thought about Cat. I wondered what time it was. It must've been nearly midnight.

24

A Meeting in the Park at Midnight

I closed my eyes and leaned my head back to let the stars wash onto my face. A breeze rattled the trees, forecasting a change of weather, and I imagined a figure walking towards me along the avenue.

'Hey.'

'Hello, Butterfly.'

'I'm glad you're here.' She sat down on the bench next to me. 'I mostly come to this place to be on my own, but tonight I was thinking of you,' she said.

'I thought you got on a plane this afternoon.'

'I changed my mind at the last minute.'

'How did you know I'd be here?'

'I didn't; I just thought you might be,' she said.

'Good guess.'

'Are you going to ask me loads of questions?' she said.

'No. I don't think anything you could say would satisfy me.'

'I love you, Ben Constable.'

'Well, that's nice. I don't really know what it means, though.'

'It doesn't mean anything, it was just something I wanted to say.'

'I had an adventure, Tomomi Ishikawa. I discovered a new and amazing city and it was fiction-worthy and very bizarre, but an adventure nonetheless. My life is richer for it.'

'That's what I wanted for you, not that I think you lack adventure, but I wanted you to do something that I could be involved in. I wanted to show you my New York. I wanted you to see where I lived and where I grew up.'

'You could have just said, "Hey, let's go on holiday. I'd like to show you New York." I think I would have been quite tempted.'

'Well, this is the way I did it. I feel stupid. I made a big mess of everything.'

'It did get a little messy.'

'Did you like Beatrice?'

'Yes.'

'I liked the idea that you might have seduced her.'

'She didn't want to be seduced. At least, not by me.'

'Oh well.'

'You're pissed off with her, though, aren't you?' I said.

'She shouldn't have taken you to my mother's.'

'Well, I was pleased she took me. It was nice to meet your mum.'

'That's good. I don't think it was a particularly pleasant experience for her, you know, what with you saying I was dead and everything.'

'Yes, sorry about that. You put Beatrice in a pretty difficult position, though.'

'Well, you can apologise from me next time you see her.'

We were quiet for a second and then I said, 'Are you going back to Paris?'

'Yes.'

'What will you do when you get there?'

'Go underground to my grave.'

'Oh, Butterfly, are you one of the undead? That really would be an unexpected twist in this tale.'

'Ha-ha-ha. I love you.'

She slid along the bench up close to me and I put my arms around her and we stayed like that for a time, and the wind brought fat splashes of rain down on us. It was the first rain I'd felt in New York. I got out my cigarettes, lit two and handed one to her. And we stayed cuddling and smoking and she rested her head against me and the wind grew stronger, and the trees fretted, and suddenly an ocean fell out of the sky. We were soaked in seconds and our cigarettes went out. We ran up to the Bryant Memorial and squished behind the plinth out of the wind and sheltered from the rain. And once we'd wiped the water from our faces and hands, I got out two more cigarettes and lit them. Butterfly licked a last imaginary drop from her nose, more for comedy than out of need, and we laughed and then squatted down with our arms around each other and she pushed her head into my chest and shivered.

After twenty minutes or so the rain stopped. Butterfly stood up and smoothed out her damp clothes.

'Goodbye,' she said, and kissed my cheek. Then, the god of imaginary things clicked its fingers and Tomomi Ishikawa was gone—she had never been—and it was just me, by myself, shivering on the step. It was too sudden so I imagined her walking towards the carousel; she turned her head to see whether I was still there, too far for me to see whether she was smiling, and too many shadows. Perhaps she would stop by the fountain and look towards her library one last time. I walked back round to Fifth Avenue on the south side of the building (to keep things symmetrical) and got a taxi to the hotel.

PART THREE

September 2007

25

Incessant Nagging

Where to end a story is matter of choice. This feels like a mantra I've been reciting for years. But at a certain point you have to let go and just say 'And they all lived happily ever after.' And when I arrived back in Paris this was my intention. I spent my evenings sitting round dinner tables, talking and drinking wine, wondering what the next thing would be to catch my attention, kind of like choosing a new book to read. But people kept asking the same questions, the same questions that were nagging at me and unsettling my sleep. Where was Butterfly? Why had she told me she was dead? Had she really killed all those people? I wrote them down in a notebook and closed it, hoping that might be the end of the matter.

Work started again. For the first few days I was just going through the motions, knowing that it would take a little time before everything seemed settled, but I imagined that, so long as I held my notebook closed, at some point the nagging questions would fade.

Beatrice and I exchanged a couple of emails and arranged to meet for a drink the following week, when she would be in Paris. There were no emails from Butterfly or Charles Streetny and that was a good thing.

I looked at my bookshelf, excited at the prospect of losing myself in a new story, but the only thing I hadn't read was a copy of Dante's *Divine Comedy* that had been sitting there for a long time, ignored. After a few pages it had me drifting off and its verses seeped into my dreams. Like it or not, I hadn't finished with Butterfly. I knew where she was.

Cat came and stood on my chest. He bapped my face with the rough pad of his paw. 'For fuck's sake, Cat, what do you want?' It was Thursday night just after I'd gone to bed early so that I could get a good night's sleep, so I could do a good day's work, so I could go out and have a good Friday night in a restaurant, and then a bar, and laugh and talk to people. But Cat wouldn't leave me be, and so on Thursday night at eleven thirty I got up and dressed, and took the lift down to the ground floor and walked to the metro. I went to Jaurès and then walked down the stairs and through corridors to the platform of the 7bis. I got off at Buttes Chaumont and waited until there was an announcement telling me that there were no more trains, and without looking behind me, without calling Cat, without giving myself time to think, I walked off the end of the platform, past the yellow sign telling me that there would be danger of death if I did, and down the narrow steps. I walked along, hugging the wall into the tunnel. No one shouted at me, no one chased me, and I brushed my hand on the plant, the only plant in the metro. Butterfly's chalked writing and the arrows had been rubbed out, but I knew where to go. I found the doorway to the left with the stairs running down and turned into the dark, carefully feeling each step with my foot before allowing my weight to fall fully.

Where to end a story is a matter of choice. I know I should have ended it in New York and lived happily ever after. But I didn't; I carried on writing, each word, each step down taking painful seconds, and after a few minutes I was still in sight of the dim light at the top of the stairway behind me. I found flat ground and a passageway to my left. It was pitch black and there was nothing for my eyes to adapt to. I tried to walk forwards but my body wouldn't let me. I found my notebook in my bag and ripped out a page, rolled it up and lit one end. I was in a tunnel a metre wide and two high with stone walls, not bricked, but carved out from the pale rock. I hadn't got more than ten paces before I needed a new torch and tore out more pages to burn. I started with the blank pages and then moved through my notes on New York; things written in cafés, names of streets and squares, three questions about Butterfly. Would I remember without my notes? Would it all still exist without these pages to remind me?

Now I was facing east, or maybe southeast, and moving slowly forwards. When I'd burned the notebook (including the cover) I moved on to *The Divine Comedy*. It was a shame as I'd only read the first canto. Dante burned more quickly than my scribbled thoughts and I tried to work out the passage of time by the number of pages burned, but it wasn't easy. So long as I was home by four that would be fine. I wouldn't burn more than half *The Divine Comedy* and I'd be sure to have enough pages to light my way back to the metro tracks, and I could get a few hours' sleep before going to work. The passage forked. OK, I'd be able to remember this junction. I had to go one way or the other so I turned left.

I thought the tunnel might be veering gently, though it was

hard to tell so now I was probably going east, or maybe northeast, and then I came to a T-junction. I turned right, probably towards the south. I came to an intersection. How many turnings could I remember? It would only take one mistake to be lost. I thought of Theseus and the Minotaur; I needed a ball of string. I picked at the zip-up jacket I was wearing, trying to pull a thread that I could attach to something, and then, like a cartoon, my jacket would un-ravel and get shorter and shorter as I walked, and one by one the sleeves would disappear and I'd be left with two pockets, a collar and a zip, and a line to follow to get me out of this place. However, the special weave of the textile used for my jacket meant that it didn't unwind so easily (in fact, not at all). I decided to go straight on. The tunnel was blocked off, bricked up. Back at the intersec-tion, straight on would be the way I'd come from. I turned right, back towards the east.

I'd already burned a good hundred pages of *The Divine Com-edy*, which was what, seven hundred pages long? Maybe it's two in the morning. That's fine. So long as I'm home by six. The path forked, but this time there was no choice because the right-hand passage was blocked by a steel door with a lock. I tried to recall my route so far, saying the directions I'd taken over and over in rhythm: left at the first fork, right at the junction, left at the inter-section, left at the second fork . . . Then I came to a spiral stair-way. I counted the steps. Thirty. And each step was say, thirty degrees, so twelve steps was a full circle. So I was facing in the di-rection opposite to the one I had come from. Maybe. Left at the first fork, right at the junction, left at the intersection, left at the second fork, down the stairs. Of course, if I went back after five thirty, then the metro would be running and I'd have to walk back to Buttes Chaumont with trains rushing past me. The tunnel turned left and right and I came to a big chamber with several possible exits. Dante wasn't bright enough to light the whole room at once so I walked round, counting the passages. Was this the one where I came in? Six. I left a page by one of the exits and walked round to the beginning to see whether I'd counted correctly. I hadn't. Seven passages then, although the page had moved slightly, which meant there was air movement to blow it, or maybe it was just my walking that created a current. I was tired and feeling delirious. What the hell was I doing here? Had I gone mad? It was time to get out.

I set off back the way I'd come, but there was no spiral stairway, or at least not yet. I thought about cities and maps. I thought about Venice and Havana and plodded on, getting lost in the rhythm of my feet. Half the book had gone. This was the wrong way. I had to turn back a couple of times because of water too deep to wade through and one time I found a fast-flowing stream. I should go back to the chamber with seven doorways and then I should sit down and get my head clear. I came to a new chamber. It was misshapen with a large rock in the middle, flattened off at table height, and a single pillar to the left made from large stones cemented together. There was no point in being cross with myself for having been so impulsive to walk down into this subterranean mess without any preparation or a map. I was coming to find Butterfly. That's why I was here. This was a heroic and noble deed of friendship and love and I was far from dead. My feet were wet, though, as were my jeans up to my knees. I lay down in a loose foetal position on top of the rock and waited.

'Wake up.'

I was trying to remember something about Dante telling me to take another route. It all seemed to make sense.

'Wake up!'

Somebody was touching my shoulder. I opened my eyes, but it didn't make any difference; I couldn't see anything.

'Hey, wake up, Ben Constable.'

'I'm fine,' I said, trying to work out where I was and why I couldn't see. 'Is that you?'

'Yes.'

'Can you see in the dark,' I said, 'or have you got special night-vision spectacles?'

'I've got a flashlight, but I turned it off so it wouldn't hurt your eyes when you opened them.'

'That's funny. Normally I sleep with some sort of light to stop me being disorientated when I wake.'

'Sorry.'

'It's OK. I hardly ever know where I am whether there's a light or not.'

'You're in the tunnels underneath Paris.'

'I recognised the dark. What time is it?'

'Twenty past three.'

'Can you turn the light on, please?'

Tomomi Ishikawa shone her torch around the chamber so I could see all its dimensions and then at herself in case I was in any doubt as to who she was (although her voice was a much more reliable method for me to identify her than her face).

'How did you find me?' I asked.

'By accident. I walked in and saw you lying here like an effigy. You scared me. How long have you been here?'

'I don't know,' I said. 'What time is it really?'

'I don't know; I don't do time.'

'No.' I was unnecessarily dry and regretted it when I heard my voice. But she ignored me.

'Or days for that matter.'

'Well, I left my flat at about eleven thirty on Thursday evening. I came down here, wandered round for a couple of hours, got lost, fell asleep and now I'm awake and I'm hungry and still tired and probably late for work.'

'We can probably presume it's Friday then.' She turned the torch off. 'I don't want to waste the batteries.'

'You should get rechargeable ones.'

'Oh, they are,' she said. 'You can turn this handle thing and charge them up.' There was a whirring sound as she frantically whizzed the lever round. 'Cool, huh?'

'Butterfly, turn the light on.'

We were shy for a second and I watched her standing a couple of metres from me, wearing a simple top, a calf-length skirt gathered at the waist and flat shoes like a ballet dancer. She smiled and swung the torch around without thinking, hurling monstrous shadows on the walls and ceiling.

I lit a cigarette because that's what happens with smokers when they're not sure what to do with their hands.

'What are you doing here?' she asked.

'I came to find you.'

'Do you have a map?'

'No.'

'What about a torch?'

'No.'

'Wow, that's cool. This place is really hard to navigate if you don't know your way around. People get lost and die. They can't get out and they just starve to death, I guess.'

'Saves you the effort of killing them.'

'I suppose so.' She sighed. Then giggled. 'Killing them's the best bit, of course.'

'I liked your stories of killing everyone, you know,' I said. 'Not at the time, of course, but in retrospect they were quite funny and scary.' She didn't answer and the lightness evaporated for a moment and we went back to shy. 'I thought there would be arrows and clues and stuff to follow,' I said.

'Oh, there were. I went round and rubbed them all out.'

'Why?'

'I didn't want you to find me anymore.'

'Why?'

'Things change.'

I sighed and thought for a second. Things felt heavy inside me and I wanted to be on my own all of a sudden. I really wanted to be on my own.

'Butterfly?'

'Yes?'

'I want to go now. Can you tell me how to get out of here?'

'You said you were hungry. We should eat.'

'I'm late for work. I should go.'

'OK. Come with me.' She turned and the beam from the torch disappeared down a tunnel. I couldn't see. I thought about just staying where I was. I remembered what I'd thought in Bryant Park on that last night in New York: in real life there is no dénouement. No matter how far I travel and to what lengths I go to find Butterfly, I will never be satisfied. There was nothing she could say that would make me understand, nothing that could make it all right. Frustrating as it was, the story was already over.

'Come on,' she said.

'I can't see.'

She turned and shone the light at my feet. I put my cigarette out on the floor and she walked back towards me, bent down and picked up the filter. 'You mustn't leave trash,' she said, and I was

embarrassed. Then she raced carelessly into the dark, shining the
light backwards for me.

'How can you walk without the light?'

'Oh, I can see a tiny bit, but I'm used to it. I know my way
round pretty well.'

'How long have you been here?'

'Since I died.'

'So you are one of the undead after all!'

She looked over her shoulder at me and grinned.

I was silent and we walked on.

'So, did you like New York?'

I smiled a bit and pouted at the same time. 'Yeah, I did.' She
shot a glance back at me, pointing the light up at my face to see
my expression and blinding me. 'It was kind of difficult sometimes. But I liked it.'

'Hey, I'm sorry it turned out like that. It was meant to be fun.
It was your adventure; my present. I was proud to show you round
my wonderful Gotham Town.'

My head raced for a second. I'd already imagined this conversation in Bryant Park. This wasn't the same, though. There
was nothing sweet here. I felt like I could see her madness. Had
it always been there? I didn't say anything and we walked on in
silence. There were junctions and passages and we turned left
and right. Butterfly never hesitated, never needed to look or
check.

'Are we in the catacombs?'

'They call them catacombs, but mostly they were quarried for
the stone. This is what they built Paris out of, until they dug up so
much that the world they were constructing up there started sinking back into the ground it had come from. Whole buildings and
streets collapsed.'

'How much of this tunnelling is there?'

'This side of the Seine, not much.' Tomomi Ishikawa was always happy giving tour guide information.

'It feels like a lot to me.'

'There are a fair few kilometres spread over various networks, but a lot of it has been blocked off or filled in for structural reasons. On the Left Bank it's crazy, though. There's almost as much tunnelling as there are streets.'

We reached a door and she took out a key ring and a rubber cosh. Holding the torch in her mouth, she put a key into the lock, hit it firmly with the cosh whilst turning the key and the door was open.

'Huh? How did you do that?' I couldn't understand what I'd just seen.

'Oh, it's a trick I learned. It's called bumping. It's easy with a little practice, much easier than picking, and it works with just about all barrel locks.'

'Do you mean opening locks that you don't have the key for?'

'Yes.'

'How did you learn a thing like that?'

'The Internet,' she said, and led the way into what seemed like an even darker tunnel.

'You're not showing me out of here, are you?'

'Oh, sorry, you said you were hungry. I haven't seen you for such a long time. I thought you might have questions. I thought you might like to see where I live now.'

There was something wrong. I still wanted to be on my own. I don't know what I had imagined I would find down here, but it wasn't this. My breathing went heavier, as if I were dealing with something difficult. I wasn't scared, I couldn't get scared with

Butterfly, but I'd asked her to show me out and she had led me here.

There was another door and she repeated her trick with a key and the cosh. We walked into some kind of chamber and she closed the door behind me. 'Well, it's not much, but it's home,' she said, and turned off the torch. I couldn't see a thing.

25¹⁄₂

Cigarettes and Water

She struck a match (the sound made me jump) and lit candles. There was a table against the wall and two chairs. Apart from that the room was bare, with two open doorways leading into darkness. All colours seemed to be tones of orange or black and there was the smell of candle wax and stone. Long shadows danced tiny movements on the walls like winter, her bare ankles so delicate they could snap beneath the downy skin.

My heart was pounding heavy in my chest and the hairs on my arms were alert.

'What is this place?'

'I don't actually know. When I found it there were odd things, probably from the war. I think people might have hidden here when the Nazis came.'

'I thought the Nazis occupied the catacombs.'

'They had a bunker; it's miles away, though. They stuck to their bit. The Resistance used the tunnels as well and all sorts of

other people. They couldn't fight a war down here. It was too com
plicated. Do you want some water?' she called, disappearing
through one of the dark openings.

'Please,' I said, more out of reflex than thirst.

'There isn't much to eat, I'm afraid. Can I get you a yoghurt?'

I could hear water pouring from a jug, not a tap. How could
she see?

'Yeah. Yoghurt's good.'

She put two glasses on the table and then came back a moment later with two pots of yoghurt and teaspoons. 'There.' She sat
on one chair and I took the other.

'Butterfly?' My voice had a look-I'll-come-straight to-the-point
tone to it which wasn't natural (we had never come straight to the
point).

'Ben Constable?'

'What's going on?'

'What do you mean?'

'I mean you told me you were dead and I haven't seen you for
seven months or something. You left me a trail of clues leading me
to stories where you said you'd killed people, and to the other side
of the world where you'd constructed a crazy scheme to entertain
me, and now I've followed you down here where you live like a
hermit/ballet dancer/fugitive on yoghurt and water. You are
stranger than fiction and seem mad like I've never seen you before. I can't work out why you would have done any of this.'

'Oh God. Why is complicated. You never used to ask about
why, that's what I liked about you. We spent whole evenings
drinking and talking, but you never wanted to know reasons for
things.'

'Really?'

'It's a rare and endearing quality.'

'I kind of came to save you,' I said from nowhere. I felt I should explain myself.

'Well, that is the sweetest thing anybody has ever done in my life. I don't know that I can explain why I did all those things. Even if I told you everything I know, I don't think the pieces would fit together, or that everything would make sense.'

'How about if you just told me why you said you'd killed yourself?'

She looked at the floor and I could hear her breathing.

'OK. I'll try to explain.' She peeled the top off her yoghurt pot and I did the same.

'I really was going to kill myself. I'd known it for a while and I was starting to make a plan; things were beginning to fall into place . . .'

'So there never was a terminal illness or anything like that?'

'I was depressed; depression's a sickness, and if it makes you kill yourself, then it's terminal.'

'OK, I agree, but what you wrote was misleading. You made it sound like you were in the terminal phase of cancer or something.'

'Yeah, I know. I thought that would make it easier.'

I'd already finished the yoghurt and was running my finger round the inside of the pot to get the last bit. Now that I'd eaten I was really hungry.

'So what went wrong?' I felt drunk on that yoghurt.

'I'm trying to explain. I wanted to kill myself because I was desperately unhappy. I had been brought up to do things that I would regret every waking hour of my life and I started to understand that no matter how far I ran, no matter how much I changed the way I thought, or who I was, my past was chained to me. It would never fade. Nothing and nobody would ever free me from that weight. There was no hope of any kind of honest happiness.'

'I thought you were happy sometimes when we talked. We laughed a lot.'

'We did laugh a lot. Those are good memories. But they were only ever interludes from the endless disgust at my life. And so I decided to die.'

I felt my throat constrict. She was wrong. Depression makes you think like that, but there are always other ways to think. We're not chained to our past. Her past is only stories that she made up—I mean there was a real past as well, but not the stories. They were a way of expressing something else. That's how stories work.

'So I started planning my death and organising things, in particular the treasure hunt, and it took over my brain. I thought about it all the time. When I slept I dreamed about it and when I woke I wanted to get up and carry on planning, and I was writing you letters every day and screwing them up and starting again and I was going through my journals looking for interesting things and throwing out embarrassing stuff. And I was happy. I was happy to be playing with you. For the first time in my life I wanted something to go on forever. I'd never known what that felt like before.'

Part of me wanted to hold her hand, but part of me didn't as well. I drank my water and lit a cigarette. She watched me enviously.

'Could I have one of those?' she said.

'Help yourself.' I pushed the packet towards her.

She lit one and it sat uncomfortably between her fingers as she took a deep, trembling drag. She noticed me noticing. 'Nicotine rush,' she said. 'I don't really smoke anymore.'

'So you decided that planning your death was the first thing you'd ever done that you enjoyed.' I didn't sound as if I believed her. I don't know that I did believe her.

'Yes.' She looked at the floor again.

'And so you told me you had killed yourself.'

She was silent.

'Can you even imagine how much suffering it causes when people commit suicide? Can you imagine what goes through their family and friends' brains?'

'I don't need to imagine.'

'It's not something you just say to people for a game, Butterfly. It's crazy. It's the cruellest lie I can think of.'

She didn't say anything but looked at me with wet eyes, and I could see the shadows on her throat where it was blocking up.

'I love you.'

'Is that something you just say whenever, like a way of mollifying people around you?'

'It's what I say to you and to some other people as well. Just special people—nobody else.'

I'd seen her like this before. I couldn't let her get away with hiding behind whatever mechanism she had for protecting herself. I wanted her to break down and vomit up everything, then she could be brand-new.

'Was telling me that you were dead the only way you thought you could get rid of me?'

'In a way, yes. You're a persistent motherfucker. You don't leave things alone. I tried to do it differently.'

'To do what differently?'

'I tried not killing myself. I tried to put distance between us, but you couldn't understand. Having had my attention, you wanted it all the time, so if I disappeared, you would always come looking, calling me up or texting. You just wanted to know that I was OK. You just wanted to hear my voice and laugh about stuff or tell me about your day. It was horrible because I loved it so much and it fuelled my plan to hide treasure for you. You would follow the trail into my world of clues and writing and I would kill myself and I was excited and happy for the first time ever. But I had to really do it for it to work. I had to really kill myself. I had to believe it.'

'So what changed? Why didn't you just kill yourself for real? It might have been easier than all this.'

'Two things . . .' I'd asked her a question she knew the answer to. She'd got away with it. She wasn't going to break down. 'The first was that I wasn't ready in time. I'd given myself a date. It was like a rule. I had to be ready for this deadline—March fifteenth.'

'Why that day?'

'It was the anniversary of something.'

'The anniversary of what?'

'Of my father's death.'

'Oh.' I suddenly felt as though I'd strayed onto untouchable territory. I nodded.

'And of Komori's death too.'

'Shit. They both died on the same day?'

'A year apart.'

'Hold on, you never know what date it is or what time or any-thing. I'm sure if you missed your suicide by a day or two, it wouldn't have been that bad.' I was talking as if she'd fucked up by not killing herself. Is that what I really thought?

'I just wasn't anywhere near ready. I knew it weeks before-hand. And then I found the door.'

'What door?'

'The entrance to the catacombs.'

'By the plant in the metro?'

'No. I found that later, after I'd been exploring. It was in the basement of my building.'

'What?'

'I was clearing out my stuff—every apartment in my building has its own locker-sized room in the basement, with a door and a padlock—and I saw this door that was different from the others. It was steel plated with two locks cut into it. While I was sorting through my things, a neighbour came down and I asked him whose door it was and he told me it went into the catacombs. I asked him who had the key. He said he didn't know.'

'So how'd you get in?'

'I looked it up on the Internet. It took me about four hours to get it open the first time. Nowadays, so long as I can get a blank key for the lock, I can get through just about any door in five or six seconds.'

'Where on earth do you get blank keys?'

'Friendly locksmith. Rue Ménilmontant.'

'Yes, of course,' I said kind of sarcastically.

'Coming down here saved my life.'

'How?'

'Well, at first I was excited. I thought I was going to find an elite club of militant clock repairers, and I have since met quite a few people like that, but it was the time I spent on my own that was the best. There was something about being contained underground that made me feel good, like I was wrapped up and safe, like there was a world where I could be alive and well, and not need to die. Then I went back aboveground and I wanted to kill myself immediately; I came back underground and I was cured. From then on I knew what I was going to do. I found these rooms behind locked doors that nobody had been through for generations and decided that this was a temporary replacement for my death. I had nothing to lose. If ever it got bad again, I could always kill myself, but for now I was OK. I'd just decide every day whether I wanted to kill myself or not.'

'Strangely, that does make sense. But it doesn't explain why you told me you were dead. There wasn't any need.' I put my cigarette in the empty yoghurt pot and poured the last drop of water from my glass to make sure it was out, then pushed the pot to the middle of the table for Tomomi Ishikawa to use. She flicked in her ash and it hissed, then she accidentally blew smoke in my face. She wafted an apologetic hand.

'I don't know.'

'You don't know what?'

'I suppose I do know,' she sighed. 'Part of the plan was for you to find my notebooks. I knew I wanted it to be you. You were the only person in the world who I wanted to read them. That was because you have a dark and twisted mind and I love you. And it's because I needed—I wanted—to share those notebooks. I wanted somebody else to know what was inside. They are the weight I have been carrying around all my life. But for you to read the books, you and I could no longer live in the same world. I wouldn't be able to stand your pity or your questions There just wasn't room for both of us. I had been planning to kill myself anyway. Telling you I was dead seemed like an obvious solution. It wouldn't change anything for you and it would mean that I could carry on for as long as I felt like—which I didn't think would be very long anyway.'

'Well, now I've read your books, and I know that you're living a second life, underground, after death. What now?'

'I don't know, Ben Constable. Your curious wandering mind has messed up everything, and I love you all the more for it.'

'But you wanted me to come here. You wrote "Down here, BC" by the plant in the metro.'

'That was before you'd read the books. I was pretty confused. I wanted saving and I wanted you to know me at the same time. But it was one or the other, the treasure hunt, or coming to find me. You chose the treasure hunt and I erased the signs. You weren't supposed to do both.'

And I had this vague feeling of understanding, like I could see a blurred form emerging out of the mist. 'Oh,' I said, and there was quiet for an eternity as my brain put it all together. 'I really am sorry. You are the strangest person I have ever met, Butterfly.'

'I guess I know that.'

'The thing is, once I knew you were alive, I had to know that you were all right. I had to understand. My brain couldn't just leave it at that. There were too many questions left unanswered.'

She pushed her chair back, came and stood in front of me and took hold of my hands; I stood up too.

'I really never meant for any of this to upset you,' she said. 'It was a game for you and me to play together; it was an adventure. I was just so wound up in what was going on in my own sad, twisted brain that I forgot to think about how you would feel. I'm no good at this sort of thing.' Her fingers played with mine.

'What sort of thing?'

'This sort of thing.' She put a hand behind my head and pulled it towards her and kissed my mouth. She'd never done that before.

26

A Sticky Situation

Oh. So this is the ending. After all that's happened we kiss because, contrary to everything I believed, this is just about: sex, or maybe this is love even. Perhaps it's just a story of two people talking a long and complicated route to getting it on. It's not what I was expecting, though. It felt good on my lips, but I was disappointed. A kissing end seemed almost cheap and lacking in imagination. This surely wasn't the point. Part of me wanted to push away, fight for something more intricate, something richer. But perhaps I was wrong. Maybe it was kissing that would save everything.

I kissed her back and our fingers touched again, delicately dancing round each other, and my heart thumped and my body ached. She led me through one of the doorways, left and then right, and I dragged my feet in the dark so as not to trip. I couldn't see. Nothing, just fingers touching my fingers, and a kind of sad joy that I'd found my friend and that she was alive. I wanted her to be alive. The acoustics changed and we were in another room now. She led my hands to a wall, cold, and turned me round, pushing me backwards, and her hand reached for my face and her tongue kissed my mouth again.

'Wait,' she whispered, 'I'll be back in one second,' and she stepped away from me.

Excitement. Sex. Brain. Wait a minute . . . I held my breath; I could feel her backing away. Adrenaline. *What's happening?* Panic. *Shit, shit, shit. Wait. Think clearly. No. Don't wait. Move. No noise. Move. Move now.* I reached out my hand to the left. Holding my breath, trying to keep my thoughts quiet. *OK, a few small breaths. Small, don't move the air.* I bent my knees slightly, shifted my weight. I stepped, one tiny step, and another. *No noise.* I could hear her still moving away from me. My arms relaxed, they could move fast. My fingers felt the air, my body listened. *Balance. No noise.* I heard her hand brush on something, feeling the shape of something, lining up, preparing a movement. *Bend knees, no breathing, another step, diagonal towards her, to the side. Feel the air—don't forget she is small; I am lightning. Let her move, she will tell you where she is.* Sudden movement (*Sorry, Butterfly; I fight*), loud noise, metal screech, metal hitting metal, I flinched to protect my eyes, a click, I knew that sound, it was a padlock. I was standing still—*great fighting, Ben.* All that had happened was she had closed a gate and locked a lock.

'Butterfly?' She jumped; I wasn't where she thought I should be.

'Sorry,' she whispered. She was on the other side of the gate.

'That's OK,' I said, and it was. I was alive. She walked away and I wonder whether those were the most exciting four seconds of my life.

* * *

I felt my way around the room. It was about three metres by three metres and entirely empty. I could touch the ceiling with the palms of my hands if I stood on tiptoe. There was one doorway with a padlocked jailor's gate. The top hinge had been fitted upside down so the gate couldn't be lifted off its fixings. There was nothing in my pockets. Anything of interest I may have had was in my bag in the other room, plus my cigarettes and lighter, which were on the table. I paced round and tried to prepare my brain for being patient, but after two minutes I was bored.

'Butterfly!' I called out (not angry, not shouting). There was nothing. 'Butterfly, can I have my cigarettes?'

Suddenly I wanted to smoke so badly I could have cried. Nothing. How long was I going to be here? I did the thing which you should never do when you have to wait and started counting. One, two, three, four . . . conscious of every second passing, pretending to be calm. *Just wait,* I said to myself. *She'll come in a bit.* A thousand is sixteen minutes and forty seconds.

'Butterfly, I don't want you to forget about me. I'm hungry and thirsty, and a bit cold, and I want to smoke and I can't see anything, and I could do with going to the toilet, I mean I could hold that for a while, but not forever, and I think you don't want me to die here, and I wish you'd come and talk to me some more. I'm sorry I was being difficult and trying to make you say stuff you didn't want to talk about. We could talk about other stuff if you want.'

One thousand and one, one thousand and two, one thousand and three, one thousand and four . . . I needed some temporary strategy for not going mental and I feared that I was going to go mental very quickly. I hadn't even been here for half an hour and I couldn't trust my brain anymore. I lay down and stopped myself counting. Then I heard the door that we had come through. I heard it bang closed through the stone tunnels and the dark. To-momi Ishikawa had gone.

At four thousand six hundred and twenty-two I heard her bump the lock. She came in clumsily, carrying things. I waited. She was moving around. And then she spoke, not close by, but calling to me from another room.

'I had to go out and get some stuff. I wasn't really prepared for visitors.'

I didn't reply and she carried on pottering about. Then a couple of minutes later a torch beam shone past the gate, illuminating my cell.

'Ben?'

'Yeah,' I whispered.

'Look, you won't like this, but I don't really know how else to do it.'

'Do what?'

'Come up to the gate and look. I've got a gun.'

I put my face up to the bars and there she was, smiling and waving a pistol at me. Where the hell had she got a pistol from?

'You need to move back from the gate and stand in the corner with your face to the wall and your hands in the air.'

'Jesus, Butterfly!'

'I just want to open the gate for a moment and you're bigger and stronger than me. I don't want you to overpower me, and I don't want to shoot you, so you have to do what I say. OK?'

I walked to the corner and put my hands in the air. I heard a key and her cosh before the lock clicked open. She put something in the room. The gate closed and the lock clicked. 'OK, you can move now.'

On the floor by the gate was a bucket with a lid, inside was a roll of toilet paper, a blanket and my bag. Tomomi Ishikawa backed away from the gate and leaned against the wall opposite. 'Your cigarettes are in the bag,' she said.

I don't know where the calm comes from at times like these (not that this sort of thing happens to me often), but there's a kind of resignation to not being in control that makes everything all right, once you let go of the idea that you could make a difference. It was nice having the light and it was nice having Butterfly there.

'You know you've gone mental, don't you, Butterfly?' I said. 'You can't take people prisoner. It's the first sign of being utterly and dangerously deluded.'

'I'm buying time. I need to work out how to get us both out of this.'

'That's easy. You put the gun down, open the gate, and then we walk out into the sunshine and find a nice terrace and drink a coffee. None of this will have happened. It'll be a story, just like your other stories, except in this one nobody dies.'

'You think that everything can be explained away, don't you? That eventually everything will all become clear and then we will be able to laugh and it'll all be better.'

'I'd like to understand what the hell is going on, but I've suspected for quite a while that nothing you could say would satisfy me. And when I really think about it I know that we don't need to understand stuff to move on. We can be whatever we want. We don't need answers.'

'Hey, that would be beautiful if it was true that you were so cool. But you're making judgements all the time, trying to decide what's true and what's not true. When I tell you lies you believe them, when I tell you things that happened you assume they're lies. All your behaviour towards me is based on the presumption that everything I wrote in my notebooks was made up. Right?'

'I . . .' My speech stumbled, as my ready-made answer didn't work anymore.

'Is that what you believe?' she asked.

I was certain that everything she had written was fiction. I'd had moments of doubt, but I knew it was made up. But when she shut me in this room I was ready to fight for my life. This was a major inconsistency—a smart lawyer would take me apart in seconds. What did I actually believe?

'I don't know what I believe, Butterfly. I don't think what you wrote is word for word true and that leaves the possibility that it was all fiction. I can't imagine you really killing those people. I think they're fantasies, where you put yourself in positions of power, where the boss is the small girl and she has the power to decide who will die and when. I like the idea of you taking back control in a life that was laid out for you. But I don't think you really did those things and I don't understand why you locked me in this dungeon.'

'You ask me questions like "why?" but you don't listen to the answers. To understand why you're in this room, you have to imagine that I did do all those things: suffocate, slash, stab, burn, poison . . . Imagine now that somebody knew it was me—that I'd killed six people—and that I'd successfully gone into hiding, but that person had come and found me and now wanted me to come out of hiding and lead a normal, happy life. I think even in your determinedly blind innocence, you can see that this simply cannot happen. For the first time in my life, I'm actually interested in living and you are inconveniently in my way.'

'But you told me everything was lies.'

'What?'

'One time when you were drunk you told me everything you said was lies.'

'Well, I don't remember that, but I would have thought it was perfectly obvious that it's not the case. There have been lies and there have been truths.'

There was nothing I could say to this. I had thought she might attack me. I had moved to defend myself. I must think it possible that she killed those people and if she had, and I knew about it, I could see that I actually was a very real inconvenience. I rummaged in my bag and found my cigarettes.

'Do you want one?' I held out the packet and Tomomi Ishikawa jumped back and pointed the gun at my face. 'Shhh, it's a cigarette,' I said.

'Stay back from the gate.'

'OK. Would you like a cigarette?'

'No, thank you. I don't really smoke anymore. Do you have any chewing gum?'

'No. All I've got is your bitter toffee almonds.'

'I don't think that's what I feel like right now. Maybe later.'

She stood up straight.

'What are you going to do?' I asked.

'I don't know,' she said. 'Carry on improvising until a plan comes.' Then she walked off.

While I slept she put a yoghurt inside the gate for me, and a jug of water and a glass. I didn't know what time it was or what day. I found my phone in my bag. There was still some battery left but no signal, of course. It was three twenty on Saturday afternoon. I should save the battery, just in case. I turned it off. There was nothing left to count. I was hungry and bored. I needed some substantial food; a big meal. I needed to get clever and find a way out of this situation. I smoked my last cigarette. My brain swam in circles like a goldfish and I felt miserable and stuck. The torchlight shone down the corridor. Tomomi Ishikawa waved the pistol at me and told me to get back from the gate and I did. She came and squatted on the floor in front of the doorway. She didn't speak.

'I feel stupid,' I said.

'You're lots of things, Ben Constable, but stupid isn't one of them.'

'I feel stupid for believing you when you said you were dead, and for thinking that maybe if I had done things differently, I might have been able to save you. I thought that if I had called or sent you a text that you might not have committed suicide. I felt as though it was my fault. And I feel stupid for mourning you, and for being in shock. I was so shocked, I couldn't control it. It was like being mad. And I feel stupid for believing Beatrice when she said she didn't know you. She even wanted me to not believe her, but I just carried on thinking stuff that fit neatly into my idea of how things should be. And for missing you so bloody much when I hardly even know you. Who the hell's Tomomi Ishikawa? I think I just made up an imaginary friend who happened to have your name. That makes me feel stupid. This whole story is just one long string of idiocy on my part, and now I'm locked up underground waiting for my psychotic friend to kill me.'

'I'm sorry you're here,' she said. 'This really isn't what I wish for you. I'll find a way to sort it out. I promise.'

'Funny when the person working round the clock for your freedom is your captor.' She did a half shrug and a half smile. 'And do you know what's even funnier?' I asked.

'No.'

'It was kissing that got me into this room.'

'Ha-ha-ha!' She laughed loudly. 'God, I'm so sorry about that, and really quite embarrassed. I was desperate.'

'Thanks.'

'No, not desperate like that.'

And now I laughed.

'No, no, no,' she protested.

I looked at her and she grinned at the floor. 'I didn't know what to do,' she said. 'I wasn't expecting to find you lost in the tunnels. I couldn't let you go. I had this padlock that I'd stolen, and this strange scary room with a steel gate. I put the padlock in my pocket and did the kissing trick and the rest, well . . . sorry.'

'There are so many endings I could have imagined for this story. And this isn't any of them. This can't be how it ends.'

'Why? How did you want it to finish?' she asked.

'I don't know. Would it be completely unreasonable to ask for a happy ending?'

'Like what?'

'Like we go out from here and you get help from some genius psychologist and realise that you've got your whole life ahead of you and it's beautiful and exciting and perhaps you even get it on with the psychologist because he is dashingly handsome and intelligent and in love with you.'

'And what would happen to you, Ben Constable?'

'Well, I'd go home a little wiser but just as innocent. And I would write a book and would feel very pleased with myself. And you and I might meet for coffee now and then and talk about stuff and laugh.'

'Excellent. It sounds completely boring. How about if there

was something that nobody had anticipated? Another person who had organised the whole thing.'

'It actually crossed my mind that there was some kind of grander conspiracy. I never wanted to admit it, but I kept thinking that people were following me, or looking at me in strange ways.'

'I followed you a couple of times.'

'Really?'

'I wanted to know if you were finding the treasure.'

'Bloody hell, Butterfly; that's disturbingly no good.'

'Hey, only a couple of times. Any more than that and it's your paranoia playing up again.'

'My paranoia?'

'People looking at you in strange ways? A conspiracy?' She stroked an imaginary beard and laughed at me.

'I thought maybe you were being held prisoner and had left me clues to help you.'

'No, sorry,' she said. 'But look, how about this for a grim twist? You spend the whole book hoping that everything you've read is fiction, but in fact I really am a murderer and I kill you . . .'

'But who writes the book if I'm dead?'

'This is the twist: you die here underground and I leave and go back to your apartment and I sit down and write the book from beginning to end, but in your voice. I write it under the name Ben Constable and at the end he witnesses Tomomi Ishikawa dying and so nobody ever comes looking for her—me—and I would live happily ever after. In fact, it might even be the beginning of a writing career with my new nom de plume. Who would have imagined that Ben Constable was in fact a woman?'

I laughed. 'That's the most disturbing ending imaginable. It's wrong in every way.'

'Sorry. That's the way my mind works.'

We were silent for a moment and then I remembered something 'Hey, there was somebody else, though.'

'Who?' she asked.

'Charles Streetny.'

'Oh, yes. The executor of my posthumous wishes. How funny
that you thought it was his name.'

'How did he know I was in New York? Did you trace the IP
address from my email?'

'What's an IP address?'

'It's a network address that all computers connected to the Internet have. It's encoded in the emails you send.'

'I don't know about that. I knew you were in New York because I'd given you clues telling you to go there, then you disappeared, and finally you sent me an email telling me you'd arrived.
It was pretty easy.'

'Oh, yes.' I remembered the email that I'd sent. 'I thought
maybe Streetny had specialist computer knowledge.'

'Would that he did. Sadly he was my better-organised alter
ego. I needed somebody who would be more compliant than the
awkward Beatrice.'

'Was Beatrice awkward? I thought you got her to do pretty
much everything you wanted.'

'No, not really. She was a bit unimaginative.'

'I liked her. She's coming to Paris next week. She might already be here.'

'Are you going to see her?'

'That kind of depends on you.'

Tomomi Ishikawa looked at stuff, but not at me. 'We'll have to
see. I don't have a plan yet.' Then she waved the pistol. 'Can you
get away from the gate, please?'

I wasn't even near it, but I stood up and walked to the corner.

She reached her hand through the bars and picked up the water jug and the empty pot of yoghurt. 'I'll get you more,' she said.

After a few hours alone in the dark, my brain felt completely mad. I had no more cigarettes and all I'd had to eat in (how many?) days was a few pots of yoghurt. Tomomi Ishikawa had been twice to empty my bucket and a couple of times to bring me water or just to stare at me. Each time she would shine her torch, wave her gun around and tell me to get away from the gate and I obeyed because I didn't fancy getting shot. She would have to let me go, though. I knew this and she knew it too. I was bored of being alone.

I found the stainless steel pen in my bag and tried to scrape a hole to escape through. I spent hours. Hours and hours. The pen started to wear down, and I scratched a furrow about two inches long and half an inch deep. I don't know where exactly I was planning to scratch my way to. It was looking unlikely that the pen was going to save me.

'Butterfly!' I shouted. Maybe she wasn't here anymore. I couldn't remember whether I'd heard the door. 'Butterfly! I know why you're mad.' I waited, but she didn't answer. 'It's because you only eat yoghurt. You can't live on just yoghurt and water; it makes you go mad.' There was no noise.

Dreams weren't made for remembering. We have no special equipment or capacity to keep hold of them and nature doesn't care whether they are documented or not. Like all thoughts in the dark, they just come and then they are forgotten.

'Of course, it nearly turned out very differently.'

I opened my eyes and she was sitting by the gate with a torch and a gun clamped together like something from a cop show. She was pointing the gun at my head, lining me up in the sights.

'Don't point that at me,' I said.

'Sorry. I'm trying to get used to the idea. I don't know what else to do other than kill you. I can't keep you here.'

'Butterfly, why can't you envisage a happy life for yourself? It's never even been your ambition, has it?'

'Life isn't like that,' she said.

'It could be. You could choose to aim for good things. I'm not saying it would be easy, but that could be your goal.'

'It's too late. They should have taught me that when I was a child. I can't go back aboveground and just change my past. I'm a danger to myself and others. But I can't keep you here either, you're right about that. But it was so nearly different.'

'What do you mean?'

'You came back to my apartment. You were supposed to come and get the computer, which you did, but you came back again. Why would you do a thing like that?'

'Sorry. I'd forgotten the power supply,' I said. 'For your computer. It wouldn't turn on. I had to come back to it.'

'OHHHH! Fucking fuck. Now I understand. It so nearly changed everything.'

'Why?'

'Because I was there.'

'No you weren't.'

'I was. I'd come back to pack my things and I'd had a shower and had filled a bag with stuff and was in some state of semi-nakedness when I heard your voice outside the door. I don't know who you were talking to. I panicked and grabbed the bag and climbed into the wardrobe and you came in. You nearly found me. You were inches away and you were talking to somebody.'

'I wasn't with someone.'

'You were, I could hear you both talking.'

'You couldn't hear them talking because they can't talk.'

'You just said you weren't with anybody.'

'I wasn't. I was with a cat.'

'What were you doing with a cat?'

'Look, there's something about me that you don't know.'

'What?' Butterfly barked with excitement.

'I've got an imaginary cat.'

'No.'

'Yes.'

'You're lying.'

'If only I was.'

'Have you always had it?'

'No. Since, I don't know, maybe eight or ten years ago?'

'How did you get an imaginary cat?'

'It's a long story, but basically anyone can have one.'

'How?'

'You just think of a cat.'

'I'm thinking of a cat now.'

'That's a bit like what Cat is like.'

'It's called Cat?'

'Yes.'

'You are a fucking freak, Ben Constable! I love you.'

'Thanks. Talking of freaks, what about you? You've kept me here for days. I want to go home and have a shower and cook some real food and sleep in my bed. You have to let me go, Butterfly. You can't keep people prisoner, and you can't kill people.'

'I'm stuck, Ben Constable,' she said. 'And talking to you doesn't really help me.' She shone the torch in my face for a moment, then turned it out and left.

* * *

My stubble was itching against my neck and I wasn't hungry anymore. I was thirsty, though. I dreamed of water in my mouth.
When I was awake I spoke with Cat. He was good company and
an attentive listener. I tried to explain Butterfly's situation to him
and he acknowledged the complexity of it but had no answers. We
reminisced on places we had visited and I told him about places I
would like to see. We travelled a lot. I told him that even though I
didn't know what day it was, I thought Beatrice had come to Paris
and gone. She must have thought me rude not to answer her calls
or emails, as though I was ignoring her. I wondered whether she
would stay in contact with me. And then wondering seemed futile.
Some things happen; some things don't. I took Cat's silence as
agreement. I considered doing exercise, but seeing as I didn't know
when I would eat or drink again, I thought I should conserve my
energy. Maybe she was just going to leave me to dehydrate. How
long can you go without water? It's not long. Two days maybe?
Sometimes I was mad, and other times I was more sane than I
would have thought possible. I remembered being four.

When I was four I got lost in the supermarket. The illusory
bubble burst and the mundanely comprehensible world of food
shopping was clearly endless aisles stacked with mind-boggling
repetition, strip lighting and grey vinyl floor tiles to eternity. Adrenaline coursed through my veins and all direction ceased to exist.
Another time I shut myself in a cupboard with the handle solely
on the outside. I was surprised by the total dark. The door
wouldn't open and the joy of adventure flipped to panic. I let out
an inhuman cry of self-pity. I had foreseen my own death.

27

An Ending

'Wake up,' she said. The gate was open and there was a jug of water on the floor next to me. She had a torch in one hand and the gun in the other. 'Wake up, Ben Constable. It's time to go.'

I gulped the water straight from the jug. 'Come on,' she said.

'I'll get my bag.'

She made me stand back as we went through her two locked doors and she closed them again after me.

'Do you have cigarettes?' I asked.

'No,' she said. 'Can I have one of those bitter toffee almonds I gave you?'

'Yep.' I went in my bag, got the little tin, opened it and held it out.

'Two of them,' she said. 'One for you, one for me.'

'I don't like almonds. I was just keeping them as a souvenir.'

'OK. Now listen. You walk in front and I will give you directions. But whatever happens, you mustn't look back. OK?'

'Who do you think I am, Orpheus?'

'Do as I say, your life depends on it.' I don't think I believed her. I didn't believe anything anymore.

Butterfly walked close behind, shining the torch around me. I thought of turning quickly and taking the gun out of her hand, but they don't recommend messing with armed people. So I walked on slowly; it felt as if my body needed to warm up and stretch before it would be able to walk at a normal pace. After a while, I reached out my hand behind my back and stopped. I wanted her to take it. It was my last olive branch. Let's leave together. Everything's all right.

She nudged my back with the gun. 'Keep going,' she said. I felt it touching my spine through my shirt and I understood something.

We walked left and right in silence and after several minutes, maybe ten or twenty, we came to the chamber with seven entrances.

'I know this place,' I said.

Butterfly pointed to the passage I was to follow with the torch. I could hear her dragging her feet a little and her steps became just slightly irregular. We came to the thirty spiral steps and I paced up. She seemed to find them more difficult than I did. I must have been out of her sight the whole time. I could have outrun her easily. I knew the way out from here. All her aggression was fake. Butterfly was crumbling behind me.

'What's the matter?' I asked.

'Nothing,' she said. She was controlling her voice so it wouldn't shake. I carried on and she walked behind me. But the torchlight wasn't shining past me anymore. She was falling behind.

'Butterfly, keep up.' I took a couple of steps more, but she

wasn't following. I stopped and listened. I could hear her breathing heavily. She sniffed. *What are you up to, Butterfly? What is this
plan with a gun and dark tunnels?* Then I heard her lean against
the wall. She sniffed again. She was crying. I heard her slide down
to the ground and the light went out.

'Butterfly!'

She didn't say anything. I could hear small sobs and her quick,
heavy breaths.

'Butterfly!'

Nothing happened.

'Butterfly!'

I tried walking backwards, but I stumbled. I took out the remains of *The Divine Comedy* from my bag, ripped a page out,
rolled it up and lit it. I turned and walked towards her.

I had to take a few steps before I could see her properly. She
was squatting with her back against the wall and her arms around
her knees. She unwrapped the sweet I had given her and put it in
her mouth.

'Butterfly?'

'You'd better go on without me.'

'Why?'

'I'm not coming. Here'—she opened her bag and took something out—'take this but don't look at it until you get aboveground.' She handed me a plastic bag with notebooks in it. 'Put
them in your bag.' I did.

'What's the matter?'

'I'm dying.'

'What of?'

'Cyanide.'

'How did that happen?'

'The sweet. Bitter toffee almond. It's poison.'

'And you wanted me to eat it?'

'Yep.'

'Why?'

'I don't know. I guess you knew too much. Why do you sound so surprised? I've been threatening you with a gun for days.'

'Yes, but it's plastic.'

'No it's not.' She waved it at me and I took it out of her hand. It was a cheap plastic toy; I'd understood when she pushed it in my back. I pulled the trigger a couple of times and it made a clicking sound a bit like a stapler.

'There were no murders, were there?' I said. 'None of this is real.'

'The gun's not real; I had to come up with something quick to stop you from just walking out and taking me with you. It was the only thing I could think of.'

'Well, it worked.'

'Until now.'

'Are you really dying?'

'I should be, if the poison works properly.'

'But you only just ate the sweet. What about before? Why were you falling behind and crying?'

'I was scared. I thought you weren't going to look back and I would have to go up and outside.'

'What the hell has looking back got to do with it?'

'You'll find out later.'

'Did you kill all those other people?'

'Does it matter?'

'Of course it fucking matters.'

'I'm not going to answer that question. Ask me something else.'

'You came and found me in the garden while I was asleep, didn't you?'

'I took your keys and turned your phone off to make sure no one would answer it when the Night Guy tried to call. Sorry. I hope you got back into the hotel OK and didn't have to sleep outside.'

'Why did you leave me locked up for so long, just for you to die in a tunnel?'

'The only plan I could think of to get you out was this one. It wasn't my first choice. I was hoping to have a better idea, but it never came. Hey, Ben Constable?'

'Yes?'

'Would you put your arms round me?'

'OK.' I'm a fool for that kind of thing. I sat down on the floor next to her and she rested her head against my chest in the dark. She was hyperventilating and trembling. I stroked her hair.

'Are you really dying?'

'Yes.'

Half of my heart was breaking and the other half was stone. I wasn't going to fall for any more tricks. Great, now I'm a cynic.

'Shit,' I said. 'I'm sorry I couldn't save you, Butterfly.'

'Don't worry about it,' she said. 'I didn't want saving.'

'OK, I'm sorry I fucked everything up in your subterranean utopia.'

'Oh, well. You weren't to know.'

'Surely there is a better ending than this.'

'I'm dying in your arms, what more could you want?'

'I want you to come and have more adventures. We could go and do chivalrous deeds like you said before.'

'Windmills.' Now she was crying again. 'All those giants were windmills. I think it's time I gave up chivalry.'

'No, they were real, I promise you.'

'Why do you say that?'

'If sanity comes with death, maybe you should stay insane.'

'Don't worry, at this late stage there is little chance of me sorting out a lifetime of mental issues.'

'I suppose not.'

'Will you write a book about me?' She was digging her fingers into me, holding on tight.

'Do you want me to?'

'Yes.'

'Can I use all your emails and letters and the notebooks?'

'The books I stole are in that bag I gave you.' Now her voice was cracking.

'Thanks,' I said.

'I think they've turned the lights down,' she croaked.

'They must be bringing in a birthday cake.'

'It's not my birthday. Is it yours?'

'Soon.'

'Did you sleep with thirty women this year?'

'Well, it's not quite my birthday yet, but so far, no.'

'Oh, well. Maybe next year,' she whispered.

'How about this for an ending?' I said. 'We could make a deal where I leave and go home and in the book I write I say that I was with you when you died, but really you don't die and carry on living underground. And I would never tell another living soul and I would never try to contact you or come and find you and you would be free and happy. And I would live with the lie a hundred per cent until eventually I would believe it. I swear I can do it. Don't die, Tomomi Ishikawa. Not again, please.' I squeezed her a bit, but she didn't move or make a sound.

'Butterfly?'

I put my hand on her diaphragm. She was still breathing, quick little breaths, and then they stopped. I held my breath, copying her, and just when I couldn't hold it anymore her body burst out into violent convulsions. I couldn't believe the force of it. I held on as tight as I could to stop her from damaging herself. It went on for several minutes and then calmed into occasional spasms. And then I choked and tears came to my eyes. I was scared. I didn't know what was happening.

'Shhh. It's all right,' I lied. 'Everything's all right.'

She went limp again. I put my hand on her diaphragm, but now I couldn't feel any movement. I put my fingers on her pulse. It was there. Her heart was beating weakly and with a made-up rhythm and pauses that were too long.

'Shhh.'

She was sitting on a rock by a river and a line of children crossed a low wooden footbridge towards her, stopping at a small island in the middle of the stream to pick wildflowers. As they passed they said '*Konnichiwa*' and presented her with the flowers, and she bowed her head in thanks to each one. Then she lifted herself to her feet and turned, walking slowly, following the path with the flowers in her hand, upstream along the river as it splashed over rocks, dancing in circles and rushing on. She walked upstream towards the source, back to the beginning.

I closed my eyes and held her for what seemed like a long time. I knew she was dead, but I waited anyway so that she wasn't on her own. I guess we were there for an hour like that, sitting in the dark. I felt her pulse one last time, but there was nothing.

'Goodbye, Butterfly. It's been very strange.'

I moved her to the recovery position and walked off. After a couple of steps I turned and went back. I kissed her head and smoothed her hair. 'Shhh. Everything's all right.' And it was now;

I'd already done my mourning. I felt all right, lighter, maybe even good.

I got to the metro tracks with a few hundred pages of *The Divine Comedy* to spare. When I arrived on the platform at Buttes Chaumont everything was closed and the lights were dim. I walked up the steps, but shutters blocked my way out, so I went back to the platform, found a seat and sat staring at the wall. Cat came and rubbed his cheek against my shin and then lay down on the ground, slightly covering my toes, and settled down to sleep. It was good to see him. I got out my phone and turned it on. I'd been underground for nine days. Then the phone started beeping and text messages came in. Two from my bank with my account balance, a reminder that I had been invited to dinner the previous Saturday, two from friends wondering whether I'd disappeared, and three messages from Beatrice: 'Hey, I'm gonna b 10 mins late' and then 'Where R U?' and finally 'Ben Constable?'. I felt happy.

I got out the plastic bag Butterfly had given me. As promised she'd returned the notebooks and there was a single shit of paper with her scribbled handwriting.

Dear Ben Constable,

Well, it's been quite a ride. I'm dead now and this time for real. I guess you know that, though, because if everything goes to plan, you will have been with me. I made a deal with myself: I would offer you a poisoned sweet. If you ate it, you would die and I would stay underground. If you didn't, I would follow you out, so long as you didn't look back, but if you turned and looked, I would eat the sweet and die. If you're reading this, then you looked back. I told you not to. You made me eat the sweet. You killed me. It's a trick, of course, but I just wanted you to know what it feels like to kill someone. Just so you could know something else about me.

If it has any meaning left, then I am sorry. I'm sorry for everything. Go write that book now.

Big kiss, Butterfly. X O X O X O
X I X X L X X O X X V X X E X X Y X X O X X U X X (Did I ever tell you?)
Ps. Oh, nothing . . . .

A Letter to Tomomi Ishikawa—
November 2008

Paris—November 27, 2008

Dear Tomomi Ishikuwa,

Sometimes I get so lost in the story that I forget what is true and what isn't. I don't really have any memories of you anymore, just memories of memories. You have somehow passed into my imagination and I'm no longer sure what you look like or how your voice sounds. Did we really used to sit and smoke on a tiny cobbled street in Ménilmontant at five in the morning? We surely only did that a few times. Perhaps it wasn't such a great friendship after all, but it did once seem that way.

I feel like I should apologise for the book, apologise for coming to find you when you didn't want me to, apologise for killing you off. But it's just a story and you're not dead and I didn't come to find you (and never will), and I'm pleased with the book, not ashamed. You should be too. It's written with love and good humour.

It took me well over a year to get round to putting pen to paper. I nearly let the whole thing drop. But the story kept turning round my head and it evolved and became ever more intricate, and then one day I woke up and knew that I wanted to write it, with or without your help.

Having finally got round to it, the whole thing went quickly. I wrote the first draft in a month (last June). I went away to Wales and lived in a wooden cabin in a garden full of flowers overlooking a green valley with a river where a train with one carriage occasionally passed back and forth. Since then I have been working on it a little each day. And now, in a few minutes, it will be over and I will be robbed of your company. Like your fictional counterpart, I would like to drag it out. Linger a few moments more.

Hey, you were in my dream (you've actually been in a lot of my dreams; when I get stuck with the story I go to sleep and you and Cat come and do all manner of weird things to nudge me onwards). Before I went to sleep I had been thinking about this letter and trying to work out what I wanted to say. In the dream you were the sandman (in France he sprinkles sand on children's eyes to give them dreams, but in the version I know he steals the eyeballs of naughty children who won't go to sleep and gives them to his own children, who live in the moon), but instead of stealing eyes you were stealing souls of people who were close to death. And you tugged at the souls and they stretched like invisible elastic and you pulled and pulled and then they would pop free and the person would die and you would just discard the soul because you had no use for it. The problem was that I could see this happening from my own point of view. It wasn't you at all. It was me. (I should have guessed. All those pointless murders came from my deranged brain, not yours.)

I don't really think that you deserve the honour. I made Tomomi Ishikawa a better friend than you were. But inevitably the book is, in part, a hymn of praise. You entertained me, we laughed, delighted and shocked each other, we explored dark places and said unsayable things, you captured my imagination and inspired me. This is a homage to our curious friendship that was, and whether I like it or not I think this story is already dedicated to you.

Goodbye.

Ben. X X X

THREE LIVES
OF
TOMOMI
ISHIKAWA

BENJAMIN CONSTABLE

SUMMARY

Ben Constable and Tomomi Ishikawa are friends. They meet for drinks, late-night cigarettes, and witty, imaginative and often surreal conversation. But Ben's life is turned upside down when he receives what seems to be a suicide note from Tomomi Ishikawa. Not only does the note announce her death, but it invites Ben on an extraordinary treasure hunt that takes him through the streets of Paris and New York City. There are clues and hidden treasures that gradually reveal aspects of Tomomi Ishikawa that Ben did not know. They also appear to disclose a startling revelation: Tomomi Ishikawa is a murderer. Combining cleverly funny dialogue with quirky, enigmatic characters and a fantastic premise that will leave readers guessing, *Three Lives of Tomomi Ishikawa* will undoubtedly resonate long after the last page is finished.

QUESTIONS AND TOPICS FOR DISCUSSION

1. The story opens with Ben and Tomomi Ishikawa imagining what Ben's book will be about. The use of imagination is a key element for the characters, especially for Ben. He even has an imaginary cat whose behavior is restricted by "the laws of science" (p. 17). If he is a figment of Ben's imagination, why can't Ben imagine him talking or able to jump great distances? What does that say about Ben's imagination? What purpose does Cat serve for Ben?

2. Why do you think Ben refrained from calling the police after reading Tomomi Ishikawa's suicide letter?

3. In her letter to Ben, Tomomi Ishikawa compares sleep and death, the sandman and the grim reaper. She writes, "I wake in fear because, for all I long for death, I run from it like the coward I am. I drink in the hope of one day finding the courage to let go" (p. 39). Why do you think she longs for death?

4. In a letter to Tomomi Ishikawa, Ben writes, "Ever since writing was invented, people have been documenting their brains, giving names to ideas, noting their dreams, and distorting their memories and making up new ones," and wonders, "What if nobody reads them?" (p. 165). Later he burns his journal pages from New York in order to light an underground passage in Paris and wonders, "Would I remember without my notes?

Would it all still exist without these pages to remind me?" (p. 293). What power does the written word hold for Ben? If it is a way to record memory, what happens when memories are distorted? What does Ben think Tomomi Ishikawa is trying to achieve with her letters to him?

5. When Ben searches for the treasure in front of Tomomi Ishikawa's old school, he thinks "of her, small and delicate, digging by herself in the night, touching the space that was touching my skin now, smelling the street and the dry earth, infringing on my personal space as if her memory were being projected inside me, like claustrophobia" (p. 185). Why does Tomomi Ishikawa send Ben on his adventure? Is it a treasure hunt or a confessional? What is Ben's motivation to keep following her clues? If you were in Ben's place, would you have kept following them?

6. Tomomi Ishikawa often tells Ben that she loves him. What is the nature of the relationship between Ben and Tomomi?

7. Ben suffers from prosopagnosia, a disorder where one cannot easily recognize faces. In what ways does it affect his interactions with others?

8. Do you believe Tomomi Ishikawa really committed the murders? Is she depressed as Ben suggests? Why do you think the author leaves it unclear?

9. At each death, Tomomi Ishikawa includes the last thoughts of her victims. Upon her own suicide, her last thoughts are

included, but not from her point of view or Ben's. Who has written her thoughts?

10. Why do you think the author named the protagonist after himself?

11. Ben always refers to Tomomi Ishikawa by her first and last names or her nickname, Butterfly. Do you think there is any difference in meaning between her name and nickname? Why does he never call her Tomomi?

12. In the story's final letter, who is writing to whom? What are the three lives of Tomomi Ishikawa depicted in the novel?

13. Tomomi Ishikawa suggests to Ben that she could kill him, steal his identity and write the book herself. What would be the strategic advantage for her in doing so? Are there any clues to suggest this might be the case?

ENHANCE YOUR BOOK CLUB

1. Look up Ben Constable's website, www.Benjamin-Constable. net, to find fascinating additional information about the book, including photos of places mentioned in the story, additional writing that did not make the final edit, and stories about the writing of the book. The website also features some of Ben's short stories, articles, and even music.

2. Ben Constable, the author, named his main character after himself. After reading his biography on his website, what similarities can you distinguish between Ben the author and Ben the character? As an exercise, have members of your group write a fictional paragraph or two with themselves as their main characters. Discuss how you each chose your topics, how strange (or natural) it was to write yourselves as protagonists, and note the similarities between authors and characters.

3. Tomomi and Ben often meet in Paris to drink wine, and even while Ben was in New York City, he needed a bottle of French red to solve one of Tomomi Ishikawa's clues. Bring a lovely French wine to your meeting—a Château Lafite Rothschild if you want to splurge, or a more modest bottle, perhaps at the recommendation of your wine merchant. If wine is inappropriate, consider creating a yogurt bar with different toppings. Include almonds if you wish, but skip the bitter toffee variety!